The Weatherman

Also by Clint McCown

Sidetracks
Wind Over Water
The Member-Guest
War Memorials

The Weatherman

A NOVEL BY

Clint McCown

Graywolf Press
Saint Paul, Minnesota

Publication of this volume is made possible in part by a grant provided by the Minnesota State Arts Board, through an appropriation by the Minnesota State Legislature; a grant from the Wells Fargo Foundation Minnesota; and a grant from the National Endowment for the Arts, which believes that a great nation deserves great art. Significant support has also been provided by the Bush Foundation; Target, Marshall Field's and Mervyn's with support from the Target Foundation; the McKnight Foundation; and other generous contributions from foundations, corporations, and individuals. To these organizations and individuals we offer our heartfelt thanks.

MINNESOTA
STATE ARTS BOARD

NATIONAL
ENDOWMENT
FOR THE ARTS

Graywolf Press acknowledges the generous support from the Literary Arts Institute of the College of St. Benedict along with the assistance of the DeWitt and Caroline Van Evera Foundation and the Lee and Rose Warner Foundation.

Published by Graywolf Press
2402 University Avenue, Suite 203
Saint Paul, Minnesota 55114
All rights reserved.

www.graywolfpress.org

Published in the United States of America
Printed in Canada

ISBN 1-55597-405-8

2 4 6 8 9 7 5 3 1
First Graywolf Printing, 2004

Library of Congress Control Number: 2004104185

Cover design: Kyle G. Hunter
Cover image: © Ed Dimsdale/Photonica

Acknowledgments

Portions of this novel first appeared in the online edition of *Mississippi Review*.

Many thanks to these friends for their ongoing support: Kevin Stein, Keith Ratzlaff, Dean Young, Jeff Gundy, Tom Mangan, Kit Golden, David Milofsky, Emilie Jacobson, Lee Hope, Dennis Lehane, Bob Butler, Joan Connor, Brad Barkley, Ann Hood, Elizabeth Searle, Michael White, Richard Hoffman, and the entire gang at Graywolf, especially Anne Czarniecki, who worked with me the extra year. Thanks also to Dawn Cooper, whose insights helped reshape much of what's here.

It happens to be true that I lived in Birmingham in 1963 and that fifteen years later I worked for a fledgling radio news outfit in Montgomery, Alabama. Still, this novel is a work of fiction. Names, characters, places, and incidents are either the product of the author's imagination or are used fictitiously. Any resemblance to actual persons, living or dead, events, or locales is entirely coincidental.

for Steve Reid and Rick Bridges,
the miracle boys of Smithfield

and for Caitlin and Mallie

You don't need a weather man
To know which way the wind blows

BOB DYLAN

The Weatherman

Prologue

November 1978

I know some things about spiders. For example, I know that spiders are more closely related to crabs than to insects. I know that the water spider spins its web underwater, then collects air bubbles on its body hairs and carries them down to inflate its nest like a silk balloon. I know that some spiders in South America are so big they eat hummingbirds. I know that strands of spider silk are used for the crosshairs of telescopic gun sights.

None of this information has ever done me any good.

That's the problem with most information. It's easy to learn the facts, hard to find a use for them. Still, I scan the catalogue in my brain, ransacking the files for what I know. My reason, in this case, is purely practical. Right now there's a surprisingly large *Mesothelae Antrodiaetidae* on the ceiling directly above my hospital bed. I know the markings: the hair on the cephalothorax is dark chestnut brown, the abdomen more purplish. He's almost two inches long—maybe three, counting the legs. The *Mesothelae Antrodiaetidae* is classified as an atypical tarantula and is the biggest of the trapdoor spiders. They're relatively common in this part of Alabama, but not on ceilings. Never on ceilings. They aren't good climbers—their bodies are too heavy and their legs too short. So even though I know perfectly well what spider I'm looking up at, I can't explain how he got there. All I can do is lie here and watch him. And wait for him to fall.

Or her—wait for her to fall.

It's hard to put a time frame on a thing like that, even for me, and predictions are supposed to be my business. For the last month I've been the weatherman for the Alacast Network—that's sixty-seven stations statewide plus Channel 11 in Montgomery—and even though I fell into the job more or less by accident, with no background in meteorology whatsoever, I've nevertheless learned to read a few signs along the way. I know what sorts of things can tumble from the clear blue, things more complicated than rain, or sleet, or hail. Basic precipitation is comparatively easy to foresee because it's always based on movement. One front pounds another, and something drops from the sky. Simple. But spiders have a different meteorology, and even though I've watched this one for hours, I still don't have many clues. He doesn't move.

Or she.

No, on second thought, not *she,* not *her,* not any form of the feminine. *She* is too disturbing to think about right now, even with medication smoothing out the wrinkles in my veins. *She* is an indecipherable notion. *She* with chestnut hair.

He, then. He has somehow managed to crawl out onto this open space and somehow managed to cling there. Risking everything for God knows what.

The Scottish hero Robert Bruce said he learned perseverance by watching a spider try over and over to fasten a thread to a branch. Maybe there's a lesson in my spider, too. But I don't see it.

Here's a blunt fact: a male tarantula might string together ten lifetimes and still not outlive the female. The reason is obvious: nature has made males the more expendable. Some are even killed by the female.

Nature's not infallible, though, and sometimes the female goes first. My mother, for example, disappeared from the scene before my father, though the particulars remain hazy. She left a note, but she wasn't a very good writer. In any case, my father never saw her again, and he proceeded to play out his final years of good health swearing his way around the golf course, slathered in suntan lotion and decked out like an arcade attraction in flammable polyesters.

A rope of spider silk an inch thick could support seventy-four tons—the equivalent of a locomotive and three overfilled coal cars. But if you put enough spiders together to make that much silk, they'd eat each other. Spiders have no concept of community. No family loyalties.

Most spiders have eight eyes.

Usually if a spider doesn't move it's because he's waiting for some careless passerby to make a last mistake, waiting for the tremor in the web that means another bundle for the pantry. But this spider has no web. He's the only dark disruption in a hundred square feet of smooth, white plaster. That's a poor tactic for a hunter, no matter how still he keeps. A spider without subtlety is a go-hungry spider, and there's no subtlety at all in this spider's position.

Maybe he's asleep, although it's hard for me to think of spiders sleeping. I guess they must. Everything sleeps. The tree frogs I hear singing in the palms each night are sleeping now. The crickets, too, most likely, are napping down in the cool coils of the radiator. The chameleon that strained all morning to become transparent on the windowpane is dozing now. Everything around here sleeps.

I could be wrong, of course; he could be wide awake, watching me with a cold, professional eye, wondering what giant after his own heart has snared me in this web of tubes and straps and bandages. Maybe he's waiting to scavenge leftovers.

It's too soon to worry, though. Before a tarantula bites, it gives out a warning by kicking itself a few times in the abdomen. That's one thing that separates it from politicians.

I do know something of politicians, having studied them far more closely than I ever studied the weather. For the past few weeks I've hovered above them in the visitors' gallery at the capitol building, watching them play out the formalities of their game. I wish I could have been there for today's session. The whole legislature must be in turmoil now, wondering how to untangle the calamity of the election. I tried to warn them. Night after night I predicted radical disturbances in the atmosphere. I mentioned whirlwinds, earthquakes, massive upheavals. My long-range forecast called for asteroids.

But that was before the wide-eyed look of disbelief on the assistant attorney general's face. Before the pulling of the trigger. And I have to admit I've seen nothing but good signs from that moment on. Cool fronts are warming up, warm fronts are cooling down. The rainbows refracting through my drinking glass seem more prophetic than the chips along its rim.

If Alissa were here I would hazard a forecast.

But no. Forecast implies a specific sense of the future. Even though Alissa believes in predestination, her moves are unpredictable.

Instead I have Shawnelle, the day nurse. She comes from the city side of the bay, but moved over here among the mimosas to live more quietly. She is meticulously slow—not like those pert candy-stripers who flit in and out like this is Disneyland, but slow and graceful. She is an intuitive danseuse who makes no thoughtless gesture. Even when her black hair drapes forward across her shoulders as she leans down to take my temperature, even then I think she knows where every strand will fall.

"You'll be just fine, Mr. Wakefield," she tells me, and except for the burn spots on my soul, she may be right. I think we're about the same age. I'm sure she's under thirty. I've told her to call me Taylor, but she won't do it.

I wonder what it was like for her fifteen years ago when federal troops patrolled the streets in green jeeps and camouflaged trucks. Maybe she carries some kind of hurt from back then. I know I do.

She says she thinks sometimes about leaving the state, trying life up north somewhere, but I doubt she'll ever go. Her pace is perfect here. Hers is the pulse of the region. This is the land for Shawnelles, for slow movers and syrupy talkers, for the methodical, the patient, the unconcerned. On days that crack the fields she moves without sweating. As the air thickens and shimmers in waves, she breathes it best. When katydids whir among the drowsy willows, she sips a glass of tea and rests her eyes in the afternoon shade. That's what I imagine, anyway.

She has nice eyes. They're green, a living green the color of a stained-glass pasture on the sundown side of church. They shine more as the day wears on and come to brilliance near the simmer of evening, during the shadow-gathering calm that follows the administering of the Demerol.

Demerol is a drug of detachment, which is perfect for me now. It doesn't take the pain away, but keeps me from caring about it. They gave me a hundred cc's for the operation, and if my arms hadn't been strapped to metal gurneys I might have sat up and watched. I could see some of it anyway. The doctor made a few quick cuts, stuck on some clamps, and suddenly my hand was inside out. I could feel the whole procedure—the removal of the fragments, the restitching of the muscles, the resetting of the remaining bones— and it never even occurred to me to flinch. He could have sawed off my arm and I would have found it entertaining.

That, too, makes me think of Alissa.

Chapter 1

For me it all boils down to family problems. Nothing original in that, I realize. We all own plots in that cemetery. But my case might be a little different from most in that I can trace fifteen years' worth of nightmares and paranoia—and, oddly enough, academic obsession—back to a particular moment in my life, a single instant on a summer morning at the freight yards, where I'd gone to steal coal from abandoned railroad cars.

I was eleven years old, and on that day my friend Tippy Weaver and I had hiked down to the Cahaba River like we did most every summer morning. The county had had its share of rain that spring, and even the summer had been damp, but a June drought to the north of us had left the water level low enough that we could wade long stretches with just our pant legs rolled. We each carried a mason jar for minnows, which were plentiful in the shady spots along the western bank, and which we could sell for a quarter to Andy's Bait Shop just across the trestle.

We also each carried a sharpened bamboo spear about five feet long, which we had whittled from broken fishing poles. Our intention was to use these spears to fend off any copperhead or water moccasin we might inadvertently provoke. Tippy claimed to have seen four snakes already that summer, but one of those turned out to be a broken fan belt, so in truth he might not have seen any at all. I sure never did. But we were Alabama boys, after all, and welcomed any excuse to carry a weapon.

We worked our way up to the third bend, crossing out of Cahaba Heights and into Irondale. From there we cut through the marshy

flood plain to Shades Creek and, crossing over, climbed the sandstone bank behind Blackie's Gentlemen's Club, a low cinder-block
dive on Front Street across from the Norris freight yards.

Blackie's was a mystery of the adult world to us then, with
neon cocktail glasses on the sign above the door and windows
haphazardly blackened with slapped-on coats of paint. On the far
side, across the gravelly pockmarked street, was a string of coal
cars that had sat untended for more than a year, each slowly filling
with season after season of rain. They'd long ago been emptied of
their loads, although not entirely. Most still held scatterings of coal
beneath the stagnant water in the bottoms of the cars.

Wading those coal cars was easier than wading the Cahaba, or
even Shades Creek, because the footing was firm and we had no
worry about snakes. The bottoms weren't even slimy, although
I can't explain why. Maybe the compartments were treated with
chemicals. Maybe the coal dust somehow kept the water too gritty
and poisoned even for scum. Maybe it was just too damn hot. In any
case the texture along the iron beds stayed rough enough for our
bare feet to find traction. We still had to move with care, because
the open cars were a favorite target for drunks with empty bottles.
So we slid our feet carefully through the black water, nudging aside
the shards of broken glass as we scavenged for the coal. Tippy kept
a burlap bag tied to the belt loops of his jeans, and in less than half
an hour we could pluck out enough burnable chunks to fill it.

This piecemeal dredging of the coal cars was not a pleasant
activity, especially on a sweltering summer day, when those rust-
coated sides burned hot enough to raise a blister. But we weren't
doing it for fun. Tippy's family was pretty bad off, even by local
standards. His dad was an older guy, over sixty, who'd lost his job
at the Shell station because they thought he'd been stealing empty
oil drums. Free coal was a real windfall for the Weavers because
it meant they could heat their house come winter. That might not
seem like a big deal, this being mid-Alabama where it almost never
snows. But the Weavers' house was mostly tar paper, so it didn't
have much in the way of insulation, and January, even around here,

can get cold. If the temperature drops to thirty-five overnight, that's what you get out of bed to in the morning. Besides that, the Weavers had one of those old potbellied cookstoves—the only one I've seen in real life—and Mrs. Weaver fixed all their meals on it. So the coal made a difference there, too.

In six weeks we'd lugged home nearly three hundred pounds. A couple of times Mr. Weaver gave me a nickel for my part, but usually he paid me in magazine pages. He'd tear out big color pictures of pretty women in lipstick ads and give them to me. That seems kind of creepy to me now, but at the time I thought it was a pretty good salary. So just about every day we'd bring in a full sack, which we'd then carry around back of the chicken coop and empty into one of Mr. Weaver's oil drums.

To this day, coal still seems like some kind of miracle fuel to me. It never rots, it never gets eaten by termites, it won't go bad like gasoline. It's a rock that burns. And on top of all that, it's where diamonds come from.

I assume that means that under the right circumstances, a diamond can burn, too. Not from any ordinary fire, of course. When they cut Arch Hathaway's body out of his station wagon, for example, the arm that was handcuffed to the steering wheel was burnt down to the bone. But his big diamond ring came through just fine. Even in the black-and-white newspaper photo it still sparkled like a star in the morning light.

Anyway, the coal. Tippy and I were just starting our first slow sweep through the murky water of an old Southern Railways car. Most of the coal cars were black, but this one was a dingy rust red, older, I think, than the others. It was directly across Front Street from Blackie's, close enough that I could have hit the front screen door with the right piece of coal. On other days, in fact, I had done just that. Kids throw things, that's a simple fact, and even though it had cost us some effort to collect the coal, after climbing back out of the cars, sunbaked and soggy, and filthy beyond reason from the brackish water and our own stinking sweat, we couldn't resist flinging the occasional chunk toward the tubing of Blackie's neon cocktail sign. It was a natural target for an eleven-year-old—colorful, exotic, and highly breakable.

To my secret relief, we never hit it. We barely even came close. Coal is pretty lightweight with a lot of odd facets and sheared edges. That meant the harder we threw, the more crazily each piece would carve out its own unpredictable path through the air. No big-league pitcher ever had the kind of curve or slider we achieved involuntarily on every throw. Consequently, the entire cinder-block front, which had no windows, was peppered with our impact marks. Blackie must not have cared, since, beyond putting dents in his screen door, we never really broke anything. In any case, he never washed the black marks away.

But on this day, August 26, 1963, our last day ever to scavenge coal at the freight yards, Tippy and I never got the chance to try our luck against the sign. A car with a bad muffler pulled into the gravel lot next to Blackie's. We noticed because there was seldom any traffic along this stretch of Front Street, at least not during the day. The club didn't open until sometime in the evening, and there were no other businesses along that desolate stretch, no destination but the barricaded dead end overlooking the creek at the far end of the yards. From the belly of the coal car we heard the slow, noisy approach, then the faint pop of gravel, then silence as the motor died, then the slam of the car door.

Neither Tippy nor I had ever seen Blackie. He was a late-night phantom known by reputation only. His Gentlemen's Club, a brown-bag private drinking establishment in an otherwise dry township, was famous throughout the valley as the embodiment of danger to both body and soul. Our minister at Trinity Methodist, Dr. Kimbrough, had used the word vice in decrying the activities of the place, and even though our parents rarely spoke about the specific goings-on, rumors of knife fights and drunken brawls circulated regularly through the school yard. It was said he was a bootlegger, that family fortunes had been lost at his poker table, that he rented out women for a dollar. He was the richest and most notorious black man in all the Shades Valley towns, and to those of us in bed by nine o'clock, he was a figure of underworld myth, rivaling Al Capone, or Legs Diamond, or Pretty Boy Floyd. Or even the devil himself.

"Maybe it's him," Tippy whispered, and he quickly began to untie the burlap sack from his waist. While he fumbled with the wet knots, I pulled myself up the sloping wall to take a look. A brief glimpse was all I could manage, because the rim of the car was like a stove top, so I couldn't hold on. As I slid back down, Tippy cast the coal sack aside and scrambled up the wall himself, burning his own fingers as I had done. With a sharp cry he leapt back down to the bottom of the car and plunged his hands into the dark water. After a few moments he straightened slightly and pressed his palms against his thighs. "I couldn't tell anything," he said hoarsely.

That was hardly a surprise. Tippy had poor eyesight, so poor they always made him sit up front in school. Nearsighted, I guess he was. His parents couldn't pay for glasses, though, so he pretty much viewed the world through a perpetual squint. I often had to fill in the more distant details. My eyes were fine.

"Just some regular guy," I told him. I'd seen the man for barely an instant myself, and only from behind, as he disappeared beyond the screen door. He was thin and blond, I could tell that much, and he wore cutoff jeans and a T-shirt. I noticed he was sunburned along the backs of his legs and arms.

Tippy fished around for the coal sack, which had slipped beneath the water out of sight. "I have to go home," he said, lifting up the mouth of the sack and pulling the drawstrings tight.

I took the sack by the neck and raised it from the water with one hand. "It's not even half full," I said. "Your mama couldn't heat a chili pepper with a load this small."

Tippy sucked in a slow breath through gritted teeth, and I suddenly realized that the look on his face wasn't a squint but a grimace.

"I jumped on glass," he said.

"Lemme see."

He put a hand on my shoulder to steady himself and drew his foot from the water. Blood trickled from a thin slice along the soft skin of his instep. I held his foot and carefully pressed around the edges of the cut. A fresh trickle flowed from the end nearest his heel, and I wiped it away with my fingers.

"It's a little deeper right here," I said, pointing to the bloodier half of the gash. "But it doesn't look too bad. You feel any glass in there?"

"I don't think so," he said, squeezing his foot with his free hand. "It don't really hurt all that much."

"Well, let it bleed for a while," I told him, wiping my fingers on my shirtfront. "That'll clean it out. And don't put it back in this water—no telling what kind of corruption we're standing in."

"Maybe I'll get lockjaw," he said.

"Maybe you will."

Tippy smiled at the possibility. It was always good to imagine a little drama in our lives. "I'll pour peroxide on it when I get home," he said.

"Peroxide's for little kids," I told him. "Put something on it that stings, like iodine, or methialate. That's how you kill germs."

"Alcohol," he declared. "I'll pour alcohol right down inside the wound."

"I bet you won't," I said.

"I will too." Tippy took the coal sack and tossed it over the rim of the car toward Front Street. "I ain't afraid of alcohol."

He pressed his foot carefully against the rough slope of the wall and stretched forward, hooking his fingers over the edge. He hoisted himself quickly up the incline and swung down on the other side. I followed him up over the rim and dropped beside him in the yellow dust.

"You talking about wood alcohol or grain?" I asked.

"Grain, you dope. Wood alcohol makes you go blind."

"Only if you drink it, moron. Anyway, where you gonna find grain alcohol? Your daddy don't allow it in the house. I heard him say so."

"There's other people got it," he said, but without much conviction.

"Name one," I challenged him.

Tippy looked down at the ground and shrugged his shoulders. His parents belonged to the Temperance Union and were Holy Rollers besides. Liquor simply didn't exist in their world, except as the principal villain in countless cautionary tales. Tippy had a better chance of finding a penguin in his mother's pantry than a jug of moonshine or a bottle of Jack Daniel's.

I picked up the coal sack and tested the heft—five or six pounds, at the most. I handed it to Tippy, and while he retied the sack to his belt loops I turned my attention to the minnow jars. The minnows were still moving, but instead of darting back and forth, they now cruised slowly along the curve of the jar. We needed to change the water soon or we'd lose them.

That was one lesson we'd learned the hard way. Most days we'd be lucky to snag half a dozen or so, because minnows were quick and difficult to catch bare-handed. But one day we hit the jackpot—stumbled into a whole school bunched up in a narrow stretch where Fuller Creek met the river. We could have reached in with our eyes closed and still brought out a handful. I'd never seen anything like it. Of course our greed got the best of us and we kept putting more and more minnows in the jars until finally they were packed in so tight they could barely wiggle. By the time we got them to the bait shop, they were all dead. Not enough oxygen in the water.

Today, too, we'd had good luck, finding a clotted run of minnows in a shallow pocket along the riverbank. This time we showed a little more restraint, but it was tough to resist overloading the jars when the minnows were right there for the taking. Maybe we'd been too greedy once again, though I couldn't tell yet. There's always a line between enough and too much, but it's hard to know where that line is until you've crossed it.

Tippy picked up one of the jars and, using his bamboo spear for balance, limped a few steps to the shoulder of the road. He stopped there, as if he were waiting for a break in traffic, and I noticed the small drips of blood that trailed behind him on the hard-packed ground.

"What's the matter?" I asked, coming up alongside him. "Mama won't let you cross the street by yourself?"

Tippy nodded toward the building in front of us. "I'll tell you somebody who's got grain alcohol," he said.

I laughed. "Blackie's got it, all right. And I guarantee he'll be keeping it, too. Here, gimme that." I took his minnow jar from him and handed him my stick of bamboo. "You'll shake 'em up too much, the way you're walking."

"You don't know what Blackie might do," Tippy said. "He might give us a little bit, if we asked for it. Just for medicine."

"Yeah, right." I held the two jars still for a minute to let the cloudiness settle, and then started across the street. At the edge of Blackie's gravel lot I turned back toward Tippy, who stood rooted to his spot,

"I bet he's got Band-Aids, too." He lifted his foot and rapped the shorter bamboo spear against his heel to shake loose some of the freight-yard grit. "Probably be glad to help us out." A smug smile crept across his face. "Unless you're scared to ask."

"Just get your butt across the street," I said.

At that moment, I don't know if I meant to take his dare or not. Tippy wasn't hurt that bad, but a sliced-open foot could be a legitimate excuse to knock on Blackie's door. I knew there was no chance to get any alcohol from him. No black man in the county was crazy enough to give liquor to white kids these days, not with all the trouble we'd had lately. He'd get himself run out of town, or maybe worse. But if we somehow got to talk to Blackie himself, face to face, even if it was just for a second, we could be big shots in the neighborhood from then on.

Tippy eased his way across to me, using the bamboo shafts like crutches. "What about it, Tay? Got enough guts?"

"These minnows are winding down fast," I told him.

"They ain't no worse off than I am," he said. "I'm the one still bleedin'." He spat into the gravel to show his disgust. "You're just chicken, is all."

I looked over at Blackie's dented screen door, not ten steps away, and shook my head. "Least I'm not stupid."

That was the wrong thing for me to say. Stupidity was a sore spot with Tippy because he was, in fact, stupid. He was the only kid anyone knew who had actually failed the first grade, and this year he had failed the fifth. He didn't say anything at first, but I could see from the way he tightened his jaw and stared past me down the street that I'd made him mad. I knew he was calculating his next move, but I couldn't guess what it might be. We often pretended to be cruel or tough with each other, and sometimes, without our meaning for it to happen, we'd go too far, and that familiar moment of crisis would suddenly arrive. I recognized that moment now as Tippy took a long slow breath and raised up the longer of the two bamboo spears—the one that was mine.

"I'll show you stupid," he said, and before I could make a move to stop him, he let it fly, full force, toward the doorway. It was a perfect throw, one that tore through the lower center of the rusty mesh and lodged there, half in and half out of Blackie's old screen door. We both froze, then, neither one of us believing the line that Tippy had just dared to cross.

I don't know why we didn't run. My whole life would have turned out differently if we had. But recklessness is its own kind of liquor and can swamp the mind in a hurry. Without a word passing between us, Tippy and I began to move toward the damaged door, daring each other forward with every tentative step.

When we reached the pitted concrete slab that footed the doorway, I tucked the jar from my right hand—Tippy's jar—into the crook of my left elbow and reached out to retrieve the spear. It was right then, before I'd even begun to pull the bamboo from the screen, that we heard the first muted shot. We both jumped, and Tippy's jar tumbled forward onto the stoop, shattering in a splash of dying minnows and glass. Two more shots followed the first, and Tippy broke into a run, bad foot and all, and disappeared around the corner of the building before I could even sort things out clearly enough to react. For the longest four seconds of my life I stood stranded in confusion. I needed to pick up the broken glass, I needed to scoop up the minnows, I needed to take back my spear, I needed to run. But I couldn't think or even move. I couldn't do anything but stand there in the exact wrong place at the exact wrong time, as muffled shouts and curses rolled forward from some back room in Blackie's club.

Then the sound of an inner door banging open.

Of chairs flung against a wall.

Of a table overturning.

Of the bursting clatter of things going to pieces, scattering in all directions across the floor.

Then three more shots, much louder this time, much nearer the front, and the rising up of shadows beyond the screen, and the gasping cry of the black man now barreling toward me from the shallow darkness of the club.

I thought I was killed for certain. But still I couldn't move, even as the screen door banged open and Blackie, it had to be Blackie, lunged across the threshold, stumbling through the broken glass and pitching forward, his heavy body colliding with mine in a glancing blow that sent me flying to one side as he skidded awkwardly to his knees in the gravel.

He knelt there, head down, blood drooling in strands from his gaping mouth, struggling to breathe. I don't think he even realized I was there, or if he did, he was far beyond caring. He coughed a couple of times and vomited weakly into his hands, then settled slowly back on his heels. I remember expecting him to fall over, but he didn't, he stayed slumped on his knees, his head resting on his chest, like a man in prayer. Like a statue, that's how still he was. Then it occurred to me that he was dead.

I looked toward the doorway, hoping to God the thin blond man would not be there yet, that I would still have time to run, like Tippy did, and leave this nightmare behind me. But what I saw there scoured every small hope from my heart. The screen had not swung shut—the shaft of bamboo had been knocked nearly free when Blackie forced the frame back against the outer cinder-block wall, and now the sharpened end of the spear drooped into the dirt beside the stoop, propping the door wide open. There in the entryway, with the gun still in his hand, stood the only person in the world I already knew to be afraid of.

It was my cousin Billy.

Billy was from the Hatcher side of the family. We shared a great-grandfather, James Hatcher, a blacksmith who was killed in the Spanish American War. Billy's father had died in a war, too, in Korea, which is maybe why Billy was always so wild. He and I grew up on the same street, just a block apart, but he was eight years older, so except for family reunions, we almost never saw each other. I'd been alone with him only twice. The first was when he was thirteen and I was five; he tied me to the stairway in his mother's basement and burned me with cigarettes. The other time was four years later, on a Sunday afternoon, right after Billy had come home from his second stay in reform school. He spotted me in the school yard and chased me all the way up to the roof of the gym. When he finally caught me by the arm, he laughed, like the game was over. But then, without reason or hesitation, he tossed me from the roof like a sack of trash. It was a long drop, maybe twenty-five feet, and if I hadn't caught a grip in some willow branches, I might have been hurt pretty bad.

Now here we were again. Only this time there was already a dead man kneeling in the dirt. And this time Billy was mad.

He stepped out onto the stoop and glanced quickly around. I looked around, too, hoping for some policeman on patrol, some passing car, some hobo headed for the river, anything that might somehow alter my situation. But the street was deserted—no people, no stray dogs, no birds, no presence of any kind. No sound but the soft grumbling of a distant train, no movement but the small halo of dust stirred up by Blackie when he fell. Billy calmly raised his pistol, aimed it at my face, and pulled the trigger. The empty click surprised him.

"Fuck!" he yelled, and started toward me. I tried to scramble away, but he was too quick and too close, and before I could get halfway to my feet he caught me by the back of my shirt and dragged me toward the open doorway.

But I wasn't feeling so paralyzed anymore. The monster here wasn't the terrifying phantom of my imagination that Blackie had been. The monster here was my asshole cousin Billy, a skinny punk with no more bullets in his gun, a flesh-and-blood human being with a flesh-and-blood susceptibility to pain.

As he hoisted me up over the edge of the stoop into the minnows and broken glass, I reached down with my free hand and jerked loose the piece of bamboo from the open screen door. He must have seen me make the grab, because he stopped in midstride and slammed me on my stomach against the concrete slab, smashing the second jar of minnows beneath me. I knew I was cut, but it didn't matter, and even with the wind knocked out of me, I could still maneuver. I squirmed sideways in his grip and rammed the spear upward as hard as I could, up the left pant leg of his baggy cut-offs, catching him on the inside of his upper thigh. Bamboo, if you carve it right, allows a sharper edge than ordinary wood—stronger, too, and more blade-like—and now I was able to push the narrow point deep into a knot of muscle. His whole body tightened involuntarily, and in that split second of delay, before he could react in my direction, I twisted the shaft, and shoved it further in. Billy howled and staggered sideways, dropping me before I could stab him again. He rolled onto his back in the gravel and grabbed his bleeding leg with both hands.

"Goddammit!" he screamed, and the rage in his voice was so fierce I thought he might come after me again that very instant, in spite of any damage I had done. But the wound, apparently, was a good one, and for the moment Billy stayed where he was—as did I, because the wind was still knocked out of me, and I couldn't yet run. So for an oddly calm handful of seconds we both just lay there, hurting, in the gravel, with the dead man propped absurdly between us, fighting our separate battles to regain control. Blackie's screen door, I remember, creaked on its hinges and slowly swung shut.

But soon enough my breath came back, and I was on my feet again. At first I thought to break toward the river, but Tippy had gone that way and might still be waiting for me just behind the building. Besides, the flood plain offered no place to hide and was too swampy for running, and if Billy caught me too near the river he could drown me. My best bet was higher ground.

I lit out across the road toward the freight yards, and even though I heard Billy slipping in the gravel behind me, I didn't look back, not then, because I didn't want to know how quick he still might be, or how close, or how crazy. I didn't want to know anything.

I just ran. I ran past the line of coal cars, and across three sets of empty track, and past the loading docks for the Birmingham Southern, and the Central of Georgia, and the Seaboard Line, and then I veered between equipment sheds and dodged a handcar overturned in the weeds, and raced along a drainage ditch, and jumped the ditch when it angled toward the river, and my lungs burned and my side ached, but I kept running, because I had no choice, and I ducked beneath a row of cattle cars on the Great Alabama Southern, and sprinted past the holding pens and past a switching spur, and came out, finally, on the far north side of the rails, up by the main tracks, where at that blessed moment a string of boxcars rumbled slowly along the upper end of the yards.

My legs were nearly spent, but I set the lumbering boxcars as my goal, and forced myself into a final kick, a last, desperate burst that carried me up alongside an empty car, up within reach of the iron ladder bolted to its wall. The ground was level and the train was slow, so it was a simple matter to grab a high rung and gain a foothold, and from there, to work my way up the ladder and step through the open boxcar door.

That's when I finally looked back, down that long cluttered slope toward the flood plain and the river. But there was nothing to see; Billy was nowhere behind me. Maybe I'd lost him in the rail yards. Or maybe he hadn't chased after me at all, maybe he was still on his back in the gravel. Or maybe he'd driven home to put more bullets in his gun. I didn't like not knowing, but that part was out of my hands because the boxcar came with a limited view, and Blackie's place was hidden now by too many other things, too many sheds, and warehouses, and train cars, and trees. Even the midmorning sun glared against me.

I stepped away from the opening, into the shadows of the car, and sank to the straw-littered floor, exhausted. The mild vibration of the tracks hummed in my spine, and leaning back against the cool, dark wall, I began to shake. I looked down at my T-shirt, mottled with blood, and brushed my fingers lightly across the cotton to feel for glass. A few small splinters glistened in the weaving, and I drew them out as carefully as I could.

It felt good to have something small like that to focus on, something appropriate to do, something uncomplicated. I guess I must have sensed already that complications would mar my life from that time on, that nothing in my questionable future would ever again be as simple as stealing coal from the freight yards or catching minnows in jars.

And, in fact, a further complication descended upon me even then, as my eyes adjusted to the smoky hollow of the boxcar. There were others in that stale half-darkness with me.

Chapter 2

I've been thinking lately about the edge of the universe, and what the weather's like out there. Cold, certainly. Motionless. And dark, infinitely dark because the flash of the Big Bang hasn't gotten there yet.

If, indeed, there was a Big Bang. Most astronomers think there was, and I'm willing to go along with that, as a professional courtesy. Astronomers are just weathermen working on a different scale.

The comforting thing about the Big Bang is that it binds everything together as part of a single chain reaction. Cause and effect from start to finish, and everything's a part of it, right down to the most unexpected and obscure detail in the show.

Somewhere, at a vivid point in time, one galaxy collided with another in a massive shower of nuclear sparks. Elsewhere, at an equally vivid point in time, I climbed into a northbound boxcar, afraid for my life. Both events, theoretically, might have arisen from a common ancestral moment, some shared happenstance of origin in the dim dawning of the universe. Everything that happens is linked, as any meteorologist can tell you. Otherwise, there could be no basis for prediction.

But that doesn't mean predictions come easy. Hail can still fall from a clear blue sky. Every weatherman knows what it's like to be wrong.

I heard a scraping noise at the rear of the boxcar, like someone absently scuffing a shoe back and forth across the grit of the floor, and my heart nearly stopped. I knew it couldn't be Billy, but I also knew there were plenty of other things it could be, things just as bad.

I'd heard stories about the people who rode the rails—kidnappers, and escaped convicts, and cutthroats of every kind. A fresh panic seized me, and I stared wide-eyed toward the sound, willing my eyes to penetrate the dark. As the dim outline of several seated figures began to take shape in the gloom, I heard other stirrings from the opposite end of the car.

So after all I'd been through the only thing I'd really gained, it seemed, was a new predicament, with no guarantee that this one would be any more forgiving than the last. Maybe that wasn't the most rational attitude to take, but the world had just shown me the depth of what it could do, and I couldn't help but think the worst. That may have been the bleakest moment in my life. My eyes blurred, and I convulsed into a series of deep, choking sobs.

I cried like that for a while, expecting every moment that something horrible would happen, and knowing I had no strength to fend it off. Then I felt a slight nudging of my sneakers, and heard a voice as deep as God's.

"You all right there, boy?"

I had no answer, but I did look up—slowly, still braced for attack. A large black man in a wrinkled brown suit frowned down at me. He had a jagged scar on his forehead and a scattering of moles across his nose and cheekbones. I was afraid of his face. But the suit reassured me—an escaped convict would not be so well dressed.

He squatted down beside me. "You ain't sick, is you?"

A woman's voice cut through the darkness from the rear of the car. "Put your glasses on, Lester," she said, and I looked toward the sound of her voice, but couldn't tell which of the half-dozen shadowy shapes was hers. "Sick don't make people bleed. That boy's a mess, I can tell it from here."

The big man reached into his coat pocket and carefully drew out a pair of horn-rims with a missing stem. He balanced the glasses on his nose and studied me more closely. "Huh," he said.

"Chuck him out the door, Lester," someone called out in a thin and raspy voice. "Now, 'fore we start pickin' up speed."

"Ain't gonna throw no kid off a moving train," Lester said. "What the hell you thinkin'?"

The man with the raspy voice stepped forward from the shadows. He, too, had on a wrinkled suit—this one more tan than brown, and slightly more tattered, with a spot at the right front pocket, like something had leaked through.

"I'm thinkin' the smart thing to do," he answered. He stepped over to the door of the car and leaned out to look at the edge of the track. "Hell, we ain't doing but eight mile an hour. He'll be awright—just grab him by the scruff and lower him down."

"Suppose he go under the train," said Lester, rising to his feet. "What you figure'll happen then?"

The raspy-voiced man looked back at Lester and sighed. "What you figure'll happen if we get caught on this train with a missin' white child?"

"Nothin' good," offered the woman. She was standing now, and moving forward, but she was still just a vague shape in the darkness.

The raspy-voiced man shook his head and shoved himself away from the opening. He had large, broad hands, like baseball mitts, and he pointed a thick finger in my direction. "That boy liable to jinx this whole trip."

Now the woman eased out into the slant of sunlight. She wore a purple flowered-print dress, and a small black hat with a crumpled see-through veil pinned back from her face. A shiny black pocketbook hung from the crook of her elbow. She looked like a woman on her way to church.

"He ain't no china clock, gonna break when you drop him," she said. "Just toss him out a ways from the wheels, is all you gotta do."

"Or maybe we don't gotta do nothin'," said the raspy-voiced man. He walked over beside me and crouched down low, putting his face up close to mine. He smelled of peppermint. "Maybe this boy been brought up to be scared of colored folks. Maybe we just say 'boo,' and he jump right out that door his own self."

"No," Lester said flatly. "That ain't what we about. We'll put him off the next stop, that'll be soon enough." He looked back down at me. "You got anything to say yet, boy?"

The raspy-voiced man was still crowding me, still staring into my face like he meant to frighten me, but suddenly I knew not to be afraid. I'd seen a killer's look, God help me, and this man didn't have it. When Billy first saw me lying there in Blackie's parking lot, he didn't put on some exaggerated scowl to try to scare me, because he didn't care whether I was scared or not. Maybe that's the most valuable lesson I learned that day—it's not the Halloween face a person needs to worry about, it's the Halloween heart. And right then, even up close, with all the malice he could muster, the raspy-voiced man seemed like just another normal person to me. Slightly irritated, maybe, and not naturally friendly, but normal, nevertheless. I knew with absolute certainty that the worst this man might ever do to me was drop me on my feet from a slow-moving train.

So as near as I could gather, my situation had improved. I leaned slightly forward until I was almost nose to nose with the raspy-voiced man.

"I got as much right to be here as you," I told him, although I was careful not to sound too snotty about it. No sense pushing my luck.

The raspy-voiced man's frown deepened and he bit his lip. Then he pushed himself up to his feet and brushed his hands on the sides of his pants. A swirl of dust rose through the smoky sunlight. "Cain't argue with a person's rights," he said calmly.

"Amen to that," someone said in the darkness.

He walked back to the open door and unbuttoned his coat to the breeze.

"It'll be awright, Daryl," Lester said. "We still gonna get there."

"Maybe so, and maybe not," Daryl, the raspy-voiced man, answered. He stared out the door at the run-down warehouses that lined the river along the outskirts of town. The sun slid sideways behind Shades Mountain. "But we got us dealt a bad enough hand already," he said. "Don't need no new joker in the deck."

The woman in the purple dress walked over to Daryl and rubbed his shoulders. "Relax, honey," she said. "This train don't carry no jokers." Then she laughed, and some of the others laughed, too, and even Daryl smiled and shook his head.

Lester squatted beside me again. "How bad you cut up?" he asked.

"It's awright," I said. "I'll put Band-Aids on it when I get home."

"This the way home for you, is it?"

I didn't answer. He reached out and gently lifted my T-shirt up over my stomach. Something there seemed to catch his attention—he adjusted his glasses and leaned in for a closer look. Then he lowered my shirt, studied it for a moment, and lifted it again.

"Well, that's a peculiar thing," he said, easing it back into place.

"What?" I asked, worried that maybe I was hurt worse than I first thought.

"Ain't but two cuts here, that I see. You got more blood outside this shirt than you got underneath."

I didn't doubt it. I'd been bled on by just about everybody I'd met that day. But the truth was, I couldn't bring myself to talk about it—or even think about it, for that matter. The pounding in my rib cage had finally throttled down to a nearly regular beat, and I was once more able to draw an even breath. I couldn't face stirring everything up again by trying to explain whose blood was whose, or how I came to be spattered with it. It was just too soon, the ground was still too unfamiliar. Besides, the boxcar was not a comfortable place to begin with. The air was stiffling, even with the open door, and as fresh beads of sweat burst out across my scalp and trickled down my face and neck, I became acutely aware of just how much mystery was still spinning all around me. I didn't like that. I needed the world to be ordinary again.

"Y'all must be Jehovah's Witnesses?" I said.

Lester opened his mouth but didn't say anything. The woman in the purple dress took a step toward me and put her hands on her hips.

"Be careful what kind of label you put on strangers, boy," she said. "Some folks might take offense being called something they ain't."

Daryl snorted. "We witnesses, all right. But not for no Jehovah. Jehovah ain't done shit."

"We Baptists," Lester said quietly.

"Montgomery Baptists," Daryl added, as if that carried some particular weight.

Lester laced his fingers and propped them under his chin. "I guess I been mistook for a lot worse," he said. "But what on God's earth made you think we was Jehovah's Witnesses?"

"You wearin' suits on a weekday," I said. "And you keep your coats on even in this boxcar heat."

Lester laughed. "We always put our coats on when we roll through a rail yard," he said. "Case we gotta leave in a hurry." He looked toward the open door, where the broken red-clay fields of the Alabama countryside now passed evenly by. He stood up and removed his jacket and folded it across his arm. Daryl, too, took off his coat and hung it on the inside lever of the door.

"But why are y'all dressed up in the first place?" I asked.

"We dressed up 'cause we got someplace to go," said the woman in the purple dress. "That's all you need to know about it."

So they had their secrets and I had mine, and the whole conversation wound down to its natural end. Lester leaned over and patted me on the shoulder, like he was my Little League coach and I'd just struck out for the hundredth time. Then he tucked his glasses into his shirt pocket, stretched, and walked back into the shadows at the rear of the car. The woman in the purple dress followed after him, and I heard them settle awkwardly to the boxcar floor. Daryl stayed by the open doorway, keeping cool in the breeze and watching intently for whatever lay ahead on the tracks.

Chapter 3

Traditionally, bad weather is the province of God. You'd think it wouldn't be that way, that the devil would get the blame for thunder-storms, and floods, and tornados—not to mention the even greater cataclysms that shake the world from time to time. But the Bible, especially the Old Testament, never allows the devil that much power. Catastrophe never seems to bubble up from Hell, it only descends from Heaven.

That probably suits the devil just fine. Why should he care if God wants all the credit for raining fire on Sodom and Gomorrah, or drowning Noah's unworthy neighbors, or bringing famine, or pestilence, or drought? It doesn't matter whose name goes on the story. The important thing is that the work gets done.

Of course, that makes justice a fairly iffy proposition. Einstein said that God does not play dice with the universe—but tell that to Job. What did he ever do to become the luckless victim of a cruel side bet on God's crap table?

What did any of us do?

No, that's not fair. I know exactly what I did, and when I did it. On August 26, 1963, sometime in the early afternoon, some-where in the Beaver Creek Mountains outside Gadsden, Alabama, I walked to the open door of a boxcar, took off my blood-spotted T-shirt, and threw it out into the high weeds alongside the track.

Without that shirt, I knew, there was nothing to prove I was there when Blackie came through the door, or when Billy followed after. I could be as innocent and ignorant as Tippy, with no story to tell but that I had heard some gunshots and had run away.

I wish I could say that Billy had made me do it, that he had threatened to kill me and all my family if I ever told the truth about that day. But this plan was all my own, a bargain hammered out between me and the devil under that bright blue morning sky.

I guess some people would have turned to God for support at a time like that and put their trust in doing what was right. But by that point in my life, I'd already come to think of God as a less-than-reliable figure. Oh, I knew He could help me if He wanted to, but I also knew how unlikely that was. I'd gone to Sunday school and church almost every week of my life, and I'd learned all about Jesus, and Peter, and John the Baptist, and all the rest of them who died horribly. Through all those stories, all those gruesome accounts of torture and death, one thing had become abundantly clear: God liked martyrs more than he liked survivors.

The devil, on the other hand, had a reputation as a deal-maker. This for that, that for this. The devil could be reasonable, and I was willing to negotiate.

About two o'clock the train stopped in Gadsden to take on a load of feeder hogs, and while the Montgomery Baptists crowded further into the dark corners to keep out of sight, I stepped forward into the hot sun and, ignoring the ladder, leapt down into the gray cinders of the rail yard. A few minutes later I was in one of the freight offices, standing in front of a big window air conditioner, making a collect call home. It felt like I'd been away for years, but there was no trace of worry in my mother's voice on the line, only surprise at hearing from me in such an unusual way. Nobody had even realized I was gone.

I was dutifully retrieved later that day by my father, who quizzed me pretty closely on my ordeal and concluded, finally, that there was nothing he could get angry about, even though he'd had to drive all the way to Gadsden to fetch me home. He did think I'd overreacted—hopping a freight out of town because I'd heard a few gunshots seemed unnecessarily extreme to him—but he allowed as how fear could make people do some pretty crazy things. My father, and everybody else I lied to in the days following, seemed to have an automatic respect for what appeared to be my minor brush with a newsworthy event: I had heard gunshots at Blackie's. That was important, my father informed me, because now Blackie was missing.

Apparently, a lot had gone on while I was sweltering in the boxcar on my way to Gadsden. Tippy had panicked, to begin with, because I never showed up back at the river. So he found a policeman at the Krispy Kreme and convinced him to drive over to Blackie's to check things out. The police don't normally listen to kids, but I guess Blackie was notorious enough that even Tippy seemed like a credible witness. Once he got there, the officer found plenty of things to be suspicious of. The only thing he didn't find was Blackie. Eventually, more policemen became involved, and before long a full-scale investigation was underway. There was speculation, my father said, that Blackie had killed someone and fled the county. There were bloodstains, after all.

After he'd brought me up-to-date about the mystery and cautioned me about the dangers of playing around railroad tracks, my father had little else to say. So we rode in silence beneath Blackjack Ridge, across the Cahaba River and back down the heart of Shades Valley, through Irondale, and Mountain Brook, and finally, out to Cahaba Heights, where we pulled into our driveway just about dusk.

I scanned the yard, the street, the neighborhood, but Billy didn't seem to be around. I sat there quietly as the motor coughed itself out and waited for my father to make the first move toward the house. But he just sat there, too.

"I meant to ask you," he said at last, "if you heard how yesterday's golf tournament turned out."

"No, sir," I told him.

"Arnold Palmer took second," he said significantly. When I didn't respond, he tried again. "Second in the American Golf Classic. That's a big-money event. You know where that puts him?"

"No, sir," I said.

"Over a hundred thousand dollars in prize money for the year. No golfer in history ever did that before." He adjusted his grip on the steering wheel and stared straight ahead, as if the car hadn't yet made it home. "Young people today have got opportunities my generation never thought of," he said. "Maybe you ought to work on your golf game."

"Yes, sir," I said, and he nodded, evidently satisfied that his message had come across. But in fact I was baffled. I had no golf game. I'd never touched a golf club in my life.

∕

When the police came out to our neighborhood the next day for a second round of questioning, trying to pin down what exactly Tippy and I had both been witness to, Tippy happily volunteered the information that there had been a car in the parking lot, light blue, maybe, or sea green. He couldn't tell them it was Billy Hatcher's 1956 Plymouth. I envied him the limits of his vision. For my part, I verified everything Tippy told them, but offered no details of my own. I never even mentioned the Montgomery Baptists.

Billy, meanwhile, had decided to lie low. At first I looked for him behind every tree and beyond every doorway, worried that he might be too much even for the devil to control. But with every minute that passed, I felt more secure, because I knew that eventually Billy would figure out that he was safe. Once Billy felt safe, I thought I could feel safe, too.

By the morning of the third day, when the newspaper still supported the rumor that Blackie might have committed some heinous crime and skipped town, I guess Billy finally realized that I'd kept my mouth shut, and that no one was after him. That must have astonished him. Or maybe not, maybe he expected it. Maybe it was part of his own deal with the devil. In any case, I got a telephone call.

I heard the ringing, and a moment later my mother summoned me into the kitchen, which was in complete disarray. The kitchen was where my mother worked on her craft projects, and she was now in the last stages of assembling a mosaic-tile coffee table for the living room. She'd been working on it for weeks, following the pattern exactly, cementing each tiny piece of tile in its designated place to create an authentically random look.

"It's your cousin Billy," she said, offering me the heavy black receiver. She wore yellow rubber gloves, crusted with dried mortar, and she had to hold the phone carefully to keep it clean. "I bet he wants to hear about all the excitement."

I took the phone and put the receiver to my ear. My mother returned to the spot she had cleared for herself on the linoleum and continued sorting through the ever-diminishing heap of colorful glazed tiles.

"Hello," I said.

"How you doin' there, Taylor?" he asked.

"Doin' okay," I said.

"Seems like this town's missin' a rich nigger."

"I don't know anything about it," I told him. "I just heard some shots and took off."

My mother smiled at me and held up a blazing golden tile for me to admire.

There was a pause.

"That was a bad thing you did to my leg," Billy said. "But I know how sometimes people do things in the heat of the moment. I might be willin' to let it go."

"I'd appreciate it, Billy."

"I'm not Billy anymore," he said, his voice tightening, "not to you, anyways. I don't ever want to hear you say my name again, not till the day you fuckin' die. You understand me?"

"Yeah."

"Awright, then." A pause. "I'll see you in church."

And he hung up.

The devil had kept his end of the bargain.

✧

Later that day I found myself sitting in the smoke-filled waiting area of the Irondale police station with my mother, who had brought me in for a last official questioning. Tippy had been called in, too, but he'd come by himself, four miles on foot, because his father was at work and his mother didn't drive. She didn't walk much either, from what I'd seen. Anyway, my mother and I sat on a brown wooden bench, and Tippy sat across from us on a gray metal folding chair, tapping his bare heel on the cement floor and fidgeting with a red rabbit's foot. He didn't like being called in to the station. He thought we were in trouble for stealing coal.

We had to wait a long time to see the officer in charge of our case because there was other stuff going on, stuff that involved a lot of black people getting arrested. Half a dozen or more were brought through in handcuffs while we sat there. They were young men, mostly, although one was an angry old woman who swore a blue streak at the officer who guided her past us.

My mother didn't quite comprehend the situation.

"I don't know why they let all these coloreds go ahead of us," she whispered. "We were here first."

"Yes, ma'am," I said.

"I'm just glad we're not downtown today," she added.

By downtown my mother meant Birmingham, even though, strictly speaking, that wasn't where we lived. Cahaba Heights was a small semirural community of truck farmers and traveling salesmen a couple of miles to the southeast.

Birmingham had a lot of satellite towns like that—Homewood, Crestwood, Edgewood, Irondale, and many more—nestled safely in the lush woodlands on the Shades Valley side of Red Mountain. These were the mostly white, suburban sister communities, with tidy elementary schools and tree-lined streets and sleepy outdoor shopping centers. Across Red Mountain to the northwest lay the city itself, the real Birmingham, with its mostly black neighborhoods and steel mills and factories and large government buildings and crowded sidewalks and famous department stores.

And on the ridge between these two divergent worlds, perched precariously on the crest of Red Mountain, stood the enormous statue of Vulcan, god of the forge. Vulcan was very nearly the largest statue in the world, second only to Liberty, and he held a burning torch high above the mountaintop. Sometimes the torch was green, which meant nobody in Jefferson County had been killed in a traffic accident that day. Sometimes the torch was bright red.

"Why shouldn't we be downtown today?" I asked.

She leaned in close. "They're *protesting* again," she whispered.

"Protesting what?" I asked. There had been so many demonstrations lately it was hard to keep track. There had been the problem with the buses, and housing, and the schools. Even Ollie's Barbecue had regular picketers now because they'd refused service to somebody.

My mother fluttered her hands and frowned. "Oh, who knows," she said. "Some people just don't like the way things are."

"It's about integration," Tippy whispered across to us.

My mother stared at him in surprise. "Why, Tippy Weaver, wherever did you learn a word like that?"

"My daddy said it."

My mother straightened herself up to her lecturing height. "Well, that's fine for your daddy to say," she chided. "But it's not a word we tend to use in polite company. It gets people too stirred up." She looked at me and raised her eyebrows. "It means mixing the races."

My mother must have thought I lived on the moon.

Of course I knew what integration meant, and segregation, and discrimination, as surely as I knew that Tom Tresh had a slugging percentage of .441 in his first full year with the Yankees. Once the Cuban Missile Crisis had subsided, the Civil Rights Movement had become our spectator sport of choice, and the last five months had given every kid in the Birmingham area a crash course in race relations. Every day brought new tensions, new stories of battle, and we reveled in the secondhand excitement of it all, rooting for or against whoever made the headlines on any given day. Our city was the talk of the nation, and had been since early April, when the Reverend A.D. King's older brother Martin got arrested, along with sixty others, for leading a protest downtown. That was the first real flash point, the one that grabbed our attention, and we'd all followed the daily skirmishes from that moment on, watching the slow escalation of violence with a perverse sense of hometown pride.

It didn't matter that we were only kids. We'd been taught to pay attention to the world, because the world was out to get us. We'd been taught to fear communism, and the Russians, and UNICEF. We'd been taught that the dominoes were falling in Cambodia, and Laos, and Vietnam, and that soon we might have to put a stop to it. We'd been taught to crawl under our desks in case of a nuclear attack. By the time Civil Rights took its turn in the spotlight, we were veterans of crisis and paranoia. We knew to keep our eyes and ears open.

So even though my parents might not have kept track of the particulars, I sure as hell had. I knew the time line as well as any national newscaster.

I knew that on April 25, President Kennedy had sent his brother, the U.S. Attorney General, to meet with Governor Wallace about the crisis and ask him to intervene in the trial of the Civil Rights protesters, but that the Governor had told him to get lost.

I knew that the very next day Martin Luther King Jr. and eleven others were found guilty as charged.

I knew about the demonstration on May 3, when Police Commissioner Eugene "Bull" Connor used fire hoses and dogs against 250 protesters.

I knew about the subsequent demonstration three days later, involving thousands.

When Martin Luther King Jr. was arrested again two days after that for conducting a parade without a permit, I knew as well as the mayor how close we all were to disaster. King was turned loose later that day as a peacekeeping gesture, but within the week his brother's house was bombed.

That was when President Kennedy sent in federal troops.

Then on June 10 two students were admitted to the University of Alabama, and the Governor swore to stand in their way.

Then on June 25 the Supreme Court ruled that prayer was illegal in the schools.

I knew there were bound to be killings. I just didn't expect to see it firsthand.

"Would you like to read the comics?" my mother asked, picking up the day's paper from the low table beside the bench and depositing it across my knees. I felt immediately uncomfortable. The paper, I knew, would have a story about Blackie in it somewhere, and it disturbed me to know how wrong it would be. I'd always believed in what the newspapers told me, but now I saw that newspapers relied on stories from people as clueless as Tippy and as unreliable as me.

For the first time I saw how prejudice could shape its own surreal version of events; how, in the absence of a body, the easiest theory to believe in was the one in which Blackie had committed his own murder and then fled the scene of the crime.

I sighed and unfolded the paper. Filling the front page was a story about a massive march in Washington, D.C. Two hundred thousand protestors had rallied there to demand changes in our segregated lives. Two hundred thousand, and I realized with a pleasant sense of amazement that the Montgomery Baptists had almost certainly been among them. Martin Luther King Jr. had been there, giving a speech at the Lincoln Memorial. The article didn't say what the speech was about, but I gathered it had made an impact on the crowd.

I felt somehow reassured reading the account, and I hoped that things might keep on track, that there might not be any more bad turns in the road. I even considered praying for it, although I wasn't sure how well that would work, given my current deal with the devil. I decided to wait until Sunday and play it by ear.

I didn't know, of course, that the next Sunday would plunge us all into the darkest chaos yet, that someone would bomb the 16th Street Baptist Church and kill four Negro girls about my age.

But for the moment things looked brighter, even in my world of lies, and I felt lucky to have rolled for a few miles through the Alabama countryside with people who had someplace serious and worthwhile to go.

The train really had been bound for glory.

I was the fool who jumped off.

Chapter 4

His name, it turned out, wasn't Blackie. It was Arvin Wilson. He was twenty-six years old, the same age I am now.

Chapter 5

There's a hot, dust-laden wind that blows from the deserts of Libya called a *sirocco*—although the alternate spelling of *scirocco* is also acceptable. This wind, usually of cyclonic origin, blasts against the northern Mediterranean coast, reshaping, bit by bit, the exposed features of Italy, Malta, and Sicily. It's the harshest of winds, sometimes unsurvivable. It can scour the face from a clock.

Sirocco, I might add, appears in the dictionary just above *sir-reverence,* which has an interesting pair of meanings. It's a contraction of an expression from the sixteenth century, *saving your reverence,* and is used as a preemptive apology before a statement that might sound offensive. But it's also a term for a lump of human feces.

I know about dictionaries. After the death of Arvin Wilson, all through that fall and beyond, I lived in dictionaries. Or hid there.

My mother had finished tiling her coffee table, so now she was looking for a new project, and there I was. I'd been trying my best to disappear into my schoolwork, handing in assignments early and then taking on more for extra credit. If I was told to do half the problems on a math worksheet, I did them all. If I was told to write five pages on George Washington, I wrote ten. What I wanted was to keep my mind busy so I wouldn't have to think—but that had the unfortunate side effect of raising my grades, and my mother mistook me for a scholar. She entered me in the National Spelling Bee and installed herself as my coach.

What we discovered was that, in spite of my many other shortcomings, I did have a talent for remembering things. I won't say it was easy, memorizing column after column of words nobody ever heard of, words that had nothing to do with real life. But real life had no appeal for me then anyway, so I plunged in with full concentration and spent much of that school year sitting at our second-hand dining-room table spelling things out for my mother.

Once I'd mastered the official lists, my mother put together her own supplemental regimen of 500 likely words, and she drilled me on them until I became infallible. It paid off. By the middle of May, I was one of America's seventy-two regional champions, and my school sent me to Washington, D.C., for the finals. My mother and I traveled there by train.

Apart from the spelling bee itself, which turned out to be another big domino in my life, there was only one other moment of real consequence on that trip. My mother and I went to Arlington National Cemetery, because it was around Memorial Day and she said I had dead relatives there. My great-grandfather, James Lee Wakefield, for one, plus three great-uncles and a whole regiment of cousins twice removed. My mother's older brother Harold was there somewhere, she said, and her brother-in-law John Hatcher. That was Billy's father.

We didn't see their graves, but we saw President Kennedy's. The earth was still fresh and mounded and marked with only a temporary plaque on a steel post—this was before they enshrined the spot in granite and marble. It was raining, a slow drizzle, but not many people had their umbrellas open, I guess as a sign of respect. A big wreath of flowers lay on the lump of reddish brown dirt.

As I stood there in the quiet huddle of sightseers at the graveside, I wasn't thinking any deep thoughts. I was thinking about stealing a handful of the dirt to take home with me. Suddenly, there was a hand on my shoulder, and a large white man in a brown hat and overcoat pulled me back from the edge of the grave and shoved me roughly aside. Apparently, he wanted a better view, and since I was the smallest person in the front row, I was the one he removed. But my mother had seen what he'd done, and as he shouldered his way in to fill my spot, she walked up behind him and elbowed him in the kidneys as hard as she could. He cried out sharply and stumbled forward, tangling his legs in the low velvet ropes. And while every tourist there watched in horror, he flailed his arms and toppled face-first onto the sticky mound of mud on the president's grave. The honor guard—two marines who seemed to think this was another assassination attempt—leapt inside the ropes and grabbed the man by the legs. The crowd gave way at once, and the soldiers dragged the man from the grave and flipped him over. Then one of them stomped on the man's forearm to make him let go of the wreath of flowers. He was caked in presidential dirt, and he was screaming angrily now, but not in English, so it didn't do him any good.

But he wasn't the only one in trouble, since there were a number of witnesses who quickly spoke up to implicate my mother. Within three minutes, the foreign man, my mother, and I were all escorted from the Arlington National Cemetery grounds under armed guard.

It was my second most humiliating experience in Washington.

The most humiliating, of course, came later, at the spelling bee itself.

They stood us up on an auditorium stage in front of all the parents and some low-level reporters for the local papers and the wire services. At first everything went the way it was supposed to. I was my mother's automaton, tonelessly spelling out one useless word after another. *Xerophthalmia. Gnomon. Zyzzyva.* And gradually the little mob of mirthless children dwindled, down, and down, and down, until the end of the day, when only two contestants remained standing beneath the glare of the blue and amber stage lights. I was one of them, and a gorgeous twelve-year-old girl from Pensacola, Florida, was the other. She had almond eyes and a dark, exotic tan. Her name was Alissa.

We had the longest showdown in the history of the competition. For two full days we watched each other mouth letter after letter until we'd worked our way through the entire vocabulary booklet, plus the secret auxiliary list they kept on hand for bee emergencies. But nothing derailed us. Near the end of the second day the television-news crews came in and trained their cameras on our faces, waiting to catch the slightest quiver of a mistake. It went on and on. Five hundred words, a thousand words. And the longer we spelled, the more I seemed to love the soft, shy tones of her alphabet, and her chestnut brown hair, which shone under the harsh camera lights like ancient bronze, and her slender fingers, laced nervously in front of her, and her bright, bright eyes, which shifted involuntarily at the start of each word toward someone beyond the lights in the auditorium crowd. I worried for her, for the flawed life she must be living, the life so capsized by guilt or loneliness or fear that it drove her all the way to the finals of the National Spelling Bee. Because none of us, I then believed, could arrive at this place undamaged.

But as long as we kept every letter in its proper place, we were safe, together, floating in our own cloudless sky. That, I guess, was my first glimpse of peace in nearly a year, and I wanted us to go on eternally spelling words to each other while the whole country stood by in awe. I wanted it so much I couldn't think. And then I didn't think.

Responsibility.

So simple a word, it defies all logic that I could have stumbled over it. But I did, and Alissa disappeared from my life, back into the mystery of her own unspellable world.

I was crushed, of course, as was my mother, albeit for a different reason. But when we got back to Cahaba Heights, we discovered there was a thriving market for such high-profile failure as mine. A representative from one of the big cereal companies came to see us about doing a radio show. He said the country couldn't help but take me to its heart after I'd embarrassed myself so spectacularly on national television.

"You'll be the Sugar Puffs Kid," he said. "We'll get you a cowboy outfit."

"Why do I need an outfit for the radio?" I asked.

"Public appearances," he said.

"Why do you want me to be a cowboy?"

"Because we sponsor about a dozen of those Saturday-morning Westerns. Jesus, kid, don't you watch television? Anyway, the cowboy angle plays perfectly with the spelling bee."

I looked at him blankly.

"That kid who beat you was an Indian," he explained.

"She was?"

"Full-blooded Seminole. I thought everybody knew that."

Maybe everybody, but not me. Before the finals, I'd been too busy studying to pay much attention to what was going on around me, and afterwards I couldn't bear to turn on the news, for fear I'd see a painful rerun of myself imploding in the spotlight.

The premise he proposed for the program was simple. As the Sugar Puffs Kid, I would be the sole and permanent contestant on a phone-in quiz show. Every week I'd study up on a different topic and then go on the air as a crash-course expert. People would call in to try and stump me with obscure questions, and if they succeeded, they'd win a case of cereal. The man from the company said people would tune in and root for me because I'd already established myself as an underdog. I would be like General Custer, he said, if Custer had ever had a second chance in radio after being slaughtered by the Sioux.

So I did the show. Why not? It was easy enough to shift from dictionaries to reference books.

That's when I learned about spiders. That's also when I learned about Etruscan art, world cities, the golden age of radio, stock-car trivia, astrophysics, and the history of cheese. Sometimes I did pretty well. We taped the show locally in a suite of offices on the top floor of the Dinkler-Tutwiler Hotel in downtown Birmingham. The local version was two hours long, but then the tape editor would package it down to less than thirty minutes for the syndicated version. That allowed me three minutes of being stupid for every one minute of being smart. It was a margin I could live with.

The cereal people liked me at first, even on my bad days. And there were bad days. We tried chemical formulae once and the company had to give away forty-three cases of Sugar Puffs. But overall they seemed happy with the job I was doing. They sent me out to do public appearances at shopping centers and charity events, dressed in a cowboy outfit that came complete with red boots, a mongrammed fringed shirt, a string tie, and a chrome-plated six-gun, the Mattel *Fanner-Fifty*. Once they even worked me into a TV commercial with Sugar Puffs Pete, their cartoon groundhog. They were going to have us sing the cereal jingle together, but then they heard me sing. My end of the dialogue was finally reduced to "Yep!" "Every morning!" and "You said it, Pete!" I forget what Pete said. We never actually met.

So for a while I was a hit. My debacle at the spelling bee brought me the same wave of public sympathy that goes out to those tiny girl gymnasts when they fall off the balance beam and blow the gold medal in the Olympics. But people don't hold onto pity very long unless you keep proving yourself more and more pitiful, and the editing process saved me from that indignity. I quickly devolved into just another obscure cultural footnote, and before long I wasn't worth all the cases of Sugar Puffs it took to keep me on the air. The final blow came when a vandal broke into the studio one night and destroyed thousands of dollars' worth of equipment. Whoever did it seemed to have a particular grudge, because *The White Man spells disaster* was spray-painted on the studio walls. No one was ever arrested for it, and no radical groups ever claimed responsibility, but because this was Birmingham the cereal people feared the break-in might have been racially motivated. The last thing they wanted was a Civil Rights controversy, even if they weren't sure how Civil Rights might be involved. Shortly after my thirteenth birthday, I was canceled. They even took back their cowboy suit.

So that was that. For the next thirteen years, I lived a perfectly normal life.

Chapter 6

Normal is a relative term.

Once my show was canceled and the spotlight had dimmed for good, Billy began to make himself a subtle presence in my life. Hardly a week went by without my catching an unnerving glimpse of him lurking along the periphery of my world. Some Tuesday nights, when I played intramural basketball beneath the same gym roof he'd once thrown me from, I'd see him sitting in the stands, watching and smoking cigarettes no one dared tell him to put out. On days I mowed the yard, he'd cruise by slowly in his beat-up Plymouth, giving me a slight nod and a smile. A few times I spotted him loitering in the parking lot outside the YMCA, where I took lifeguard training on the weekends. And every now and then he'd show up in line behind me at the Jack in the Box or the Krystal, relaxed and nonchalant, as if he were only there for the burgers. He never spoke, but he always made sure I knew he was still around.

Some of these could have been chance encounters, I suppose. We all have to go places and do things, so maybe our paths were bound to cross from time to time. But there was more to it than coincidence, because Billy didn't live in Cahaba Heights anymore. He'd become a full-time college student down at Auburn, so it took some effort on his part to keep showing up in the neighborhood.

It was hard for me to imagine Billy in college, but according to Aunt Marie he was a real academic standout down there. I guess reform school had taught him to apply himself. He'd kept up his studies throughout his incarceration and, in the end, had managed to graduate only a little behind schedule from Shades Valley, the same high school I attended. Now he was a political science major on the Dean's list.

I understood the appeal college held for Billy. Vietnam was looking over his shoulder the same way he was looking over mine, and as long as he remained a student, he couldn't be drafted. I learned from his mother that he'd even signed up for ROTC, which meant the government would not only give him weapons training—which was the last thing anybody should have been doing for Billy Hatcher—but it would also pay his way through law school. Law school. I almost fell over when I heard that. But I could see what a smart choice it was. Law school meant that if the war was still going on when he got his degree, he'd enter active service as an officer in the legal corps, with no chance in hell of seeing combat.

All the relatives, including my parents, applauded this new incarnation. No one had ever come right out and said so, but everybody knew Billy was the most dangerous limb on the family tree. Now he'd become a poster child for self-improvement, a straight-A student with a legitimate future on his newly landscaped horizon. I could almost hear the collective sigh of relief.

Then suddenly he stopped coming around. I didn't notice right away. Absence doesn't announce itself the way presence does. But there was a moment one summer night just after I turned fifteen when I thought I saw him in a back booth at the Dairy Queen. When I got closer, I saw it wasn't him at all, just some skinny redneck out for a banana split. That's when I realized I hadn't seen Billy in maybe a month or more. For some reason that put me more on my guard, and I began to look for him everywhere I went. But he was gone.

My first thought was that he might be in jail or on the run. If anything like that were the case, no one in the family was likely to talk about it around me, which meant I'd have to drag it out of somebody. My mother seemed the logical choice. She and Aunt Marie talked on the phone an hour every day, and even though my mother was far less religious than her older sister, they organized church projects together nearly every weekend.

I joined her at the kitchen table one afternoon where she was working on her latest kit from the hobby shop, a ceramic-tile mosaic of a pirate head, which she planned to hang on the dining-room wall.

"Look how deep the color goes," she said, holding up a dusky gold-flecked piece of the pirate's cheekbone.

"Nice," I said.

She squeezed a drop of glue onto the back of the tile and carefully nestled it into place. "I love the milky ones especially. The glazing gives them more dimension." She smiled down at the half-completed project. "I believe I could do this for the rest of my life."

"That might get old," I suggested.

She puckered her lips and shook her head. "Why should it? Golf never gets old for your father." A slight coolness flattened her voice, but she kept her eyes on the pirate. "And you can be certain this is a far more productive use of time. I'm creating art here, Taylor. It'll still be around long after we're all gone."

I leaned in and pretended to scrutinize the mosaic. "Yeah, it's real pretty," I said, although it looked to me like the kind of project you'd give a fourth-grader on a rainy day. The notion that it might outlast me on the planet was slightly annoying.

"It's more than pretty," she corrected me, holding it up before her like a mirror. I expected the freshly glued piece to slide from its nook beneath the pirate's eyepatch, but it held fast. "This is my boon companion," she proclaimed.

My mother had no talent for art as far as I could tell, but she definitely had a gift for leaving me lost in a conversation. I had no idea what she meant, though her voice carried determination, as if she'd reached some decision about her pirate's unfinished face. She carefully set the mosaic back down and began to separate the remaining loose tiles into color groupings.

"That reminds me," I said, though nothing had, "I haven't seen Billy Hatcher around in a while. I wonder what he's up to this summer."

For the first time since I'd sat down my mother pulled her attention away from her mosaic and looked at me. Her eyes held a heaviness I hadn't noticed before, and as she stared at me, I felt transparent as a ghost. She bit her lower lip and leaned back from the table.

"Billy's taking care of his mother," she said. "Your aunt Marie's got breast cancer."

Guilt crept over me at once. I knew I was supposed to feel bad for her, but under the circumstances I just couldn't. Aunt Marie was a fundamental Baptist who regarded most everyone but Billy and my mother in terms of their transgressions, and in my fifteen years, she'd rarely said a word to me except to point out whatever I'd done wrong. I guess that was her way of improving the Christian community, but she could be pretty hard to get along with. I don't mean to say I was glad Aunt Marie had cancer. I wouldn't wish that on anybody, and especially not her because she was my mother's only sister. But my fear of Billy was overwhelming, and I couldn't help thinking that anything keeping him preoccupied was some kind of blessing.

"How bad is it?" I asked.

"It's gone into her bones," my mother said. "She's down to sixty-five pounds. But Billy's right there with her. At least she's lucky in that."

"What'll he do when school starts back up in the fall?"

"It'll be over by then," she told me and returned to sorting the tiles.

*

The graveside service took place in early August on a day so hot the men had to take off their suit coats to avoid heat prostration, while the women perched together on metal folding chairs in the shade of the funeral canopy, fanning themselves and cooing over my mother. Billy stood apart, near the cracked granite headstone of an ancestor, silently watching his mother's casket, which rested on a steel bier above the grave.

The service itself was brief because the chubby, balding minister was a substitute who'd never met Aunt Marie. He talked in boiler-plate terms about the power of Christ and how those who believed in Him could never die. Then he asked people to open their hymnals to page 432 and lift up their voices in song. A rustling murmur passed through the crowd, which I guess he took to be the sound of obedient page-turning, but, in fact, it was the sound of confusion because there weren't any hymnals. That detail escaped him, and he plowed ahead, launching into the hymn by himself, expecting everybody to follow. He got about three words in before he realized his mistake, but by then it was too late, he couldn't just stop singing. If he'd picked one of the standard hymns, there would have been no problem, people would have jumped onboard, but instead he'd chosen some obscure song about asking Jesus to be the stone wall against the darkness, which nobody had ever heard before. A couple of people tried to hum along out of politeness, but that just made it sound like he was being accompanied by cattle.

After the service we all moved to the picnic area between the cemetery and the church, where large bowls and platters of food simmered beneath waxed paper on a long utility table brought out from the Sunday-school room. I loaded my plate with chicken legs and potato salad and joined my parents at one of the card tables set up in the lee of the church.

I'd barely settled onto the webbing of the aluminum beach chair when Billy walked over with his own plate of food and sat down in the chair across from me. It was the closest I'd been to him in years. I filled my mouth with potato salad and tried to concentrate on a carpenter ant running zigzag patterns on the red-checked tablecloth.

"Fine turnout," my father said, gesturing to the crowd with a forkful of baked beans. "A lot of people thought highly of your mother, Billy."

"Yessir," Billy said quietly. "And Jesus heads the list."

"No doubt," my father agreed.

My mother hiccupped a small sob and squeezed Billy's hand.

"Marie was my tether," she said. "I'm afraid I'll drift away without her here."

"Christ is our tether now," Billy told her.

The sincerity in his voice made me look up, and what I saw was disorienting. This was not the Billy I knew. No cocky smirk, no threat in his eye. His hair was combed, parted neatly on the side. He looked meek and tidy in his starched white shirt and tightly knotted tie. His shoulders were slumped forward, rounded, as if they'd just that minute shrugged off a tremendous weight. He could have been an encyclopedia salesman.

I didn't dare speak, and since neither of my parents had ever been able to regard Christ as anything but a conversation stopper, we all just ate in silence under the cloud of Billy's last sentence.

Finally, when I'd eaten enough chicken to justify leaving the table, I took my plate to the garbage barrel and dumped it inside. A thick swarm of flies rose above the metal rim, slow and lazy in the afternoon heat. As I turned toward the dessert table, I found Billy blocking my way.

"I need to speak with you, Taylor," he said, reaching past me to drop his empty plate in on top of mine.

A fly landed on my cheek, but I was too frozen to react. Billy brushed it away for me.

"Let's get away from this garbage," he suggested. He put an arm around my shoulder and guided me along the gravel driveway toward the rear of the church, into the shade of a drooping hemlock.

"Far enough," I said, forcing myself to a stop. I shrugged free of his grip and took a step away.

"All right, we'll talk here." He looked around and smiled. "Between the church and the cemetery. That's a good spot for us, Taylor. It tells the whole story."

"What story?"

"The story of my redemption," he answered. "I've been washed in the Blood of the Lamb."

I'd pretty much fallen away from religion when I was eleven, thanks to Billy, but I knew the basics. Jesus saved the wicked, giving new life to anyone who asked, no matter the crime. From crooked tax collectors to crucified thieves, everybody had an equal shot at paradise. Still, Billy Hatcher was the least likely candidate I could imagine for a conversion experience.

"I didn't know you even went to church," I said.

"I didn't used to. But the Lord knew how to hunt me down," he said. "He found me at a drive-in movie."

"You got redeemed at the drive-in?"

"Yep." He lowered his head sheepishly. "It was one of those spiritual-uplift movies put out by the Southern Baptist Crusade. I saw it the very first night I came home from school to take care of Mama."

I'd heard all my life that the Lord moved in mysterious ways. But still. The idea that a movie could turn Billy Hatcher into a Born-Again Christian was more miracle than I could ever have hoped for.

"What was it about?" I asked.

"It was about me, Taylor—some young asshole headed straight to Hell until he found his salvation in Christ." He glanced toward his mother's grave, where mortuary assistants had begun disassembling the canopy. "When it was over, some fella came on the loudspeaker and said anybody who'd been changed in his heart ought to come down front and testify. So I did. Then they signed me up, and I've been on the straight and narrow ever since."

The fly from the garbage barrel buzzed between us. I blotted my forearm across my brow.

"That's. . . good, Billy."

A sudden wrenching noise made us both turn again toward the cemetery, where the grave-diggers had somehow botched the job of lowering Billy's mother into the ground. The bier had collapsed on one side, dumping the coffin headfirst into the hole. Now one gleaming blue end protruded obscenely above the red dirt pile. The chief mortician, who had been overseeing the procedure, swore loudly at his crew as they scrambled to haul the fumbled coffin back out of the grave.

Instinctively, I braced myself for some sort of explosion on Billy's part, but he offered no reaction at all, which was even more chilling.

"I know it's hard for you take in," he said, his voice smooth and reassuring. "I've been an evil person, and nobody knows it better than you. But all that's over with. I've found God's grace."

"But what about . . . what about what happened?"

He shook his head and let out a long breath. "I'm not that person anymore, Taylor," he explained. "I'm still guilty, I understand that, and I'll have to atone for my sins. But from here on out I'll be doing God's work."

"You're gonna be a minister?"

He squinted up at the steeple for a moment, then looked down at his shoes. "There's other ways to serve. I'll be whatever God's got in mind." He looked up at me again. "You know, Moses killed a man once," he said softly. "Look how he turned out."

"I guess that's right," I said.

"But here's the thing, Taylor." His voice turned worried and apologetic. "God's willing to give me a clean slate. But that won't hardly matter unless you're willing to do the same."

Whether this trap had been set by Billy or by Jesus, I saw no way out of it. He sounded like a true convert—his tone was gentle and his demeanor was calm. His words seemed infused with remorse for what he'd done and who he'd been. But if my parents had taught me anything, it was that people tended to backslide.

"I won't say anything," I told him.

The relief in his smile was almost poignant, as if he believed I'd just saved both our lives. He hugged me tightly, and I felt the genuine warmth of the gesture. But there was something spiderlike about it, too, and I couldn't keep from shuddering.

"We're family," he said, not yet letting go. "We know how to stick together."

Over his shoulder I saw the grave-diggers wrestling with Aunt Marie's coffin, shoving it finally below ground.

Chapter 7

But family ties weren't what they used to be. The Old South was disappearing. The tendrils of kinship that bound most Bible Belt communities were breaking down, and each succeeding generation was more likely than the last to cut its losses and move on. Billy's mother had blamed it on the twin evils of television and the automobile, which she claimed encouraged wanderlust in the teen-aged mind. I couldn't really say she was wrong. My own mother was less specific, as was her nature, saying only that one certainty in life was that we would eventually disappear from one another's lives. I thought she was just being philosophical. It turned out she was serving notice.

She left us in March of my freshman year of college. I came home from Tuscaloosa for spring break, and she was gone. Her clothes were missing from her closet, her Picasso print of *Don Quixote* was missing from the bathroom, and her Studebaker was missing from the driveway. I pointed all this out to my father, who merely shrugged and settled deeper into his easy chair with the evening newspaper.

"But she's gone," I said.

"The note's on the refrigerator."

The handwriting was so tiny it barely looked like writing at all.

"What the hell is this?" I said. The note was three or four sentences, but except for the last two words, which seemed to be *down under,* I couldn't make it out.

"I think that second word is *dying,*" my father called from the other room. "And there's a word that might be *drowned* in that third line. The police couldn't read it either. They asked me if I thought it was a suicide note."

I rejoined him in the living room. "The police?"

"Oh, sure," he said, lowering the paper. "I called them right away, just as a formality."

I looked back through the doorway at the note, still stuck to the refrigerator by a magnet shaped like a Siamese cat. *"Dying? Drowned?"*

"Relax," he told me. "I'm pretty sure she was just being metaphorical. She took her passport."

"You don't find any of this upsetting?"

He paused to think the question over. "No," he said finally. "I guess I don't. That's probably one reason she left."

"But you're my parents," I protested.

"Taylor, you must have noticed that your mother and I never spoke to each other."

"That's how parents are," I said.

"I can see how you might think that. But your mother's had one foot out the door for a long time. Now that you're all settled in college, I guess there wasn't much left to keep her here."

"You should have done something."

"I tried to get her interested in golf, but she didn't want any part of it, and I wasn't about to start doing art projects. They call that irreconcilable differences." He raised the paper between us. "But don't you worry—I'm sure we'll hear from her again."

He turned out to be right, of course. When I came home at the end of the term, he met me at the door with a fresh development.

"Your mother's divorcing me," he announced cheerfully.

"You saw her?"

"Nope. I was at work. But she left another note."

I checked the refrigerator, and there it was, fixed in place beneath the same magnetic Siamese cat, next to what looked like a big ragged nail hole. This second note was quite a bit longer than the first, although the handwriting still verged on the microscopic.

"Why does she write like this?" I asked. "She never wrote this way before."

"I think it's meant to be a reflection of the diminished state of her self-esteem," my father said.

"What makes you think that?" I asked.

"Says so in the note." He handed me a magnifying glass, and the third sentence seemed to bear him out. I could also decipher the phrases, *nothing to live for,* and *dock of a bay.*

"She's got Otis Redding lyrics in here," I said.

"That's the way I see it," my father agreed. "The police are back to the suicide theory, though."

"She says *down under* again."

My father nodded. "I'm guessing Australia."

"And it looks like there's a name here," I said.

My father chuckled. "Yeah, I think it's Martin Luther."

"King?" I asked, studying the script closely.

"No, just Martin Luther. She nailed the divorce papers to the refrigerator door."

And that was the penultimate word from my mother.

✴

My father, on the other hand, was just getting started. He'd built up a great stock portfolio, having bought a lot of IBM and Xerox in the early days, and even after the divorce he was in reasonably sound financial shape. He quit his job with Ray-O-Vac, where he'd been the top salesman in the flashlight-battery division for the last twenty years.

I don't think either of us realized what a stabilizing influence my mother had been in his life. Now that she was gone, he was rudderless, with only a vague and unrealistic sense of who he was and what his limitations were. Now that all his battery- selling days were behind him, his new dream was to become a professional golfer, and he pursued that goal with a sort of desperate fervor that transformed him from a bland, brown-suited businessman into a flamboyantly attired cartoon. He spent countless hours reading golf magazines and instruction books. He mowed a small circle in the backyard and buried a tin can in the middle of it to practice his putting. His vocabulary narrowed, so that everything he had to say about the world now came filtered through incomprehensible golf clichés. He set his sights on the PGA-qualifying school.

He had the dedication; the problem was he had no ability. On his best day he couldn't have made the local high-school team. Nevertheless, golf did alter his life. One overcast afternoon, while working on his chip shots at the par-three course on the Greensprings Highway outside Homewood, he met Lucy LaVonn, who sold cosmetics for the Mary Kay company, and who had just taken up the game herself.

It was love at first sight. God knows why. My father was a delusional, balding, potbellied, freshly divorced, unemployed, bad golfer who had recently developed a slight stutter. Lucy LaVonn was a plump, giggling, heavily made-up technical-school dropout with a tall bushel of curly black hair and a signature Mary Kay lip line drawn thickly in pencil around her mouth. She was two years older than me.

He brought her home from the golf course for dinner one night. I kept quiet until the hamburgers were gone and Lucy had excused herself to go to the bathroom to delineate her mouth.

"What the hell's wrong with you?" I asked him.

"Lucy thinks I'm deep," he said. "Nobody ever t-t-told me that before. I feel like I eagled a par five."

"Maybe she's a moron," I suggested.

"Oh, I th-think she probably is," he said. "But that works okay for me."

"You're more than twice her age," I pointed out.

He shrugged. "It's not how you dr-drive, it's how you arrive."

There was nothing I could say to that, so I just refolded my napkin and carried my dirty plate to the kitchen.

A week later they got married.

It wasn't one of those happy-ever-after deals, though. The occasional stutter became more pronounced, and eventually he couldn't get a sentence out in under a minute. His golf game deteriorated from awful to God-awful, and he developed tremors in his hands. He couldn't keep his balance when he walked on sloping ground, and his neck became so stiff he had trouble looking down at a golf ball.

He checked himself into the new research hospital in Birmingham and they practically turned him inside out trying to come up with a name for what he had. Finally, they found one: progressive supra-nuclear palsy. And though the disease would take its own sweet time picking him to pieces, stretching out the devastation across half a dozen more years, the prognosis was certain. In slow motion the dominoes of his nervous system would fall, one by one. First he would forget how to speak. Then he would forget how to walk, how to move, how to urinate, how to swallow. Finally, he would forget how to breathe.

He would not, however, forget who he was. The body would fall away, but the mind would stay clear, a mute prisoner in an ever-diminishing jailhouse. Memory would retain its pristine polish, and he would still know every detail of his own identity, and of his past. But with each new day he would become more and more a frustrated spectator, a soul evicted from the present moment of its life, a ghost locked just outside the world's front door, banging soundlessly to be let back in.

In my father I saw reflected one of the most complete forms of crippling. Unable to say what he knew, unable to do what needed doing. Of all the fates available to us, that may rank among the saddest.

In the early stages of this long decline, I developed an unexpected appreciation for Lucy LaVonn Wakefield. She was loyal as a lapdog, and though she often cried hysterically, she still tended to all my father's needs. At first it was just a matter of finishing his sentences for him, and she could do that because she knew all the golf terminology. Later, she happily changed the television channels for him, and later still, she did a good job of mashing up his food for easy chewing. But things just kept getting messier, and when my father stopped hitting the toilet bowl, she decided it was time to call in the professionals.

I couldn't really blame her. At that point he was essentially a 200-lb. infant in constant need of supervision and care.

What Lucy needed was a beefy male nurse, someone with medical training, but also someone who could lift my father out of bed and carry him wherever he needed to go. She interviewed five or six likely candidates, but only one was willing to live on the premises, and that was what Lucy preferred. So she hired Steve Rigotoli, a bulked-up and hairy angel of mercy fresh out of nursing school.

It was love at first sight. God knows why.

*

As for me, after a low-key, low-profile career as a history major at the University of Alabama, I settled into a low-key, low- profile job right there on campus. I worked as an assistant research librarian, and my primary responsibility was to look things up for lazy or dim-witted students. If someone wanted to know how many horses died in the Battle of Gettysburg, or who the Secret Service agent was who jumped on the back of Kennedy's limo in Dallas, I was the person to ask.

No one did ask, however. Most undergraduates were too uninformed even to realize I was there to help them, so very little of my time was spent doing actual research. Most of my day involved operating the microfilm camera, turning the current events of daily newspapers into miniature celluloid images, and then packing them away for the future. That was the part of the job I loved, the part that let me choose which details of our collective recorded life were worth saving. I scanned the pages for informative articles, significant events, remarkable people. From a historian's point of view, mine was a position of great power. If I didn't put the news on microfilm, it decomposed as quickly as the paper it was printed on. Without my intervention, news eventually stopped being news and faded instead to a dim and unreliable recollection. I was the informational gatekeeper of the times. In a hundred or two hundred years, I told myself, researchers would comb through my files to rediscover the spirit of the age, and what they would find there was entirely up to me. Whatever I left for them to sift through and puzzle over would be called history.

So that was the life I'd settled into, a life so academically hermit-like I might as well have lived in a cave. Since I'd skipped the frat scene as an undergrad, I had no ongoing social connections in Tuscaloosa, and all the Cahaba Heights kids I'd grown up with had scattered themselves across the country searching for careers. Even Tippy Weaver had moved on. For him, finishing high school had been a challenge, but he'd made it. The last I'd heard his uncle had landed him a job doing minor public relations work for the railroad. So just about everyone in my peer group—if I could call it that— seemed to have found a path more productive than my own.

I was slow to realize it, though, because the delusion that kept me going was so seductive. I'd convinced myself that the act of selectively recording history was equal to the act of making history. I thought that by putting my thumbprint on the world's archival records, I was shaping the future's perception of events and therefore making a difference in the world. What I failed to see at the time was that making a difference after the fact is the same as making no difference at all.

My moment of epiphany came on a Tuesday at about ten in the morning. I was alone in the camera room casually scanning the artifact of the moment, a copy of the previous day's issue of the *Montgomery Ledger*. It was early election season—the primaries were a couple of weeks away—so there was a lot of garbage to sort through. Everyone running for office was trying to manufacture headlines, but most of the press conferences and news releases and speeches and announcements were nothing more than blatant bids for publicity. It was tough to separate the nuggets of real news from the slag heap of political rhetoric and public-relations strategies. But the news was always there, if you looked for it.

On this particular day it was easy to find—page one, right-hand column, leading headline:

> *Attorney General's Office wins conviction*
> *in 1963 Civil Rights slaying*

By that time I'd learned that some news stories appeared simply because they contributed to the public record, others because they highlighted some sort of oddity, and still others because they shed light on some larger issue. The stories I tended to rescue from oblivion were the ones that fit all three categories, and this one was an obvious candidate. The resolution of a fifteen-year-old murder case was definitely a strange blip that belonged in the public record. Throw Civil Rights into the mix, and you had a story with legitimate historical potential.

I admit to being biased in that regard. The Civil Rights Movement, I had come to believe, was the most far-reaching story of my lifetime—more enduring than either war or technology, and more relevant than space exploration. What people did to one another on a daily basis was the real measure of a civilization, not the grandstanding ability to put a golfer on the moon.

I was so certain the story belonged in my files I almost didn't bother to read it. But as I brought the camera lens into focus, details inadvertently emerged, bits and pieces caught my eye, and soon I found myself reading and rereading the entire world-altering account.

After years of dead-end investigations, the attorney general's office, it seemed, had somehow located five witnesses who were willing to come forward and give testimony in a long-neglected case. The legwork was credited to an enterprising assistant attorney general who had made the case his own personal crusade for justice. His determination had paid off. All five witnesses had identified Clay Hartsell, a seventy-year-old white supremacist, as the man who, in the summer of 1963, put four bullets into the back of a black businessman and then dumped his body along Pinchgut Creek, at the mouth of Shades Valley east of Birmingham. Mr. Hartsell himself never denied the charges.

The victim had been the owner of an after-hours establishment called Blackie's Gentlemen's Club. His name was Arvin Wilson.

The assistant attorney general was William R. Hatcher.

Mr. Hatcher, the article pointed out, was now emerging as a front-runner in the race for attorney general.

Chapter 8

Billy had been busy since I'd seen him last. He'd earned his law degree and, after a couple of low-profile years as a captain in the army, had landed a job as a union negotiator with the steelworkers in Birmingham, where he won a reputation as a fierce crusader for the working class. That led to a job as a prosecutor in the state attorney general's office, and before long he was the rising protégé of the attorney general himself.

On my twenty-fifth birthday, I'd even received a card from my great-aunt Edith with the news that *Reader's Digest* was about to do a profile on him, a puff piece, it sounded like, portraying him as a prototypical American success story. Their take on Billy was pure Hollywood: he was the plucky youth who, after a few early mistakes in judgment, had now dedicated his life to serving the greater public good.

It bothered me that such a stalwart publication could be on Billy's side. I'd always had a fondness for *Reader's Digest*. My parents used to keep the current issue displayed on the coffee table and the back issues stacked neatly on a shelf above the toilet. They'd been loyal subscribers, and sometimes my mother had read articles or features aloud to me, things like "I Am Joe's Liver," or "It Pays to Increase Your Word Power." I always felt nostalgic whenever I saw a copy. What was I supposed to feel now? If I couldn't count on *Reader's Digest* to know the whole story, where did that leave me? If the printed word could be so unreliable, even in the upper echelons of journalism, then history itself was on shaky ground.

Now, of course, I'm more flexible in my views. Now I can say without the slightest sense of alarm that recorded history is as unreliable as the weather.

But on the day I read about Arvin Wilson's ancient murder and Clay Hartsell's fresh conviction, I still believed in microfilm and the need to get the story straight. Over the objection of Mrs. Pullman, the head research librarian, I left work early and made the three-hour trip to Montgomery, to the office of the *Ledger*.

The man I came to see, the author of the article, was Arch Hathaway, and when I asked a woman at a tidy counter near the front of the office where I could find him, she seemed surprised, as if no one had ever asked to see him before. But she did point him out to me, at the back of the room, slumped over his desk, with his face pressed against the grillwork of a small electric fan and his mouth hanging open. Even from a distance, I could see the heavy sweat stains radiating from his armpits and spotting the front of his shirt. The strange thing was that the office was air-conditioned.

The picture didn't improve as I got closer. Arch Hathaway was a disheveled man, with scraggly, slept-on hair and one side of his white shirttail hanging out of his pants. His checkered sport coat, which was balled into a heap, rested in the OUT box on his scarred walnut desk. The front edge of the desktop was covered in package-wrapping tape, presumably to keep the splintered veneer from tearing holes in his clothing or scratching his thick arms. He was seriously overweight, and the folds around his neck had the dingy gray cast of half-scrubbed ink stains, as if he'd used a newspaper to blot away his sweat.

As I arrived at his desk, he lifted his left hand to acknowledge my presence, but kept his face to the fan.

"I'm Taylor Wakefield," I said. "The lady up front said you're Arch Hathaway."

"News or human interest?" he asked. His voice was reedy and higher pitched than I'd expected, and he sounded somehow disappointed, as if he'd already decided to be bored by my answer.

"I'm not sure what you mean," I said.

He turned his head slightly toward me and frowned. "I only do hard news," he explained. "If you're here because Lassie saved some fuckin' kittens from the well, you need to talk to Elliot." He pointed toward a desk on the other side of the room, where a slimmer, neater young man in a blue blazer was furiously typing away. "Elliot handles all the warm-and-fuzzy crap."

"I'm here about Arvin Wilson," I told him.

"Who's Arvin Wilson?"

"You did a story about him."

He pulled his face from the fan grate and leaned back in his chair. A checkerboard of red indentations marked his forehead. "I just write the news, pal, I don't fuckin' memorize it."

"He got killed fifteen years ago. There was an article in yesterday's paper."

He laughed. "Damn, we're slow." He swiveled his chair toward an elderly man pouring coffee from a percolator at a table against the wall. "Hey, Durwood," he called, but the man didn't respond. He lobbed an art gum eraser onto the tabletop. It bounced around crazily, knocking over a stack of Styrofoam cups, but the man pretended not to notice. "Hey! This guy here says it took us fifteen years to write a story. Sounds like one of your screwups."

The man peered at us over the top of his wire-rimmed glasses. "I imagine he means the Clay Hartsell case. It was yesterday's lead, for Christ's sake. It had your name on it."

"Clay Hartsell—oh, shit, yeah, the hobbyhorse story." He swiveled his chair to face me. "I know what you're talking about now." He narrowed his eyes. "But look, sport, if you're one of Mr. Hartsell's relatives come to tell me what a good ol' boy he is, I don't need it."

"No, I'm not related to Mr. Hartsell," I said. "I'm related to the other side."

Arch Hathaway snorted. "Kid, I've only seen Arvin Wilson in photographs, but I gotta tell you, I don't see much family resemblance."

"No, it's the prosecution I'm connected to. My cousin's the assistant attorney general. William Hatcher."

He eyes widened and he nodded his head. "Hatcher, huh? Well, then I'll be sure not to call him an asshole."

"I don't care what you call him," I said. "I'm just here to tell you the story got it wrong. Clay Hartsell's not guilty."

He sighed and lifted his shirtfront to let the fan blow across his stomach. "Five witnesses say different. I've talked to the man—he's an old-time racist, pure and simple. A dyed-in-the-wool bigot. Half the guy's wardrobe is bedsheets."

"He still didn't do it," I said.

"So why don't you go tell your cousin?" he asked. "I'm sure he'll straighten it all out for you."

I couldn't decide whether I'd told him too much or not enough. Arch Hathaway didn't inspire confidence, and I couldn't quite make myself spell it all out for him.

"I can't really talk to my cousin about it," I said. "It's complicated."

He smiled. "Oh, I get it. A conspiracy in the attorney general's office."

I hadn't thought about it in those terms until I heard him say it, but that's what it was.

"What if there were another witness?" I asked. "Somebody who said it happened some other way."

"Then it's five against one, sport. You do the math."

In all the years I'd failed to tell the truth about Arvin Wilson's death, it had never once occurred to me that I might be powerless to set things right, that if I did finally speak up, it would make no difference.

Arch Hathaway slid open his bottom drawer and took out a bag of miniature powdered doughnuts. He daintily plucked one from the bag and popped it into his mouth.

"So you won't do anything?" I asked.

He took another doughnut from the bag and examined it. "Sorry, pal." He pushed the second doughnut into his mouth and licked the powder from his fingers. "I won't shit where I eat." He leaned forward in his chair and spoke in a softer voice. "Let's say you're right. All you see is one bad story. But I'm in that building every day—I get a hundred stories a year from the attorney general's office. I rely on those people to keep me informed so I can do my job. If I break their frickin' hobbyhorse, they'll never talk to me again."

"What's a hobbyhorse?"

"It's their high-profile news story, sport. The headline-maker. The one they're gonna ride all the way to reelection. I'm sure as hell not about to piss everybody off just because you heard a different version of events from fifteen years ago."

"I didn't hear a different version," I told him. "I saw one."

He put one last doughnut in his mouth and replaced the bag in the drawer. Then he laced his fingers across his stomach and sat there breathing noisily as he chewed.

"You and who else?" he asked.

"Nobody. Just me."

He shook his head. "Well, you see, there's the problem. We get about ten people a week in here with crazy stories. I don't just mean the weirdo stuff, although we get our share of that, too—UFOs in Aunt Gussie's cornfield, or some crap like that. But we also get a lot of dangerous stories, the kind that could mess up people's lives. Maybe somebody tells us the governor is a child molester, or the state treasurer just robbed a liquor store, or the mayor was a Nazi war criminal. You'd be amazed at what people come up with just to get their names in the paper. That's why we ask for two sources. It's the only safe way to rock the boat."

"So without a second source, you won't lift a finger—is that it?"

He grinned. "Oh, I'm always willing to do that." He held his fist up between us and flipped his middle finger in my direction. It bore a thick gold band with a large diamond set in the center.

"What if one source is all there is? I mean, sometimes that's the way things happen."

"Maybe that's the way *things* happen," he said. "But that's not the way *news* happens. Not for this paper, anyway." He swiveled back and forth a few times, gazing around the room as if he were looking for an idea. Then he stopped suddenly and smiled. "What you need is an outfit with lower standards." He leaned over his desk and scribbled something on a small yellow notepad. "And I think I know just the place. Here," he said, ripping out the sheet and handing it to me. "Go fuck up somebody else's career."

I looked at the slip of paper. "What's *Alacast?*" I asked.

"The Alabama Broadcasting Network," he said. "They run a whole butt-load of radio stations around the state and Channel 11 television here in Montgomery. If you want to get a piece of news out far and fast, Alacast can definitely do it."

"You think they might run the story without a second source?"

He clasped his hands behind his head and licked the sugar from the corners of his mouth. "Hell, sport, these guys are innovators," he said. "Sometimes they'll go without any source at all."

Chapter 9

In my childhood radio days, I once did a show on Christian martyrs, and though I can't say why, much of that information has stayed with me.

The first Christian martyr was Stephen, who was stoned to death for being too critical of local priests and politicians. He called them "stiff-necked people, uncircumcised in heart and ears."

Saint Sebastian had two bouts with martyrdom. He began by offending Emperor Diocletian, who had him tied to a tree and shot full of arrows. By some miracle, Sebastian survived. He returned to face the emperor and told him that arrows were no match for the grace of God. Diocletian was impressed and promised not to make that mistake again. Then he took Sebastian to an amphitheatre and had a troop of soldiers club him into a number of small, flat pieces.

I think the lesson in that, from the traditional Sunday-school point of view, was supposed to be something about unswerving faith and the courage of one's convictions. But here's what I got from it: *Don't push your luck.*

Maybe I just don't get the whole martyrdom thing. Martyrs all have a bulldog tenacity that holds them to an idea, whereas my mind drifts like partial cloud cover. I could never stand up before an official mob and summarize my proof of their stupidity because I know the consequences too well. Organized lunatics are notoriously bad sports. I wouldn't tangle with them any more than I'd try to thread a cobra through my belt loops.

If somebody tied me to a post and piled up the kindling, I could become pretty flexible with my doctrines. Like Galileo. When he got hauled up before the Inquisition, he took the reasonable way out, swearing the whole thing was a simple misunderstanding, that his telescope didn't really work, that the world was as flat as an untuned harpsichord, that stars were angels winking in the sky. I admire that kind of practicality.

Martyrs have been variously burned, boiled, skinned, crucified, drowned, stabbed, dismembered, thrown from high places, dragged behind horses, trampled beneath horses, pulled between horses, hanged, poisoned, eaten by lions, eaten by dogs, eaten by ants, and eaten by other people.

My meeting with Arch Hathaway got me thinking along these lines, and by the time I reached the offices of the Alabama Broadcasting Network, I was having second thoughts about what I was doing. Maybe I should have gone to the police. Maybe I should have stayed home.

The network building was hardly reassuring. It was a squat yellow cinder-block complex in a run-down residential neighborhood just two streets behind the state capitol building. A Rambler jacked up on blocks dripped oil by the curb, and the small plot of yard, though pleasantly shaded by large elm trees on either side of the buckled sidewalk, was overgrown with crabgrass and thistle. There was no evidence at all that this was the nerve center of a media empire. The place looked more like an abandoned dentist's office.

The inside was no better. The network didn't even have this eyesore to itself, but shared the office space with two chiropractors, a father/son periodontal team, an optometrist having a going-out-of-business sale, and a discount urologist who specialized in venereal disease. The urologist, in fact, had a framed newspaper article mounted on the wall outside his door with a headline saying exactly that: *Discount urologist specializes in venereal disease.* I didn't stop to read the story.

The plain balsa door at the dim end of the hallway was the only one without a nameplate glued to it, and at first I thought it might open to the janitor's closet. But slivers of light leaked out around the loose-fitting frame, and easy typing filtered through the door, echoing along the Masonite walls like a steady rain. I pushed open the door and leaned inside. A slight, middle-aged woman with heavily rouged cheeks was hunched over a humming Smith-Corona. She didn't notice me at first, so I kept still and waited for her to break stride.

She never did. She was the most consistent typist I'd ever seen, so smooth, so measured, she didn't even stumble at the carriage return, but inched her way down the page, word after word, line after line, monotonous and perfect. Around her the windowless office was lined with filing cabinets, and the floor was so littered with stacks of unopened cardboard boxes that her desk seemed haphazardly adrift in the middle of the room. Her brown dress was the color of the paneled walls. In one corner, an electric bug-zapper dangled at eye level from a metal crosspiece of the suspended ceiling, and the dried remains of a dozen moths lay scattered beneath it on the linoleum tile floor.

"Excuse me," I said as she rolled a fresh sheet of paper into the machine. She looked up quickly, a number-2 pencil clenched in her teeth. "I'm not sure I've got the right place . . ."

She took the pencil from her teeth and waved it vaguely toward the corridor behind me.

"The urology clinic is across the hall."

I blinked, and she was typing again. "I'm sorry to interrupt," I said. "But is this the Alabama Broadcasting Network?"

She raised her delicate hands from the Smith-Corona and leaned forward on her elbows, palms up and fingers twitching.

"Who wants to know?"

"I'm Taylor Wakefield," I said, taking a step forward. "I've got some information I need to talk to someone about."

"Through there," she said, indicating the narrow inner hallway to her left. "Just poke around until you find somebody. But don't open the broadcast closet if the red light's on."

I stepped tentatively through the opening. To my immediate right stood a door covered with black soundproofing tiles. A plastic reindeer head brooded above the frame, its nose glowing a bright red. At the opposite end of the hall a second soundproofed door seemed to double as a bulletin board, displaying a jumble of envelopes, notebook pages, and black-and-white photographs. In between, two other rooms branched off the hallway. The first was a bathroom with no door on it; the second was a large windowless workspace flooded with pink fluorescent light.

This second room was apparently the hub of the operation. Six or seven large Ampex reel-to-reel tape machines sat jammed together unevenly on the long tables that lined the cinder-block walls, giving the place the look of a small, crowded repair shop. Two floor-model reel-to-reelers, tall as refrigerators and obviously homemade, stood wedged into two of the corners. There was no finished casing on either machine, just gray metal plates bolted to the front frame where the reels were mounted; colored wires dangled from the open sides. Four bulky manual typewriters and three telephones filled most of the remaining table space, along with a coffeemaker, a few stray food wrappers and blue plastic cups, countless wads of yellow paper, and a tottering stack of tape reels. Just inside the doorway, a ticker-machine printed steadily onto a roll of newsprint that unspooled slowly to the floor.

Two men sat perched on wooden stools at the least cluttered table. The larger of the two, a middle-aged man with his white shirtsleeves rolled to his elbows, was bent low over the table, studying some minute piece of intestine from a tape recorder that lay disemboweled in front of him. The other man, dressed more neatly in a coat and tie, sat typing something onto a small sheet of yellow paper.

"Excuse me," I said, leaning through the doorway. Neither man turned around.

"Talk to Alf," said the older man, the one working on the tape machine. "I'm busy." Then he sighed and ran his fingers through his shiny black hair.

"Deadline minus forty," said the younger man, who paused in his typing to hold his left arm over his head. A large digital watch flashed numbers at the end of his coat sleeve. Thirty-nine, thirty-eight, thirty-seven. Then he lowered his arm and resumed typing.

"Are you Alf?" I asked him.

"I guess you don't watch television," he said, still focused on his typing. His voice expanded into a resonant, self-mocking tone. *"I'm Danny Larson, Capitol Reporter for the WWII Channel 11 News Team."*

"Where can I find Alf?" I asked.

"Wait three more seconds," he said, his voice returning to normal. "He'll be the guy shoving your butt out of the doorway." He pulled the yellow sheet from the typewriter and held it up over his head.

I looked into the quiet hallway behind me, and as I did, the door beneath Rudolph's glowing nose swung open and a thin man with a bushy brown mustache rushed from the broadcast booth. He was dressed in jeans and a denim work shirt and looked more like a ranch-hand than a network executive. I stepped aside as he rounded the corner into the workroom.

"Is it ready?" he asked as he snatched the yellow sheet from Danny Larson's hand.

"Nope," Danny Larson told him. "We're half a minute short. You'll have to fill."

"What about a public service spot?" he asked, glancing through the text on the yellow sheet. "Sarge, what's handy?"

The older man, Sarge, picked up a tape cartridge from a stack on one of the reel-to-reel machines. "School bus safety," he said. "It's a fifteen-second cart."

"That'll do."

"But check the machine, Alf," Sarge cautioned him. "The swimming-safety cart might still be cued up from this morning."

Alf grabbed the cartridge and hurried back to the booth, which was, I could see, nothing but an oversized closet outfitted with a control panel, a reading lamp, a microphone, and a metal folding chair. He slammed the door behind him.

Danny Larson shifted his attention to some sort of log sheet taped to the wall in front of him, while Sarge continued to study the pieces of his tape recorder. There was nothing for me to do but wait, so I stood quietly in the doorway, listening to the soft clack and whir of the ticker machine.

Five minutes later, Rudolph's nose blinked off and Alf emerged from the broadcast closet carrying a stack of tape cartridges.

"How did it go?" Sarge asked absently as Alf walked by me into the workroom.

"That depends," he said, shoving the cartridges onto a shelf just inside the door. "How tall does corn get?"

"Seven, eight feet maybe," Danny Larson told him.

"Then we may get phone calls. I promised twelve."

Sarge finally looked up from his work. "What do you mean you promised twelve?"

"The tape broke on the Magic-Grow-Fertilizer spot. I had to do the commercial live."

"How the hell could you think corn was twelve feet high?" Sarge demanded.

"Blind optimism, I guess." He turned to me. "Who's this guy?"

"I'm Taylor Wakefield," I said.

Danny Larson turned from his log sheets and stared at me.

"You're Taylor Wakefield?"

"I need to talk to somebody about a story."

Alf opened his mouth but didn't say anything. The sudden confusion on his face was so apparent I wondered if I'd been sent here as a joke. Then he looked at Sarge, who rose from his stool and took a cautious step toward me. Sarge was a tall man, several inches taller than me, but he craned his neck down to scrutinize my face. At first he seemed as perplexed as Alf. But then he slowly smiled and extended his hand.

"I'm Jim Presley," he said. "You probably don't remember me, but I used to be your engineer."

I shook his hand and smiled back, but I had no idea what he was talking about. I was here to break my deal with the devil, and the only engineer I could think of was one I'd never met—the one who hauled me from the freight yards in Irondale, the one who took the Montgomery Baptists to their own sure place in history. Jim Presley was obviously not that guy.

"It was my first job after the army," he added. "You used to call me Sarge. We put a pretty good show together."

Then I remembered. Fourteen years earlier, using spare parts from countless junked and obsolete machines, Sarge Presley had rigged up a functioning sound studio at the Dinkler-Tutwiler Hotel so I could do a radio show. He had maintained all the equipment, he had run the control board, and he had handled all the incoming calls. He had even edited the final version of each week's program, trimming out as much of my stupidity as the time slot would allow. Sarge was the wizard who had kept our show on the air.

"My God, Sarge, it's great to see you," I said.

Danny Larson stood up and tucked his shirt more tightly into his waistband. "I'm Danny," he told me again, smiling. "I used to listen to your show all the time. You were awesome."

"Sarge knew how to edit," I said. "He could have made a squeak-toy sound smart."

Sarge put his arm around my shoulder and gave me a hug. "What's a parsec?" he asked, slipping into the deeper tones of his radio voice.

"Three-point-two-six light-years," I answered, somewhat reluctantly. The trained-chimp aspect of the show had always bothered me a little.

"When was the word *technology* coined?"

"Eighteen-thirty-eight."

"Who was Andrew Jackson's personal physician during the War of 1812?" He was feeding me leftovers from some of our old shows. I was surprised he remembered the questions.

"Charles Clinton McKinney."

"Who was the only civilian casualty in the Battle of Gettysburg?"

"Jenny Wade."

"Why are manhole covers round?"

"It's the only shape that can't be accidentally dropped through the hole."

The brain is a basic binary computer. If you put garbage in, you get garbage out.

"I've got a question for the expert," said Alf, leaning back against the wire-service machine and folding his arms. "What are you here for?"

Similar to the sirocco is the *harmattan,* which is a seasonal version of a simoon wind along the west coast of Africa. It's hot, dust-laden, and violent. Natives of the region know never to face it directly. It can drive a piece of grit straight through to the brain.

I sighed. "That's a complicated question. I think I'm here to screw up my life."

Alf looked at me for a long moment, and nodded his head. "You've come to the right place," he said. "We know all the shortcuts."

I had no doubt about that. I had no doubt about anything, in fact. I was on the verge of reconnecting myself with history, and history is not an altogether bad place to be. Most people think of it as stagnant, a fixed record of events, but that's wrong. True history is pure motion, a river of independent moments sweeping us through time. New doors open unexpectedly, new lines of migration charge across the land. Opportunity is never more than a single revolution away. And so, in the twenty-five-minute gap between broadcasts, I settled onto a stool in the Alacast workroom and told Alf, Jim, and Danny the story of Arvin Wilson's murder.

They believed me. Simple as that.

The word *martyr* comes from the Greek. It means witness.

Chapter 10

Radio waves. Wherever we go they're with us, bathing us in a cascade of signals, passing ceaselessly through our bodies as if we weren't even there. The right receiver, tuned properly, can pick up "Louie, Louie" on the polar ice cap, "Wild Thing" in the remotest heart of the jungle. There's no escaping the programming of our own terrestrial broadcasts. All night long, the frequency spectrum reflects off the ionosphere in a crisscrossing of sky waves. We're awash in the secret languages of unheard music and talk.

But there's more to it than that. Not all radio signals are terrestrial. Most, in fact, originate elsewhere. Some come from the outer layers of the sun, flaring up erratically in massive black eruptions. Some seep mysteriously from nearby planetary atmospheres or from gas clouds deep inside the Milky Way. Some waves arise from rapid pulsations of neutron stars, or from the exploding nuclei of distant galaxies, or from quasars. Some radiate from leisurely chain reactions among the drifting hydrogen atoms of interstellar space. They come from anywhere, essentially, bombarding us from infinite sources, from every angle in every time. And as near as we can tell, each unearthly wave carries the same unvarying load: static.

That's a lot of dead airtime.

Or maybe it's not dead air at all. Maybe static is a language in itself, spelling everything out for us in a round-the-clock universal broadcast. Maybe the problem is we aren't tuned in.

In any case, Alf del Tasorian had strong opinions about the primary function of a news network. Under his direction, Alacast specialized in generating static.

"We're the junkyard dogs in this town," he said, as he pounded on the cork-covered door at the end of the Alacast hallway. "It's our job to bite government in the ass."

That sounded a little extreme to me, and I said so.

Alf stopped his pounding and looked at me with what could have passed for wide-eyed innocence. "Sometimes extremism is the only logical option, Taylor. That's what civil disobedience is all about."

"I'm not here to start a revolution," I told him.

"Revolution's the natural state, kiddo," he said. "You want to stop a bad guy, we'll give you a shot at it. But keep in mind that bad guys come in bunches. Sometimes you have to forget the rules and improvise."

This was not reassuring. I'd steeped my life in academic protocol, in the careful connecting of dots that creates an organized filing system. Plunging off into the quicksand of improvisation was no way to conduct proper research.

"I thought reporters had to stick to the facts," I said.

"Reporters don't write from the witness stand, Taylor. We're storytellers. We create narratives to help people make sense out of random events. We make movies out of snapshots."

"Events aren't random," I said. "Every fact leads to another." I felt confident of this. The cause-and-effect streamline of history was clear proof.

"Wrong," he said curtly. "Every fact leads to a *million* others. But we can't include a million facts, so we pick the most interesting handful."

"What if they're the wrong ones?" I asked.

He shook his head, and I could see he was annoyed by my slow learning curve.

"It doesn't matter which ones you pick," he said, the impatience creeping into his voice. "Facts are just a starting point. Imagination is what shapes the news. The weather, too." He grabbed the brass knob and rattled the door in the frame. "If you want to be a weatherman, that's the first thing you'll have to learn."

Weatherman. That wasn't a job I'd ever imagined for myself. Who would? Weathermen were famously unreliable, always getting the blame for ruined picnics and rained-out ball games. But that was the job he was offering, and for some reason it sounded right for me, though I couldn't say why. Maybe just the oddity of it. Maybe the timing. Their current weatherman was stepping down to run for office, they told me, and they had to fill the spot right away. Alf was convinced that my leftover celebrity would appeal to their core audience. I knew he was overestimating my status, but Sarge and Danny urged him to take me in to see the president right away.

It wasn't as if I had any better options. My career in the library basement in Tuscaloosa seemed to have gone about as far as it could, and being on the radio was something I was used to. Besides, I'd been in hibernation long enough. Now that I'd spoken up about my cousin Billy, it seemed appropriate to be here in Montgomery, close to whatever might happen next.

"Weather isn't a story you make up in the newsroom," I objected.

"The forecast is. Nobody's got the facts on tomorrow's weather— too many variables. Every prediction you've ever heard was just some guy's calculated guesswork. Fiction. We could probably have a chimp pick forecasts out of a hat and nobody would know the difference."

Alf probably meant this as encouragement, but I now had more misgivings than ever. I'd reached a point of radical change in my life, and I was willing to do just about anything to make up for past transgressions. But I had no idea how to present myself for a job as their weather chimp, and I began to feel grateful that President Wilderman wouldn't open his office door.

But then, of course, he did open it, and my misgivings multiplied.

"This better be important," President Wilderman said, squinting out at us both. He was younger than I'd expected, about the same age as Alf, though better groomed. His cheeks were flushed, and as he focused his attention on me, his whole face turned wary, a little confused, like a man opening the door to strangers in the middle of the night. This impression was heightened by the fact that he was wearing pajamas, light blue and neatly pressed, maybe fresh from the package. Over these he wore a smartly tied dark blue silken bathrobe, also neatly pressed, suggesting that he was an immaculate sleeper. His left arm hung casually at his side, where in a loose grip he held a blue-steel handgun, which he tapped absently against his thigh, the barrel toward the floor.

"Good news for a change," Alf said, seemingly oblivious to the odd particulars of his boss's appearance.

"Bad news is more interesting," President Wilderman replied, but he stepped back from the doorway and motioned us inside with his gun.

The office was small but obsessively neat—no errant papers cluttering his gleaming mahogany desk, no leftover coffee mugs on the windowsill, no dust on the blinds. On the paneled walls hung a tidy array of framed photographs of President Wilderman shaking hands with men in business suits, some of them politicians I recognized. The bookcase below the window held no books, but displayed an impressive collection of trophies and plaques, presumably attesting to his phenomenal success in the news business. His desktop, too, seemed more a display area than a work space, and featured an eclectic assortment of souvenirs and keepsakes—among which were an autographed baseball on a small stand, a clear-plastic case of Civil War bullets, a shining silver railroad spike, and a minutely detailed model of a three-masted schooner.

President Wilderman walked around behind his desk and sat down, while Alf and I perched on the two straight chairs across from him. He eyed me more closely.

"So what's this about?" he asked.

"I've found your replacement," Alf told him.

"I'm a hard man to replace." He propped his feet on the edge of his desk, careful not to disturb any of his knickknacks. I got the feeling he was trying to look relaxed, but it wasn't working. There was something artificial in his pose, as if he'd never had his feet on the furniture before. Not that he looked awkward—he was smooth all the way. Every hair was in place, and every movement was well timed. The man was an eight-by-ten glossy of himself. Even the bottoms of his slippers were clean.

"This is Taylor Wakefield," Alf said. "He's the best weatherman in the mid-South."

President Wilderman frowned. "After me, you mean."

"Right," Alf agreed. "Taylor, this is Rusty Wilderman, president of the network."

"No need to call me Mr. Wilderman—I'm just regular Rusty." He touched the gun barrel to his forehead in a small salute.

"Taylor's been in broadcasting for years," Alf continued. "We're lucky he's available."

Rusty narrowed his eyes and studied me. "You think he's got the right look?"

"Absolutely."

Rusty nodded. "Okay, then. Welcome aboard, Taylor."

"You mean I'm hired?" I asked.

Rusty looked puzzled. "Sure. Why not?"

"He thought you'd want to hear more about his credentials," Alf volunteered.

Rusty smiled. "Waste of time. We like to move fast around here." He leaned forward and set the gun on the desk next to the baseball. "Did Alf give you the job description?"

"Not exactly," I said.

"Good. I don't believe in job descriptions. We're a small outfit— a mom-and-pop network, you might say. We all pitch in wherever we're needed, any time of the day or night."

"News is a full-time proposition," Alf agreed.

"So's the weather," Rusty added. "We're not clock-punchers here. Twelve, sixteen hours a day, six or seven days a week, that's the kind of commitment it takes." He was struck by an afterthought. "But don't put in for overtime."

"Don't worry," Alf said. "He's not in it for the money. He just loves the weather."

"I know how he feels." Rusty took his feet off his desk and swiveled toward me. "I trust you'll take good care of it."

"Like it was his very own," Alf assured him.

"That's fine, then," he said. "So, Taylor, any questions before you get started?"

"Why are you wearing pajamas?" I asked.

Rusty nodded approvingly. "A sharp eye for detail." He ran his palm across the shiny sleeve of the bathrobe. "This is a costume," he explained. "I've been rehearsing for a commercial."

Alf's watch began to beep softly.

"Gotta go," he said. "Taylor, see me before you leave and we'll iron out the details." Then he bolted from the office, leaving me suddenly alone with Rusty, who looked at his own watch and chuckled.

"Alf's on the air in eight seconds," he said. He picked up the model of the three-masted schooner and turned the tiny wheel at the helm. I heard a click, followed by the staccato electronic beat of the Alacast theme music. Rusty set the novelty radio down between us and stared at it as the music faded away and Alf's crackling voice emerged from tiny speakers in the ship's portholes.

"News is pretty easy to do on short notice," Rusty continued, easing the prow of the ship toward me for better reception. "You can just go though a recap of whatever you can remember from the last report. Weather's easy, too, as long as you take a look out the window before you go on the air. Sports is the only tricky one, because you can't just make up scores—that's something we learned the hard way."

His gaze settled on the baseball, and he smiled. "Know what this is?" he asked, lifting the ball ceremoniously from its display perch and offering it to me. I took the ball and examined it. There was a scribble of writing between the parallel seams.

"An autographed baseball," I said.

Rusty's smile broadened. "That, my friend, is a Jackie Robinson home-run ball."

"You saw Jackie Robinson play?"

"No, no, I bought it from a guy."

I examined the signature closely.

"This says *Pee Wee Reese*."

"They were teammates," Rusty said, as if that explained it. I set the ball back onto its stand.

Then Rusty turned up the volume on the schooner and we listened as Alf moved smoothly through brief news stories about a single-engine plane crash outside Dothan, an illicit love affair in the office of the registrar of deeds in Jefferson County, the accidental electrocution of a power-company lineman in Mobile, and an unverified sighting of the Pope in downtown Gadsden.

"Get yourself a watch with an alarm on it," Rusty told me. "We live by the clock. Sixty-seven radio stations out there depend on us to feed them a five-minute broadcast every half hour. Every second we miss is dead airtime all over the state."

"Thanks for the advice."

"If you were a news reporter, I'd also suggest you get one of these—" He held up the gun for my scrutiny, presenting it sideways, like a pitchman holding up the preferred deodorant or the best bar of soap. "But you might not need one to do the weather."

In my early radio days, I'd done an hour-long show on the special features and idiosyncrasies of popular handguns, and I recognized this one as a Walther PPK. Rusty took a holster from his desk drawer and shoved the Walther snugly into place.

"Why would anybody need a gun to do the news?" I asked.

"Sometimes people don't like what we say," he said, wrapping the leather belt around the holster and placing it on the desktop between us. "For the inarticulate, guns are an alternate means of self-expression. It helps if they know you can shoot back."

I could see the muzzle gaping toward me through the bottom of the holster, so I shifted sideways to remove myself from the potential line of fire. Meanwhile, Alf, speaking from the tiny ship, launched into a commercial for an insurance company, telling us we couldn't afford to put off that kind of protection any longer.

"So everybody around here carries guns?"

"I can't speak for everyone. But I carry a nickel-plated Smith & Wesson 38. Darla carries the snub-nosed version. The shorter barrel lets it fit in her purse."

"Who's Darla?"

"My wife. You probably saw her at the desk out front. She's our first line of defense."

"So what about the PPK?" I asked, pointing to the Walther.

"Piece of junk. Jams every time I use it. But it looks good on TV, so I'm putting it in my commercials."

"Change your ammunition," I said.

A voice other than Alf's lumbered into a gravelly prerecorded promotion for highway safety, and Rusty turned off the radio.

"What?"

"Walthers don't jam without a reason. The problem's usually in the ammunition. Some companies use a low-grade powder that doesn't have enough kick to eject the first shell from the chamber."

"Is that right?" he asked.

"My guess is you've been buying Japanese bullets from discount houses. Upgrade your ammunition and you won't have any problem."

He nodded. "I'll give it a try." He swiveled back and forth a few times, then waggled a finger in my direction. "By the way, we do have a dress code. You'll need a proper outfit for the TV segments."

"Something conservative, you mean."

He shook his head. "Conservative is for anchormen." He pulled open his center drawer and rummaged for a moment, then drew out a pink sheet of paper and handed it across to me. The heading read, *Clothing Guidelines for Alacast Employees.* "Stay away from those blazers with insignias on the pockets—they're for sportscasters. Weathermen need to look more jaunty. A plaid, or a check, maybe. Something you might wear to a Rotary Club barbecue. The idea is to look avuncular."

"Thanks," I said, folding the dress code and tucking it into my hip pocket.

"No dark plaids, though," he cautioned me. "Anything dark reads as sedate, and sedate clothing suggests a person who sits down a lot, a person who spends his time indoors. That's the wrong image for a weatherman."

We sat in silence for what seemed a long while after that, both of us staring stupidly at the gun and holster. Then it occurred to me that if I waited for Rusty to restart the conversation, he might ask me something technical about weather.

"What did you mean about using the gun in commercials?" I asked.

He brightened at once. "For my campaign. The gun, the pj's— they're part of an ad concept for my TV spots. I'm still polishing the script, but the premise has great demographic appeal." He put his arms out to the side, inviting me to take in the full picture. "See, it's like I'm so dedicated I got up in the middle of the night to arrest somebody. Voters respond to that kind of dedication." He smoothed the lapels of his robe, ready for the camera.

"What are you running for?" I felt obliged to ask.

"Didn't Alf tell you?" A smile broke out across his face. He slid open the bottom drawer of his desk and fished out a campaign bumper sticker, which he held across his chest like a warning label:

RUSTY WILDERMAN FOR ATTORNEY GENERAL

"That seems to be a popular office," I said.

"Yeah, there's a bunch of us running. I've got the edge, though. I know how to sell an image."

"Why do you want to be attorney general?"

He shrugged. "Gotta start somewhere."

Another silence settled over the soundproofed room. I cast about for some new source of conversation.

"What's that?" I asked, pointing to the silver railroad spike.

He brightened again. "Public service award from Southern Railways. We did a series on derailments." He leaned back in his chair and plucked a framed photograph from the wall behind him. "That's me shaking hands with the governor," he said as he handed the frame across to me. I had no interest in the photo but looked anyway to be polite. Right away I noticed two remarkable things.

The first was that it didn't fit Rusty Wilderman's description. The governor was in the picture, all right, but he was sitting off to the side, not shaking hands with anybody.

The second was that I recognized the man who really was shaking hands with Rusty Wilderman. He wasn't a politician at all, he was a young public-relations rep for the railroad, and even though he'd already faded from Rusty's memory, he stood rock steady in mine. Tippy Weaver grinned broadly out at me from the souvenir photo, the silver spike gleaming in his raised left hand.

I should have known right then what kind of storm was coming.

Chapter 11

Tell the truth and take what comes, that was the decision it had taken me fifteen years to make. In those fifteen years I'd had time to imagine virtually every consequence that might befall me as a result of my overdue confession, the dark options ranging from jail time all the way to sudden death. A job as a weatherman was one outcome I never would have predicted.

Naturally, I had reservations, most of which stemmed from the fact that I was unqualified in the field of meteorology. As far as the next day's weather was concerned, my guess was no better than anybody else's, and I assumed this would prove a liability.

I was wrong. Rusty Wilderman had already lowered the bar considerably in that regard. He knew next to nothing about cold fronts or tropical depressions. For him it was all about appearances, looking the way a weatherman ought to look, and that part of the job came naturally to him. Projecting the right image was Rusty's stock-in-trade. He'd spent his twenties working as a male model, which was how he'd made the business contacts to finance his network. Those trophies and citations I'd seen in his office hadn't been for anything he'd done in broadcast journalism, they were awards from the advertising industry. He'd sold everything from used cars to hair coloring, and for him the weather had been just one more product to pedal. In Rusty's world, actual knowledge was less important than a lint-free sport coat and a happy-go-lucky brand of patter. Making people believe in his sincerity was all the job required.

Now he was in his mid-thirties, and looking like a weatherman wasn't enough for him anymore. Instead he wanted to look like a politician, and that meant he had to get elected to something. After a careful analysis of the way various statewide races were shaping up, he'd set his sights on becoming attorney general. He had no qualifications for the office, but he did have high name recognition among potential voters, and that alone made him a viable candidate.

But there was a stumbling block. The FCC had rules about broadcasters running for office. Even though he owned the network, he couldn't use it to promote himself in the race unless he was willing to donate equal time to every rival candidate. He was far too cheap to take that kind of hit in revenue, and because he understood appearances, he realized it would look bad for him to continue as an on-air personality during the campaign. People would think he was unethical. So the logical course of action was to find a temporary replacement and step down as the network's weatherman. I happened along at an opportune time.

That's one theory of history, of course—that someone always happens along at an opportune time. Or inopportune, depending on who gets shot. For better or worse that someone becomes a point of intersection where larger forces culminate. Where opposing forces collide.

I didn't know quite what to make of the fact that Rusty Wilderman and my cousin Billy were both running for attorney general. Neither one would get my vote. They were like different sides of the same counterfeit coin.

But at least I now had a team to play for. The Alabama Broadcasting Network. Alacast. I could scarcely believe that I'd blundered into such a high-profile job with such a high-profile organization.

"I don't know a thing about operating meteorological equipment," I told Alf as we sat in the newsroom filling out the necessary paperwork to make my hiring official.

"No problem there," he said. "We don't have any. All you've got to do is read the zone forecasts that come in over the AP wire."

"That's all?"

"For the radio spots, yeah, that's pretty much it. The TV broadcasts are a little more involved because you'll be on camera and there's more airtime to fill. But I'm sure that won't be a problem."

"Why not?" The hourly radio broadcasts didn't worry me, but television was new territory.

Alf looked up from the stack of papers. "Because we really don't care how you fill it."

"As long as I talk about the weather, you mean."

"No, once you get the forecast out of the way, you can talk about whatever you want. Send out birthday wishes to old people. Congratulate couples on their golden-wedding anniversaries. Quote famous philosophers. Rusty used to tell stories about his vacations. Hell, Taylor, you were a radio whiz kid. You could fill three minutes in your sleep." He put the completed application form in front of me and handed me a ballpoint pen.

"But I don't know how to work the broadcast equipment, either."

"Details," he said, dismissing my ignorance with a wave of his hand. "Sarge can bring you up to speed in two hours. It's not that complicated. I'll give you a complete schedule of your duties so you can stay on track."

"I just wouldn't want to make the network look bad," I told him, carefully writing my name beside the X.

He barked out a laugh. "Taylor, I don't think you understand the mission statement here yet."

"What is it?"

"We don't have one." He scooped up the signature page and stuck it into a manila file. "We're a disreputable experiment in outlaw journalism."

He then proceeded to fill me in on all the pertinent history of the network. It was a disturbing account, but I suppose in some sense the success of the Alabama Broadcasting Network lay in the very fact that it had no normal standards, no past to live up to. Or very little, anyway. Channel 11 TV had been around forever, but the radio branch of the empire was only nine months old, and that was nine reckless months of fly-by-night muckraking, of going out on all the wrong limbs, of not caring how many retractions had to be broadcast later. Alacast was an anomaly in the journalism industry, a brash upstart of an organization with a kamikaze approach to gathering and dispensing information. As news director, Alf had already been fined twice by the FCC for violations of standards and practices. Several court actions were in the works, including two initiated by the governor's office.

But people were listening, that was the mystery of it all, and ad revenues were high. Alacast had become the odd darling of the moment, the tabloid of the airwaves, offering hourly updates on everything sleazy or grotesque that may or may not have happened around the state that day. Crooked politicians, gruesome crimes, sex scandals, UFO sightings—Alacast reveled in it all. The point was not so much to inform people as to leave them feeling vaguely uneasy, no longer certain of those bland bureaucracies that ran the civil aspects of their world.

So that was the outfit I'd signed on to work with. Alacast was a bottom-feeding news operation known for its gross inaccuracies and its growing number of pending lawsuits. Its president was oblivious, and its receptionist was armed.

"You'll catch on soon enough," Alf assured me. "Just give people something to talk about, and you'll do fine."

Something to talk about. Sure, I could do that, I could be that kind of weatherman. I'd always been a quick study, so it wouldn't take me long to learn the basics. After that, well, I'd do what Alf suggested—I'd improvise. I'd say things no weatherman had ever said before.

Chapter 12

As I mentioned, I majored in history. My specialty was Medieval Europe, which was the subject area for my senior honors thesis. Most students will say they arrived at a major because of a natural interest in the material, or because they were inspired by some gifted scholar. I blame my eighth-grade English teacher, who made me memorize that poem about two roads diverging in the woods.

Take the road less traveled by, that was the gist of it. Maybe that's good literature, but it's not good advice. If every time the road splits you take the narrow fork, pretty soon things are bound to start closing in. Before you know it, there's no room left to turn around.

That's how I got to be a medievalist. I mean, in college if you keep taking the road less traveled by, sooner or later you end up in Medieval Studies. It's the elephant graveyard of the humanities.

I don't mean that in a negative way. It's just that most of the material that survived from the period was written by philosophers and clerics, and most of their works were dry religious tracts aimed at resolving the contradiction between free will and preordination in the providential universe. For a span of almost nine hundred years, from St. Augustine to Thomas Aquinas, virtually everything written dealt in one way or another with this single issue, which was delineated by the two overriding questions of medieval dialectical theology:

1. *What the hell am I doing here?*
2. *Who the hell is responsible?*

For years I'd sided with free will, believing I was the culprit, the sole architect of my own guilt-ridden predicament. But now that I'd begun to take action, to set wheels in motion, as it were, the more I noticed larger wheels that seemed to be encompassing my own. Yes, I was finally attempting to do something. But that didn't mean I was in control of the situation, and I had no idea what the outcome might be. Gears were turning all around me, setting both my pace and my direction. I was a passenger inside a mechanism much larger than any I had known.

Or not. Which is always the definitive rebuttal in the argument between free will and determinism. That was the insight four years of tuition had bought me.

So whether it was my own idea or something ordained by the cosmos, when I left the network that afternoon, instead of driving back to my apartment in Tuscaloosa, I decided to head for my father's house in Birmingham. His place was an hour and a half closer, after all, and I was supposed to start my weatherman duties the following dawn.

On the way out of Montgomery, I stopped at a pay phone to call my boss to tell her I wouldn't be working at the library anymore.

"That's great," she said. "We were cutting your position anyway."

I hadn't dropped in on my father in over a month, so I was a little apprehensive about seeing him. The disease was relentless in dismantling his abilities, and each time I came to visit, a few more building blocks had disappeared from his personality. He was like a fading photocopy of himself, and sometimes it was difficult to pinpoint whatever level of communication was still open to us. Every reunion required that I gauge some new degree of loss.

The front door was locked, as usual. Lucy LaVonn Wakefield was skittish about intruders and kept all entryways secured even when everyone was home, and even in broad daylight. I had a key to the side door of the garage, so I let myself in that way, carefully avoiding the infrared beams of the new alarm system Lucy had recently installed, which she said was to guarantee her peace of mind. Total waste of money. Lucy did have her good qualities—she was cheerful, hard-working, frugal, considerate, and in her own way, loyal. She was a good cook and a tidy housekeeper. But she spooked easily, having little more fortitude than a hamster. She would never feel completely safe.

Lucy was in the family room, cuddling on the sofa with Steve. They were watching a game show, something with a big spinning wheel that determined all the prizes.

"I'm here," I said from the kitchen doorway, and she jumped, her terror reflex easily outmuscling Steve's beefy arm, draped protectively around her shoulder. Popcorn went everywhere.

"My gracious, Taylor," she laughed. "You just about scared the life out of me."

"Sorry," I said. "Hey, Steve. How's it going?"

"Not too shabby," Steve answered. "I'm getting pretty used to her jumps." He held up his beer can. "Looky there—didn't spill a drop."

"Good man," I said.

He twisted around to face me. "Say, Taylor, there's a box of fried chicken in the fridge, if you want any."

"Yeah, thanks."

"But don't touch the Jell-O," Lucy warned. "That's for your father."

I pulled out the glass dish and looked into the bright unnatural green of my father's standard dinner. There were only pear pieces suspended in the gelatin, which was a bad sign. It meant his throat muscles had degenerated too much for him to handle the stringy fibers of a pineapple chunk or a wedge of mandarin orange.

"You want me to take him a bowl?" I asked.

"No, honey, it's not chilled enough yet," she said. "I just put it in awhile ago."

I took out the red and white box of chicken and closed the refrigerator door. "How's he been doing?" I asked. I put the box on the table and looked inside. All the breasts and legs were gone, so I plucked out a damp wing and carefully pulled it apart to expose the two good bites of dark meat. It wasn't much of a dinner, but at least it killed my appetite.

Steve pointed the remote control at the TV and turned down the sound. "Bob's a fighter. He keeps hanging in there." He stood and stretched, then picked a stray piece of popcorn from the neckline of his blue hospital scrubs, his choice of uniform around the house. "I gave him a bath about an hour ago. If he's still awake, he'll be real happy to see you."

"What if he's asleep?" I asked, dropping the bones into the garbage pail. "Should I leave him alone?"

Steve puckered his lips in thought. "Nah, go ahead and wake him up. Don't know what good sleep'll do him."

"It's coming up on prime time anyway," Lucy added. "Thank God he's still got television." She settled back into the sofa, her attention snared once again by the spinning wheel of prizes.

Steve rubbed his biceps. "I can bring him down if you want."

"That's okay, I'll just go stick my head in for a minute." I rinsed the cold grease from my fingers and headed for the stairs.

"Ignore the mess," Lucy called after me. "I'd have straightened up if I knew you were coming."

"Messes don't bother me," I called back, and in this case it wasn't a lie.

My father's room was dim in the twilight. I turned on the television at the foot of his bed, and the soft blue glow washed over him. The volume control was broken on this particular set, stuck forever in the mute position. Lucy was saving up for a new Sony Trinitron, but for now silent programming was my father's only option. In the early stages of the disease, Steve had suggested that the volume problem might even be therapeutic, that the lack of sound would force my father to work his mind more, to pay closer attention to what was happening on the screen.

But as I looked at my father's semiconscious face in the pale flood of half-light, I realized how useless that tactic had become. His mind was finished jumping through hoops, at least as far as the external world was concerned. His decline had now carried him across too many borders even to look back from. As he stared disinterestedly at both me and the TV set facing him from the rising darkness, it occurred to me that he may not have been able to tell which was the machine and which was his son.

"Hi, Dad," I offered, softly. "It's Taylor. Thought I'd drop by for a visit." I stepped around to the side of the bed and patted the bedspread at the bump of his knee. The gesture felt odd to me, but I didn't know what else to do. My father kept staring toward the television.

"It smells pretty good in here," I said, noticing the lavender-like fragrance enveloping the bed. That was one of many things I had to give Steve credit for—he kept my father's room clean and fresh, free of any sickroom odors. Little bowls of his homemade floral potpourri were placed strategically around the room. Steve really did seem to care for my father, and I felt lucky that Lucy had found him.

My father breathed a barely audible sigh.

"I got a new job," I told him. "I'm going to be a weatherman. Maybe you'll see me on TV."

His eyes drifted shut, then reopened fully and froze there. I waited, thinking he might try to speak, but he just stared ahead, wide-eyed and still, like a woodsman startled by an unexpected sound beyond the campfire. Maybe a pain had shot through him, or more likely the ongoing breakdown of his nervous system had triggered a simple reflex. Random muscle action was common to the disease. But maybe he was signaling me, letting me know he was there.

"I thought I might stay with y'all for a while, maybe move back into my old room in the basement. Just for a few weeks, until I can get a place in Montgomery. If it's okay with Steve and Lucy."

Steve and Lucy. They'd been a loving couple for half a year now, and that was one piece of knowledge my father had taken with him on his long descent. He never told me what he thought about losing Lucy to a young, healthy mesomorph like Steve, but somehow I don't think it bothered him. Emotional attachment had never been his strong suit. He and Lucy had been anchored by the golf they played together, and once that dropped out of the equation, all they had left was the mutual burden of his illness. Lucy still had a few good decades left, and it was inevitable she would find someone else to drive the golf cart. My father understood that, I feel certain. It might even have been a relief to know that someone else had become the center of Lucy's wobbling universe.

His muscles began to relax again, and the craggy furrows disappeared from his forehead. His eyes settled into a more neutral gaze, as if one more tiny light had just gone out. I stood for a while looking down at the unreadable expression on my father's face, thinking how normal it was to see him like this. Our relationship at that very moment, with him nearly comatose and me standing idly by, was not significantly different from what it had always been. In some ways this current version of my father was the purest expression of who he really was. He'd always been present, without being attached.

And there I was, my father's son, waiting at the head of the line, ready to carry on the tradition.

I didn't want that, I didn't want to become the world's most perfect rerun of my father. Avoiding it would be difficult, though, because the transformation was already pretty far along. My father had let a single obsession—golf—replace all the deeper human content in his life. History had been my hiding place, my golf. For fifteen years I'd kept a constant, focused eye on the past, fearful of being overtaken by whatever harpies had been born for me that bloody day in Birmingham. Now those harpies had broken through into the present, the beating of their wings was all around me, and one way or another, my obsession with Arvin Wilson's death was about to resolve itself.

But then what? Assuming I was still alive, what would be left for me after I'd done my civic duty and betrayed my born-again cousin? The only thing I seemed to have staked a meagre future on was talking to strangers about the weather, and that sounded dull even by my standards. A sudden tiredness poured through my arms and legs like sand. I slumped onto the edge of my father's bed, and stared with him blankly at the soundless blue glow of the game show.

The program seemed elementary and slow, but something about it intrigued me. The contestants took turns spelling things out, one random letter at a time, piecing together the parts of an arcane riddle. Bit by bit, the clues piled up. Letters became words, words became phrases. Eventually, the answer made itself known.

The stiff-haired woman who first deciphered the code began to jump and clap her hands in spontaneous delight, and all at once I felt a surge of hope. I understood this show, and what it offered. The providential universe was taking on all comers. The message hidden in the game had been there from the start, preordained and waiting. Free will lay in the guesswork that uncovered it, that revealed it to the patient folks at home.

Free will. If choice were something real, there might yet be a way to sidestep the fate of my father, to reanimate myself, to reconnect with the emotional current or whatever it was you might call that jazzed pulse of longing that makes the heart thrive.

I wasn't incapable. I'd felt the lightning once already in my life, briefly, at a unique and isolated moment in my otherwise dingy past. Maybe what I needed was to go back into the alphabet of my own sorry history, back to the only time in my experience when the words were all spelled right, and stake a claim on that one flutter, that one unfettered pang of happiness.

As crazy as I knew it seemed, I had to find Alissa.

Chapter 13

In some ways, I was a natural choice for weatherman. The motions of the sky had always intrigued me. When I was in Sunday school and too young to separate the figurative from the literal, I got the idea that the sky was one big holding tank for God. I learned early to keep an eye on the happenings overhead, to watch out for sudden shifts in God's demeanor, every puff of cloud appearing as an inscrutable manifestation of the divine. Ultimately, that put me outside the realm of the Baptists, Methodists, and Presbyterians of the neighborhood. I was more inclined to count myself among the Druids, who took every quirk of Nature as a sign.

But even as a Druid, I was a backslider. Technology got me, as it gets almost everyone. That's why it's tough to be a Druid in the world today. The sky has its moments, but television puts on more reliable shows.

I don't think the Druids were particularly opposed to technological progress; they just weren't any good at it. Take Stonehenge, for example. The outer circle was originally made up of thirty sandstone blocks, each one thirty feet long and weighing over twenty-eight tons. Thirty more stones were balanced on top of them. Inside that first circle was a second ring of sixty stones, and inside that were two more sets forming two large horseshoes, one inside the other. At the center of it all lay a sixteen-foot sandstone slab, and eighty yards to the east stood a single stone monolith. This intricate and precisely calibrated setup was surrounded by an earthen wall three hundred and twenty feet in diameter. And what was the purpose behind this almost imponderable feat of engineering? It was a calendar. At dawn on the summer solstice the shadow of the eastern monolith would fall across the sandstone slab—assuming, of course, a bright, clear English morning. When rain was in the forecast—or mist, or fog, or haze, or even low clouds on the horizon—the whole thing was a bust. Better luck next year.

So for all its modern success as a tourist attraction, Stonehenge was essentially just a one-day calendar with a weather-dependent design flaw. That's an amazing imbalance between form and function. In practical terms, that pile of rocks might well be the most embarrassing expression of technology on the entire time line of human history. It's no wonder the Druids let it fall into ruin. The first time some Hittite trader brought a desk calendar up from Phoenicia the whole thing became obsolete.

The point is not that the Druids were stupid. They simply operated under a different set of assumptions. Their priorities were strictly pre–Industrial Revolution, so they had no concept of mechanical refinement, mass production, or even obsolescence. To the primeval Druid, the notion of technological progress did not exist.

Broadcast journalism, on the other hand, was a favored godchild of technology. The field was a haven for mechanical tinkerers, for lovers of gadgetry. I was fairly certain my Druidic sensibilities would put me at a disadvantage. There would undoubtedly be complex pieces of equipment for me to operate, and I was someone who could barely work a toaster.

I arrived at the network that first morning early. The hog report, which was ancillary to my weatherman duties, was supposed to air at 5 a.m., so I showed up at a quarter past four and waited on the outside steps. Sarge drove up around 4:57.

"Amateurs come early," he said, unlocking the building. I followed him down the corridor to the office door, which he opened without any fumbling of keys. He walked quickly through all the rooms, turning on lights, then checked the wire-service machine in the inner hall closet. It had been typing out news all night, and now a long roll of newsprint lay unfurled around the base of the stand.

"As soon as you get the Farm Show tape going," he said, "you'll have to tend to this." As Sarge turned away from the machine, it clicked itself on and began typing again, feeding more paper onto the floor. "Now watch closely," he said, turning on the light in the broadcast booth.

The booth, like everything else at the network, was an improvisation. It had originally been a spacious walk-in closet. Now black soundproofing tiles covered the walls. Various tape machines, microphones, and modular control boards filled the waist-high shelves that lined the booth. A bare bulb hung low from the ceiling over the metal swivel chair. A paper-filled clipboard dangled from a nail on the rear wall, and next to it was a large round clock. The time was thirty seconds before five o'clock.

The hog-report tape was already mounted on one of a pair of breadbox-sized reel-to-reel recorders. Sarge wound the tape forward by hand until he heard a deep distorted beep that apparently meant the show was cued into position. Then he flipped two toggle switches—one on the tape machine and one on the control panel—and the booth came to life. Equipment began to hum, colored lights flickered along the control board, needles jumped in their gauges.

"Now we're online," he said. "Whatever we send out, either through a tape machine or a live mike, feeds into all the stations in the network."

At ten seconds before the top of the hour, Sarge turned on the tape player. A high-pitched beep sounded loudly in the booth. Sarge immediately twisted a large knob on the control panel, and another beep sounded, much softer this time. "These adjust the sound levels," he said, indicating the large knob and three others next to it. "But don't trust your ears. Check the gauges. If the needle swings into the red, the level's too hot."

"Good morning!" someone boomed in a deep, jovial voice. *"It's time to talk about livestock! I'm your host, Frank Landerman!"*

Sarge twisted a large red knob, and Frank Landerman fell silent. But the needles continued to bounce gently back and forth, well within the safety range. "That knob shuts off the audio in the booth," he explained, "but still feeds it out to the stations."

"What were the beeps about?"

"Every prerecorded show is cued up with a ten-second lead-in. The beeps warn the stations that we're about to transmit." He left the booth and returned to the wire-service ticker. "But here's where the real work starts," he said, tearing off the long stream of newsprint. He measured off a few yards for himself, then scooped up the rest from the floor and shoved it into my arms. "The commercials have already been spliced into the Farm Show tape, so you've got ten free minutes to catch up on yesterday."

"I have to read all this in ten minutes?"

"Not just read it. Boil it down. You've got to get three and a half minutes of good stories out of this mess for the World News wrap-up at 5:15." He began to scan his own long piece of newsprint.

"You mean a live broadcast?" I started to feel queasy.

"Sure. But you've also got to record it while you're doing it live, so you can rebroadcast it at 5:40."

"Okay," I said, trying to get things clear in my mind. "So I've got fifteen minutes to put the World News report together."

"Well, actually you've only got until the Farm Show tape runs out at 5:10."

"What happens then?"

"First you've got to rewind the tape so you can rebroadcast it at 5:45. That won't take long. But then you've got to send out the zone forecasts for the state, and that'll keep you busy right up to World News."

"Where do I get the zone forecasts?"

Sarge tapped the mass of paper I was still clutching to my chest. "It's all in there." He looked at his watch. "You'd better get started."

I glanced quickly through the long train of unrelated paragraphs on the unrolled sheet. There were dozens of stories, wired in from all over the world, each relative crisis reduced to a blip of information a few sentences long.

"How do I know which pieces to put on the air?" I asked, noting a minor crash landing in Chicago followed by a mild volcanic eruption in Peru.

Sarge tore a narrow strip from his share of the printout and handed it to me. "Use your worst judgment."

The story was about a sheriff in Mexico who'd been raping all the women prisoners in his jail. They'd somehow caught him with his guard down, and he wound up with a cell door closed on his genitals. He was in critical condition.

"Sex and violence," he said. "That's always the lead."

"What about this kind of stuff?" I asked, showing him a longer paragraph about labor negotiations in England.

He shook his head. "Nothing bureaucratic unless it bleeds, and nothing that takes longer than fifteen seconds to explain." He checked his watch again. "By the way, when the World News is over, you've got sixty seconds to rewind it and cue up the Sports Report. Barry—he's the sports guy—usually leaves the tape somewhere in the booth." He walked back into the broadcast closet and looked around. "Yeah, here it is," he said, picking up a reel of tape from the top of one of the machines. "This airs at 5:21. That way the local stations can slip a couple of their own commercials in between World News and Sports." He paused. "Think you can remember all this?"

"I've already forgotten most of what you've told me."

"Too bad, because it gets more complicated. When the Sports tape ends at 5:25, you've got to do five minutes of National News."

"Culled from this," I guessed, holding up the leavings of the wire-service machine.

"Right." Sarge tore off a piece of newsprint and tucked it in my shirt pocket, while I scanned back up the page for the air-crash story. I missed it, somehow, but I did spot a piece about cracks in a nuclear power plant that looked disturbing enough.

"I suppose the National News has to be recorded for rebroadcast?"

"Right, at 5:45. You're catching on."

It wasn't a matter of catching on, it was a matter of assuming the worst. He tore another story from the sheet, then wadded up his portion of the wire-service remains and tossed them back into the closet. "After National News," he went on, "you've got to put together the Alabama Report. That's the hard part because you can't use anything from the wire service."

"Why not?" I asked, puzzling over whether an American Embassy bombing belonged to the National or World reports.

"Because the only local stuff they run is what they get from us."

"Then how do I come up with a report?" By now I was scanning my own snake of newsprint so quickly I was barely seeing the words. But I could feel the time evaporating, and I couldn't slow down. It was like someone had cut my brake lines.

"You'll have to rewrite a couple of yesterday's stories. There's a good chance somebody'll phone in something you can use. This time of year, we get a lot of early-morning calls from campaign managers telling us their candidates' schedules for the day. It's just filler, but you can still use it. If you come up short after that, pull something out of the futures file." I followed him into the newsroom where he opened a metal file drawer underneath one of the tables. "This is where we keep track of upcoming events. Anytime we get a press release, we file it here for future reference."

I reached the end of my newsprint. Between us, we'd probably found enough material for National and World news, but I still hadn't located the zone forecasts.

"So local news runs from 5:35 to 5:40?"

"Yep, with a rebroadcast at 5:55. That'll bring you back to the top of the hour."

"Then what?"

"Then you start the whole thing over again. We follow the same format all day long. It'll be second nature in no time."

"Just how long am I supposed to keep this process going?"

"You'll get some help about the middle of your third cycle."

"That's ridiculous. I can't run an entire radio network by myself for two and a half hours." I held up the shreds of newsprint. "I can't even find the zone forecasts."

Sarge reached into my shirt pocket and pulled out the scrap of paper. "Right here," he said smiling.

"But I'm just the weatherman. I can't be responsible for this much stuff."

"Did I mention about commercials?" he asked.

"Yeah, you said they were already spliced into the tape." I stuffed the mass of newsprint in the closet behind the wire-service machine. A new roll of information was already inching toward the floor.

"That's only true for the Sports Report and the Farm Show. And of course the zone forecasts are a closed-circuit non-commercial feed, so there's nothing to worry about there. But when you do a live broadcast, you've got to insert the commercials yourself." He led me back into the booth and showed me a tall stack of tape cartridges on a rack just inside the door. "This is the eight-track cart library. We've got about forty commercials on the active list." He pointed to a clipboard on the wall. "That's the commercial log. It tells you which ones to play and when to play them. That's important because some of the affiliates run their own commercials in place of ours, so we've got to be perfectly synchronized on all our breaks. In every five-minute broadcast, we break for sixty seconds at the two-minute mark and thirty seconds at the four-minute mark." He picked up a tape from the top of the stack and inserted it into a quadruple-decker eight-track tape player. "All you have to do is punch it into the machine and hit the START button. They're all infinite loop cartridges with automatic recuing and cutoff, so there's nothing else to worry about."

"Sarge," I said, "there's no way in the world I can handle all this."

"Are you kidding?" He closed the door to the broadcast booth, shutting us inside. "I've seen you memorize the batting stats for every player in the major leagues. You'll do fine. It's really pretty mindless—like filling out a crossword puzzle when you've already got the answers. All you've got to do is go through the motions."

I knew it wasn't that simple. Mindless motions were always the most difficult to remember, or at least they always had been for me. Of course, he was right about me and numbers—I had an *idiot savant's* talent for absorbing long columns of statistics. But this was different, this was performing a sequence of procedures. I'd never been any good at that sort of thing. In high school I got cut from the basketball squad because I couldn't remember how to run the basic plays. I got kicked out of the chorus for the senior musical because I couldn't learn the dance routines in *The Music Man*. It took me seven years of piano lessons to memorize Mozart's *Minuet in G*, and even then I drew a blank halfway through the recital. I can't cook without a cookbook. I can't tell complicated jokes because I leave out steps before the punch lines. I can't even adjust my stereo without rereading the owner's manual. So from where I stood it seemed pretty doubtful that I could ever keep this network on the air.

I looked at the sweeping second hand of the wall clock as it climbed toward the final moment of the Farm Show. Sarge, I think, recognized my panic.

"Tell you what," he said. "I'll handle all the details for today. You just watch. Take notes if you need to."

He eased into the metal chair, and as the second hand crossed the proper mark, he flipped a couple of switches and began the first live broadcast of the morning.

So that's how the first day began. Sarge performed all the necessary duties while I watched and made an exhaustive list of everything he did and the exact time he did it. I even clocked his bathroom break. I did read the zone forecasts to the affiliates, but apart from that I was just an amazed spectator to Sarge's timing and precision.

About seven o'clock the phone calls began to come in, and Sarge put me in charge of taking messages. Some were from listeners who'd missed the Farm Show and wanted to know how soybeans were doing, or what the closing price had been for yesterday's hogs. All I could tell them was to listen to the next broadcast. One woman was a fan of Frank Landerman's and wanted to know if she could speak to him. I told her no.

But most of the calls were from political underlings who wanted to tell us about their candidates' upcoming press conferences. Sometimes the candidates themselves called, and when that happened I was supposed to keep them talking while Sarge tapped into the line with one of his tape recorders. Since I had no idea who these people were or what the issues might be in their campaigns, I had a hard time thinking of questions. That didn't seem to make much difference, though, because they already knew what they wanted to tell me. No matter what question I asked, they could turn it into whatever question they wanted it to be, which I guess is a talent most politicians develop. Afterwards, along with everything else he had to do, Sarge lifted bits of their conversations from the tape and spliced them into his news reports, but only if the bits were juicy enough. If a candidate made some levelheaded observation about a school-bond issue, it never made the airwaves. But if somebody said something libelous about another candidate, or made some outlandish charge against a corporation or a government agency, that got rushed into the very next broadcast.

Splicing these last-minute segments into the report was a delicate procedure involving two reel-to-reel machines, a roll of Scotch tape, and a razor blade, but Sarge handled it with ease. If a candidate called as late as three minutes before a broadcast, Sarge could work him in.

None of it was easy in my estimation, but Sarge made it look that way, just as he'd done in the old Sugar Puffs Kid days. I was lucky to have him there to guide me through the routine. The panic of knowing I'd soon have to run things by myself began to subside. As long as I kept one eye on my notes, I could go through all the necessary motions to keep the programs up and running. Maybe I wasn't a natural like Sarge, but with written instructions to follow,

I could at least function well enough to avoid a catastrophe, and that was good enough for me.

For the first time I began to realize that I was doing the network a favor by taking this job. Looking at it objectively, I could understand why they'd be willing to hire someone of my inexperience. This weatherman job was entry-level at best, fleshed out with more responsibility and busywork than any veteran broadcaster would tolerate. The pay was lower than what I'd been making as a research librarian, and the hours were ugly and long. True, I was still a sham as a meteorologist, but I didn't feel quite as guilty about it now.

At 8 a.m., the start of the fourth broadcast cycle, the rest of the network crew arrived. Rusty, dressed in a powder blue suit this time, walked through the offices without a word to anybody and shut himself behind the soundproofed door. Darla, as uncommunicative as her husband, slid into her place at the front desk and began typing. Barry, in thick glasses and a dark jacket, looked more like an accountant than a sportscaster, but at least he offered a brief hello before busying himself with one of the reel-to-reel machines. Alf and Danny came in last, loud and relaxed, like two guys entering their favorite neighborhood bar.

"How's the first day of school?" Alf asked me as I tore a three-foot length of newsprint from the ticker machine.

"Can't talk now," I told him. "I've got a deadline." National News needed twenty seconds of fresh material, and I had to choose between an oil fire in Oklahoma and killer bees in Texas. I went with the bees.

Alf laughed. "We've all got deadlines, kiddo." He looked at his watch. "You've got a big one in half an hour."

I thumbed quickly through my notes to see which deadline he was talking about: 8:35 was a live broadcast of state and local news, with a rebroadcast at 8:55.

"Sarge is doing the on-air stuff for me today," I corrected him. "I'm still learning the timetables." One of the phones rang in the newsroom, but Danny was in there now so I left it for him to answer.

"Barry, come get the phone," Danny called out. "I'm making coffee."

"Sarge always takes over this time of the day. He's our drive-time voice," Alf said. "Your first shift's already over."

"I'm through?" A wave of relief swept over me.

"Not exactly," Alf said. "You've got to do another shift from two to five."

That wasn't so bad. I could handle three more hours.

"So I get a six-hour lunch break," I said.

"Well, you've got a pretty large beat to cover," Alf said, "so lunch might not always work out."

"What beat? I'm the weatherman."

Alf shook his head. "Remember when Rusty said we all pitch in around here? What he meant was we all do at least three jobs." He pulled open a file drawer and took out some stapled sheets of paper. "Danny usually keeps tabs on all the government agencies, but now he's tied up with election coverage. So his beat-list gets passed on to the new guy. That's you." He handed me the packet, a four-page alphabetized list of all the state, federal, and civic agencies in town.

"There must be a hundred organizations here," I objected.

"A hundred and sixty-two, actually," Alf corrected me. "But the list won't seem so big once you learn to prioritize. Nothing ever happens at the State Bureau of Cosmetology, for example, so you can go days without talking to those people. But you'll want to check in with the Department of Public Safety every few hours because they've always got something messy going on."

I read down the list. Some of the names were familiar, like the Department of Transportation or the FBI, but a lot of them sounded made-up or irrelevant. The Unrefrigerated Seafood Commission. The Bureau of Canals. The Textile Guild. The Bull Semen Depository. The All-Brick Association. There were no addresses or phone numbers.

"There aren't enough hours in the day," I said.

"Exactly right." He raised his eyebrows and tapped his forefinger on the paper. "That's why you have to go make friends with people who work at these places—so if something big ever does happen, you're the guy they call."

"Somebody's calling him already," Barry said, poking his head from the newsroom doorway. He held up the receiver. "Got a candidate here who needs a weather forecast for his press conference."

"That's bullshit, by the way," Alf said. "There's only one real reason candidates call here. They want more coverage." He glanced at his watch. "Make it fast, Taylor. You've got your television debut in twenty-seven minutes."

"What?"

Sarge emerged from the broadcast booth and took the length of newsprint from my hand.

"It's not all radio, remember," Alf said. "You're the Channel 11 weatherman. You do a forecast at 8:35 every weekday morning."

"And another one at 5:35," Sarge added as he disappeared back into the booth with his updates.

It was stupid of me to be so surprised. I knew being the TV weatherman was part of the package. But nobody had given me a time frame, so I had assumed they'd let me ease into the job at my own pace. Being thrown into the deep end twice in one day was more than I'd planned on.

"But I don't even know where the studio is."

Barry stretched the tangled phone cord into the hallway and pressed the receiver into my hand. Then he passed a few pages of wire-service stories on to Alf.

"Relax," Alf said. "You can ride over with me. Barry's got a press conference for the Blue/Gray Game, so I've got to do the morning sports report."

"Hello?" I said absently into the phone.

"Yeah, this is Assistant Attorney General William Hatcher. I've got a press conference at one o'clock today on the Capitol steps—sure hope you folks can send somebody, by the way—and I need to know what the weather's looking like. I mean, if it's fixing to rain, I can reschedule."

I didn't know what to say.

"Hello? You there?"

"I'm here," I told him.

"Great. Well, how about it? You got a forecast for me?"

"I'm still working on it," I said.

Harmattan simoon. The scouring wind.

Chapter 14

Typical of all Rusty Wilderman's enterprises, WWII TV Channel 11 was a low-budget operation. The station was housed in a faded blue Quonset hut on the seedy western outskirts of town, and except for the silver broadcast tower balancing crookedly over the flat country-side, the place looked more like a storage garage for farm equipment than a television studio. Even at twenty past eight, which was when we rolled into the yellow dust of the parking area, only two other vehicles occupied the makeshift lot. One was a sun-baked equipment van with *WWII TV* painted on the side. The other was a pickup truck with a hog tethered in the back.

"Not much to look at," I said as we stepped out into the morning heat. The hog began to snort loudly in our direction. He wore a bright red collar with a short chain that attached him to a small steel ring mounted on the top of the tailgate, greatly reducing his mobility. He strained against the chain as he snorted.

"The station's mostly just a relay point for syndicated programs," Alf explained. "Except for the live news reports, it's a one-man operation."

The one man, it turned out, was Frank Landerman. The morning farm show represented only a minor portion of his many chores for the Alacast-WWII network. His main job was to babysit the antiquated equipment at the station and to make sure all the syndicated programming got on the air. But he also anchored the fifteen-minute TV news broadcasts and hosted a prerecorded half-hour cooking show. His weekends were free except for Friday night, when he wrapped himself in gauze like an Egyptian mummy and climbed out of a cardboard sarcophagus to introduce Midnight Crypt Theatre. Like Sarge, Frank Landerman was a key utility player on the Rusty Wilderman broadcast team.

At that particular moment, however, he was asleep on a sofa just inside the door of the building, snoring beneath a large window air conditioner. His navy sport coat was pulled across his face, protecting him, I guess, from the chill. Alf shook him by the pant leg.

"We're live in nine minutes," Alf told him and headed deeper into the gloomy darkness of the studio. I stayed behind, in a slant of sunlight from what appeared to be the only unblackened window.

Frank sat up and blinked a few times. "Long night," he said. "Two campaign fund-raisers and another pointless speech by the governor."

"That's election season," Alf called back.

Frank looked at me. "Is my hair all right?" he asked, gently cupping his temples with both hands. "I hate to go on-air with that matted-down look."

"It's a little lopsided," I told him.

He frowned and walked over to the water cooler. He dipped his head into the arc of water, dousing his face and hair. Then he shook his head violently and ran his fingers up over his scalp.

"How about now?" he asked. Water droplets dribbled from his chin.

"Now it looks flat," I said.

He nodded. "It'll puff out once we're under the lights. Gets hot in a hurry out there. We'll be sweatin' like pigs in no time."

"Pigs don't have sweat glands," I told him.

He frowned again. "You must be the new guy. I'm Frank Landerman." He didn't really sound like Frank Landerman, though. He wasn't as booming or as gregarious as he'd been on tape.

"I'm Taylor Wakefield," I said, shaking his hand. "I heard some of your Farm Show this morning."

Somewhere in the glass-fronted booth along the side wall Alf threw a switch, and the inner portion of the studio came alive with light. There was a pastel blue news desk in front of a crudely painted backdrop of what was supposed to be downtown Montgomery. People of various races strolled the sidewalks, waving friendly greetings to one another. Everyone appeared prosperous and happy.

Off to the side stood two large weather maps, one for the state and one for the country. Both maps were littered with childish cartoon faces of smiling suns and crying clouds. Angry silver lightning bolts crowded together along the borders, waiting to be assigned an appropriate location. It all looked like a not-very-interesting game for preschoolers.

"I knew that about pigs, you know," he said, wiping his chin on the sleeve of his jacket. "I do some farming. That's my boar out there in the pickup."

"It looked like a good boar," I said, for lack of anything better.

"Nope. Supposed to be a breeder, but he's a total dud. That's why he's in the truck. I'm taking him back to the guy I bought him from, see if I can get some kind of refund."

"How long you had him?" I asked.

"Over a month."

"Maybe he just needs more time."

Frank Landerman laughed. "You a pig farmer, are you?"

"Not in the literal sense."

"Well, if you were, you'd know it's stupid to risk a whole breeding season on a disinterested boar. If he can't settle any sows in thirty of my lunch hours, he's not the boar I need."

Some people get defensive when faced with fresh information, I guess, because learning something new often requires admitting that your old position was inadequate or wrong. It was clear to me that Frank Landerman, in spite of his being a news anchor, was not particularly interested in advancing his education. So I didn't tell him anything to help him out, even though I could have. It's true I'm no pig farmer, but I do have a memory for certain things, and I once read about a study at Oklahoma State on the proper procedures for breeding swine, the details of which have stayed with me.

Consequently, I know that a mature boar can service three gilts a day, but shouldn't do more than fifteen in a week or forty in a month.

I know that the most efficient way to introduce a new boar to the herd is to isolate him for thirty days, then keep him in close proximity to the herd for another thirty before you use him.

I know that in summer the proper breeding times are early morning or late afternoon, but never around lunch because it's too hot. An overheated boar can't breed well because heat affects semen quality. The motility drops to inadequate levels.

And I know that no boar should be carted around in the back of a pickup unless he's first had a good wallow in the mud. Otherwise, he'll be susceptible to heatstroke. But there was no mud on Frank Landerman's boar. He was as clean and well groomed as a household pet, a clear sign of mismanagement.

Alf came back from the booth with a red-and-black-plaid sport coat in one hand and what looked like a conductor's baton in the other. The coat was wrinkled badly, as if it had been stored in a shoe box.

"Tools of the trade," Alf said. Until that moment I'd forgotten all about the costume requirements of the job. He tucked the baton in the breast pocket and tossed me the jacket. A pungent, musty smell came with it. I held the thing up and looked at it. Large sweat stains darkened the fabric beneath both armpits. The sleeves were frayed at the ends, and the collar was smudged with old layers of stage makeup. It looked like a bagpipe that had been run over by a tractor.

"That's Bubba's old coat," Frank said, a hint of reverence in his voice. He edged up beside me for a closer look.

"Bubba was before my time," Alf told him.

Frank ran his fingertips lightly along the lapel. "Where'd you find this?"

"Floor of the costume closet."

Alf walked over to the cameras and rolled them both forward into position, then pressed a couple of switches along the sides. One camera was aimed at the news desk, the other at the weather maps.

"Bubba used to tape a game show here on Saturday mornings," Frank continued. "Biggest moneymaker the station ever had. Without Bubba, Rusty never could have branched out into radio."

"Sorry I missed it," Alf said absently. "Taylor, put the coat on and stand between the maps. When the light goes red on your camera, you're on the air."

I put on the smelly jacket and tried to smooth down some of the wrinkles. My palms were damp, so my hands came away coated with a fuzzy residue of dust and lint. I brushed them off as best I could. Ever since I'd walked through the studio door I had tried not to think about airtime, but now the moment was closing in and a hollow nausea was rising from my stomach. The space around the set seemed slightly tilted, and I began to feel clammy in the harsh brilliance of the lights. I'd rehearsed a little in the car on the way over, so I did have some grasp of what I wanted to say. But I wasn't sure I'd be able to say it.

"Oh, you didn't really miss it," Frank said. "That game show still pays part of our salaries. Rusty keeps it going in reruns. I don't know why people would want to see the same game show twice, but apparently they do. It gets triple the ratings of any other program we run."

"How will I keep track of the time?" I asked, as I moved carefully to my spot on the set.

"I'll give you a signal," Alf said. "When you see me wave, you've got fifteen seconds to wrap everything up."

The extensive bank of overhead lights bore down as hotly as Frank had predicted, and I felt pinpricks of sweat breaking out on my scalp. The glare was blinding, and I had to squint to keep my eyes from tearing up.

"Bubba was an interesting guy," Frank went on. "Started out as a rodeo clown, but he got too banged up. Ended up here. I think he died in that coat." Frank shook his head sadly and took his seat behind the anchor desk.

Alf checked his watch. "We're on in three," he said, busying himself with some final adjustments on the cameras. "Frank, I trust you've got your script?"

"Trust is the cornerstone of our profession," he replied, his voice suddenly deep and resonant, the same voice I'd heard on the Farm Show tape. He took some folded pages from his coat pocket and pressed them flat on the desktop. Then he ran his fingers through his hair again, the final fluffing before broadcast. He looked respectable and dignified, in a small-market sort of way. Someone to believe in, if only on the local level.

The procedure was simple. With Alf operating the equipment, Frank would open the program with five minutes of news and I'd follow with three minutes of weather. During my segment, Frank and Alf would trade places, and Alf would follow my report with four minutes of sports. The operation was probably about as primitive as any you'd find in the business, but for a no-frills production, it got the job done.

Still, that first morning my eyes had trouble adjusting. I knew Frank would introduce me, so I'd at least have an approximate notion of when to begin talking, but I'd spent enough time in radio to know that broadcasting was measured in microseconds. If I didn't pick up the cue perfectly I'd look like an amateur, and that cue was a mere red blip that I somehow had to locate through the dazzling intensity of sixty high-powered overhead lights. The harder I tried to stare through the wall of glare, the more my eyes watered, until, as Frank began the introduction of his broadcast, I finally had to look away.

My gaze settled on the shadowy space behind the backdrop of downtown Montgomery, the storage area for flats and furniture. I blinked away the tears and allowed my eyes to rest in the dim coolness of that backstage alleyway. For a few comforting moments, I didn't realize what I was looking at. But as Frank droned on, spinning out his version of the same stories I'd been putting on the air all morning, my vision gradually cleared and I was able to focus on the largest shape hulking there in the shadows.

It was the giant wheel of prizes from Bubba's defunct game

show, the same wheel I'd seen spinning only yesterday in front of Steve and Lucy's couch, the same wheel I'd watched from the edge of my father's bed. Now here I was in Bubba's outlandish game-show jacket, and it was a perfect fit. I didn't know what to think.

My confusion didn't last long, though, because suddenly Frank Landerman had reached the end of his sincere account of the day's disasters, and he was now telling the audience that it was time for a look at the weather *"with our brand new weatherman here at WWII, Taylor Wakefield!"* His enthusiasm caught me by surprise. There was expectation in his tone, as if I were the newest attraction on the midway. I turned to the camera and saw the red light blink on.

"Thanks, Frank, " I said, but for the next few seconds I froze. Whatever I'd planned to say was gone from my mind forever, and my brain blurred into the giddiness of an adrenaline rush. "The weather doesn't usually matter," I said at last. "So I might not talk about it much. But if I do, you should be skeptical, because it's mostly just guesswork anyway." I paused again, and there went my first twenty-five seconds.

Alf stepped around to the side of the camera, looking slightly perplexed. Frank tossed his script away in apparent disgust and silently walked off the set.

Then I began to talk about the next day's forecast. I said I thought it might rain, but I wasn't sure. I also told people it might get hot, but I wasn't sure how hot, so we should all just play it by ear. And finally, I passed along some weather trivia, explaining why hail comes in different sizes.

Then I announced my contest.

"Now listen carefully," I said. "Fourteen years ago a girl from Pensacola won the National Spelling Bee. The first person to call in with her name and address wins my first paycheck." I spread my arms to the side. "I'll also give you this jacket."

By now Alf had moved into position for the sports report. He signaled me for the fifteen-second wrap-up.

"And here's a public service announcement," I said, measuring out the clock-ticks in my mind. "Be careful how you vote in this next election, because one of the candidates killed somebody."

Then the light on my camera winked out, and Alf began talking distractedly about a tennis tournament in Europe.

When we were all safely off the air, Alf dropped his head onto the desk, and Frank came striding out of the darkness toward me.

"What the hell kind of weather report was that?!" he demanded.

"Postmodern, I'd say."

"Now you look here, Wakefield. I don't want to hear that kind of nonsense on my show again."

"I didn't know it was your show," I said.

He flushed a deep red. "I'm the news anchor!" he hissed. "I've got to have absolute credibility out there! If you're unprofessional, it reflects poorly on me!"

If Frank had been a borderline heart case or a serious diabetic, he might have had a stroke or a seizure. From the apoplectic look on his face, I half expected him to start speaking in tongues.

Alf stepped carefully between us and clapped a hand on my shoulder. A puff of dust rose from the ancient plaid.

"Tell him, tell him I'm right," Frank demanded. Then he reached past Alf and jabbed a finger at the buttonhole of my lapel. "And that jacket is network property. It's not yours to give away. For your information, Bubba's name still means something around here."

Alf sighed. "Interesting approach, Taylor, I'll give you that."

"Sometimes extremism is the only logical option."

"I notice you didn't use your little pointer-stick," he said, drawing the baton from my breast pocket. "Or any of those plastic weather faces on the maps."

"Didn't seem natural."

"Oh, please," Frank groaned, raising his hands in the air. "There was nothing natural about anything you did. That entire display was amateurish and inappropriate. You're the worst weatherman I've ever seen."

"Which is not necessarily a bad thing," Alf interjected, tapping the baton lightly against Frank's padded shoulder. "This is television, remember. *Worst* can be good, because it makes people talk. When people talk about a show, they're more likely to tune in." He nodded his head as he thought through the idea. "Yeah, postmodern, I like that."

"Utter hogwash," Frank insisted, and I couldn't say he was wrong.

"Look, Frank," Alf said evenly. "You said yourself that most viewers would rather watch reruns of Bubba's game show than sit through your newscast. Think about that. You get lower ratings than a dead rodeo clown."

Frank Landerman's outrage crumbled as he caught this glimpse of his mortality as an anchorman. His shoulders slumped.

"It may be time for a radical departure," Alf went on. "So if Taylor wants to give away Bubba's ratty sport coat, that's fine with me. In fact, if he wants to give away *your* sport coat, that's fine with me, too."

The defeat was palpable on Frank's semitrustworthy face, and I felt genuinely sorry for the guy. He had a couple of personality problems to work out, but at least he had professional standards. I was the one soliciting true love in the middle of a weather forecast. I was the one talking about murder.

"The commercial loop is about finished," Frank said quietly. "I have to switch us over to the affiliate relay." He gave me a last frowning look, then shuffled away to the control booth.

"Now what?" I asked.

Alf tucked the baton back into my pocket. "Lunch."

"It's not even nine o'clock yet," I pointed out.

"Take it when you can get it," he said. "Besides, we've got things to talk about."

Frank threw a switch in the booth, and the stage shrank into darkness. I followed Alf's dim outline as we moved toward the front door.

Outside, the sun had already cleared the curved, corrugated edge of the building, and the last cool remnants of the morning had burned away. It was scorching hot now, unseasonably so, as hot as the studio had been beneath the lights, though far more humid. I found myself wishing I could go back on the air for another half-minute to amend my forecast, to warn people about the dangers of the rising heat, about the suffocating power of humidity.

"I hope Frank won't hold a grudge," I said.

Alf picked a small granite chunk from the weeds just outside the door and flung it toward a line of crows that had taken up residence in the scattered gravel near his car. They flapped a short distance away and settled into the branches of an old mimosa bordering the red-clay field beyond the lot.

"Frank's a throwback," Alf said. "Rusty inherited him when he bought the station. He's a useful guy to have around, though. He's got a First Class FCC license, which means he's qualified to fix the equipment. Every station's got to have somebody like that."

"I didn't mean to make him so upset," I said as we rounded the rear of the equipment van. Alf stopped short.

"He'll get over it soon enough," he said, staring at something ahead of him in the lot. "He's got his pig to worry about."

"It's not just a pig," I told him. "It's a breeding boar."

"It used to be a breeding boar," Alf said, pulling me forward for an unobstructed view of the truck. "Now it's just bacon."

He was right. The boar dangled by its neck from the top of the tailgate, its hind feet nearly reaching the ground. There was no movement, no sign of life. We approached the spectacle slowly and stood silent for a moment at the back of the truck, taking in the details. The boar's mouth was strained open, revealing two yellow rows of chipped and jagged teeth, and its dark tongue hung grotesquely from the side. The eyes bulged wide, frozen between emptiness and panic above the stranglehold of the bright red collar. Alf gingerly gripped the curly bristle of its tail and gave the carcass a slight shake. There was no response.

"Looks like a suicide," Alf said, absently wiping his hand on the hem of his jacket.

I wondered if that could be true. I wondered if animals could knowingly put an end to things, the way people do. I wondered what had gone through the boar's mind before the hot floor of the truckbed finally drove him over the wall. I wondered what choice he had.

"I'm basically a city boy," Alf said. "That's the biggest dead thing I've ever seen outside a funeral home."

He looked at me as if he expected confirmation. But I had nothing to say.

Chapter 15

It's no accident that the moon keeps a steady face trained on the earth. The phases we talk about are simple illusions. New moon, quarter moon, full moon—just tricks of light and shadow. Form without substance. The tangible parts—the rocks and the dirt and the abandoned billion-dollar lunar landing craft—all remain fixed, caught in the permanent headlock of earth's greater gravitational force. No matter what goes on in the world, the moon can never turn away.

There's nothing mystical about it. The moon simply has an uneven mass, so the side that weighs more always points down. Down meaning here, where we are. It's like those inflatable punching-clowns with the sandbags inside to make them bottom-heavy. No matter how hard you hit them, they always right themselves after the blow.

Some candidates are like that, too. In the intricately mapped cosmos of the electoral process, there are always a few lunar bodies in the sky, candidates of uneven mass, figures too minor to exert their own gravitational force. Those were the candidates I inherited with my new weatherman job. The ones nobody took seriously. The ones who had a right to coverage because of FCC regulations, but who were too peripheral for legitimate reporters to waste much time on. The ones with no party backing, no campaign war chest, no hope of winning. The ones on the lunatic fringe.

They weren't all crazy, though.

Gustav Grozniak, for example, was a bright Ukrainian immigrant with an advanced degree in electrical engineering. Somehow he had become enraged by the oil and power companies and was running for governor as a protest candidate. His English was weak, which was a stumbling block, so he generally stuck to reading prepared statements at his press conferences. But he also kept an interpreter on hand, in case anybody had questions. The interpreter was a woman named Kolsk, who was also his landlady. According to Ms. Kolsk, Gustav had a five-year plan for converting the entire state to solar power.

Wilkie Smith was a sadder case. His father had made a fortune with Bessemer Steel, and as a consequence Wilkie was sitting on a four-million-dollar trust fund. But he had a problem with his metabolism, something wasn't right about his thyroid, and even as a six-foot college senior he weighed less than a hundred pounds. He grew even thinner in the years following his graduation, and his weight somehow gave rise to an increasingly violent irritability, especially when he'd been drinking, which in turn led to numerous altercations with the law. After bailing him out on a series of very public misdemeanors, his family finally disowned him, telling him they just couldn't take the humiliation anymore. He took the rejection hard, and retaliated by getting work as the Skeleton Man in a resident carnival outside Montgomery. His first day on the job, he issued a press release about it to all the media outlets in the state, openly denouncing his parents for destroying the last vestiges of his self-esteem. But his family continued to ignore him, so now he was upping the ante by running for the U.S. Senate.

The Swelter twins were in that senate race, too. Tim and Tom. They were fairly intelligent boys, both with law degrees. But they ran their campaign on a single ill-conceived gimmick—that since there were two of them, they could get twice as much work done as anybody else. Tim was the official candidate of record, but they made it clear that a vote for one was a vote for them both. Tim would live in Washington, while Tom would handle matters here at home.

And there were plenty of others. Every race had its amateurs and also-rans. Idealists, egomaniacs, power-seekers, self-promoters—

plus a few petty criminals and sociopaths—they all had lapel buttons and bumper stickers to pass out. Of course, none of these wild-card candidates would ever be legitimate contenders in the general election. Most of them knew it coming in the door.

In some cases, that was a shame. The most interesting man in the gubernatorial race, for example, might well have been Benjamin Charles Bibberly. He was a fringe dweller who didn't have a chance in hell, but he still earned my vote. He was the one who clarified my options.

That first morning, after we found Frank Landerman's boar hanging from his truck, Alf and I differed on what to do next. I thought the polite thing would be to let Frank know what was waiting for him in the parking lot, but Alf said no. "Never waste time on anything that'll take care of itself," he said. So we went on to lunch like nothing had happened.

While we were waiting for our lunch at Grizzly's Barbecue, Alf called Sarge at the network to find out what the rest of the day's agenda might be.

"You've got your first press conference this afternoon," he told me as he slid back into our booth.

"Billy Hatcher," I guessed. I knew I'd have to step into Billy's path sooner or later, so the news didn't really rattle me. Besides, a press conference would be the safest way to go about it.

Alf laughed. "Not a chance. Hatcher's major league, and that's Danny's territory. You get the small fry."

The waitress set our plates of pulled pork and slaw in front of us. "Can I get y'all anything else?" she asked.

"I'm ready for a refill on this iced tea," Alf said, handing her his empty glass with a smile. When she left, she took away my glass, too.

"Listen, Taylor, I know we're throwing a lot at you today," he said. "But that's the best way to start. From here on out, it'll only get easier."

I knew he was wrong. All I'd learned today was how to juggle time, and that was just an empty parlor trick. The real acrobatics would come later.

"Anyway, press conferences are easy," Alf continued. "Just listen for a good quote, put it into a thirty-second wraparound, and call it in to the network."

"What's a wraparound?"

"It's a story with a quote stuck in the middle. First you talk, then you play the piece of tape, then you talk again."

"I don't have a tape recorder," I pointed out.

Alf reached into his coat pocket and took out a small Lanier microrecorder about the size of a pack of cigarettes. "Be in the senate chamber at four o'clock," he said, pushing the machine across the table to me.

"So who's the small fry?" I asked.

Alf chuckled. "Bibberly," he said.

            ✧

The Capitol building in Montgomery is an easy thing to find, even if you don't know the town at all. It sits high on a hill overlooking the massive white structures of the Department of Education and the Department of Public Safety, as well as the redbrick Baptist church of Martin Luther King Jr. Five broad white tiers of steps lead up to the double brass doors of the main entrance. Jefferson Davis was sworn in as President of the Confederacy at the top of these steps. The building itself was modeled after the Capitol in Washington, D.C., but the dome of the Montgomery version is a little smaller and has a clock in it. The front portico has six enormous columns that I first encountered on a field trip in kindergarten. They were the first columns I'd ever seen, and later, in Sunday school, when I learned about Samson pulling down the pillars of the great house of the Philistines, these were the pillars I thought of.

I didn't see the pillars, though, on my way to the senate chamber that day. The network offices, where Alf had dropped me after a lengthy orientation drive around town, were tucked away just a couple of short blocks behind the Capitol, so when I walked over for the Bibberly press conference, I came in from the rear. The back door of the building wasn't anything like the front, or even the two side doors, for that matter. Those three were all covered with ornate overlays of polished brass. On a sunny day, the glare could blind you. But the back door had no brass at all. It was set one floor below the others and opened out onto a black asphalt driveway with a green garbage Dumpster. The door itself was ordinary—a farmhouse kind of door, frail-looking against the massive building that rose around it. Its ancient paint pulled from the wood in cracked, white blisters. Now, it was propped open with a metal folding chair, and the smell of meatloaf drifted out through the black-framed screen door. A uniformed guard sat heavily on the chair, while another leaned against the cool stone wall, fanning himself slowly with his hat.

I flashed the press pass Alf had given me and pushed through the screen door into the thick heat of the back hallway. The meatloaf smell hung in the air like a hot, damp fog, and I followed it to the dingy cafeteria at the center of the building. Remnants of the afternoon coffee-break crowd still lingered over nearly empty cups. Three middle-aged ladies in beehive hairdos got up to leave through the opposite doors, and I followed them to a worn marble stairway in a side hall. From there I made my way up two long flights to the floor of the Capitol rotunda.

A cluster of tourists stood in the center of the hall, staring up at the lush murals on the inside of the dome. A floor above them, two adolescent boys raced around the inner balcony, while a third boy, maybe eight years old, dropped pennies over the brass railing. Beneath the balcony an elderly guard sat watching as the pennies bounced and rolled on the marble floor.

I showed him my press pass and asked him what time it was.

"Depends on where you mean," he said. "Out here in the hall it's three-fifty." He jerked his thumb back over his shoulder toward the senate-chamber door. "In there it's four-fifty-five." A penny struck the floor in front of him and rolled in a slow curve around the side of his chair. "The lieutenant governor did it."

"Did what?" I was obliged to ask. Another penny hit the floor.

"Froze the clocks. Waltzed in here yesterday with a pair of wire cutters and stopped 'em dead."

The boy in the balcony dropped his last penny and skipped away toward the stairwell. The guard watched the boy until he disappeared from view, then he scrambled from his chair and snatched up all the coins he could find.

"Why would he do that?" I asked.

"State constitution says the legislature cain't work past five o'clock. With the clocks stuck on four-fifty-five, he can hold 'em in session long as he wants without breaking the law."

"Can he get away with that?"

The guard shrugged. "I ain't gonna arrest him for it." He slipped the small handful of change into his pocket just as the boy ran in from the dim side hallway. "Far as I'm concerned, anything that gets more work out of the legislature is okay with me."

"Doesn't that give him more power than he's supposed to have?" I asked.

"I guess you could look at it that way," the guard replied. "There's not much happens up here that don't have two sides to it."

The boy walked slowly past us, scanning the floor for his coins. He picked up a couple of pennies the guard had missed and stood staring at them in confusion.

I thanked him for the information and pulled open the door to the senate. The chamber inside was as stately and old-fashioned as I'd expected it to be. Immediately beyond the entryway, the room was dominated by the broad overhang of the visitors' gallery, which sagged low into its support posts with a kind of decadent dignity. Along the left and right walls, heavily framed windows stretched high toward the twenty-foot plaster ceiling, where six slow fans stirred the afternoon heat. Five rows of dark mahogany writing desks curved toward the speaker's platform at the front of the room, which was set off by a finely carved balustrade. At the rear of the platform sat the enormous desk of the lieutenant governor, and above it on the wall hung the broken clock and the drooping flags of the state and the nation. The air smelled of varnish and cigars.

I sat at a desk in the front row, took out a notepad, and wrote up the story of the broken clock. It didn't fit the *sex or violence* rule, but I figured I ought to have something ready to phone in to Sarge in case the press conference turned out to be a bust. I was still timing sentences in my head when a door to the right of the speaker's platform creaked open and a slim wisp of a boy limped in carrying a tall stack of neatly folded laundry. T-shirts, it looked like, piled so high they partially obscured his face, and for a moment I thought it might be the kid who'd lost his pennies to the guard. But as he eased the pile onto the edge of the platform, I realized my mistake. This boy had thinning gray hair and a taut, weathered face, and suddenly I knew who he was. If my day hadn't been such a swamp of distractions, I'd have remembered sooner, probably the instant Alf told me whose press conference I was to cover. But now it all came back to me.

"You're Benny Bibberly," I said stupidly.

"It's tough to hide things from you boys in the press," he said dryly as he sorted the shirts into three separate stacks.

"No, what I mean is, I know you. We worked together once."

Benny's eyelids drooped low as he concentrated on my face. "Sorry," he said, "I can't place you."

"It was about fourteen years ago. We did some interview shows together in Birmingham."

"I do a lot of interviews," said Benny, refolding the top shirt from the most disheveled pile. "I'm a famous guy."

That was true. Benny Bibberly was the most well-known failed politician in the state. In his three decades of campaigning he had earned a reputation for saying exactly what he thought, even if it cost him votes. His record was spotless—he'd never sold out to any special-interest groups, he'd never publicly smeared an opponent, and he'd never compromised himself with any crooked political machinery. He'd also never won an election, but in some ways that was beside the point.

He'd first found the spotlight as a successful jockey, but a bad spill had snapped his Achilles tendon, forcing him into premature retirement. That was back in 1948. Later that year he tried to get elected to the Birmingham city council and finished last in a twelve-man race. He followed that with a write-in campaign for mayor and got so few votes he didn't even get credited with a percentage point. After that he dropped out of sight for a while, then resurfaced in 1954 to declare his candidacy in the gubernatorial campaign. That was the year Benny made political history. Against incredible odds, he stunned both the nation and himself by becoming the first candidate in a major American election to receive absolutely no votes at all. None. Not even his own. When reporters asked him about it, he said that voting for himself would have been unseemly. No gentleman, he asserted, should ever claim a victory that hinged on his own selfish vote.

The people of Alabama were proud of Benny after that, and he suddenly found himself with a groundswell of support. When he ran for governor again in 1958, he carried 2 percent of the vote, more than he'd managed in all his other campaigns combined. The momentum continued, and in 1962 Benny reached the high-water mark of his career with 3 percentage points.

I first met him in 1964 on a television interview show. Channel 6 in Birmingham was having something called "Lovable Losers Week" on its noontime talk show, and Benny and I were the special guests. We were both hot items at the time. I was fresh off the heels of my National Spelling Bee humiliation, and Benny had just published his autobiography, *Losing Isn't Everything.* I've still got a copy of it somewhere.

Benny picked a shirt from one of the stacks and tossed it to me. "Wear this as often as you can." He thumbed down through one of the other piles and pulled another shirt from near the bottom. "I'll give you one for Sarge Presley, too," he said. "What size you figure he needs? I'm guessing extra large."

"I don't know," I told him.

He held the shirt against his body to gauge the size. It hung before him like a dress. The blue stenciling across the front said, *Short and to the Point: Benny Bibberly for Governor.*

"This looks about right," he said. He deftly refolded it and placed it on the desktop in front of me.

"I'm not sure we can wear these," I said. "We aren't supposed to take sides."

Benny grinned crookedly. "You didn't seem like such a stickler on TV this morning."

I couldn't argue that. "I'm breaking in a new format," I said, shifting a little in my seat.

"Well, I liked it."

"Thanks. Some people wanted me to be a little more traditional."

"Yeah, I can guess who," Benny said, a tightness creeping into his voice. "Landerman panics if his dessert fork's in the wrong place."

"He just wants things to be professional," I said, although in fact I had no idea what Frank Landerman wanted.

Benny shook his head. "No, that's not it. He's just terrified of being looked at."

That seemed an odd thing to say about a television anchorman, but I let it pass. I looked back toward the main chamber door, hoping other members of the press corps would come straggling in. But there was no one.

"I'm not sure how these things go," I said, "but shouldn't there be other reporters here?"

"Oh, don't worry about that," he said with a dismissive wave of his hand. "We can go ahead and get started." He abruptly sat down on the edge of the platform. "I don't have a speech, so we can go right to the question-and-answer session."

He'd caught me off guard. "I'm sorry," I said, flipping pointlessly through my notebook. "I don't really know the issues yet. I don't know what to ask."

"Then ask me how my campaign's going."

"Okay. How's it going?"

"Not bad." He paused. A sly smile crept across his face. "Now ask me the name of the girl who won the National Spelling Bee in 1964."

Again he'd caught me off guard. I was afraid to ask the question. He read my discomfort instantly, and a mock sneer curled his lip.

"Boy, for a guy about to accuse some candidate of murder, you sure rattle easy," he said. "Maybe I ought to be the one asking the questions." He pointed to the tiny tape recorder on the desk in front of me. "Is that thing on?"

"No, not yet," I told him.

"Good," he said. "I want to talk off-the-record."

I tried to think what that meant. Was it that I wasn't supposed to repeat anything he told me, or just that I wasn't supposed to say where I heard it?

"Sure," I said. "No problem."

He pushed himself up from the platform and took a seat at the desk beside me.

"Why do you want this girl's name?" he asked, his voice dropping to a more confidential tone.

"It's hard to explain," I said.

He drummed his slim fingers on the desktop. "No, it's not. It's either about love or it's about something else."

He was right, of course—every issue could be parceled out that way. But I still wasn't clear on the answer.

"It might be about love," I told him. "But it might be about something else."

He thought it over for a minute, then nodded. "Well, for the time being, let's say it's about love. I'd feel better that way." He took a slip of paper from his wallet and passed it across to me. "Her name's Alissa Powell. She lives down in Fairhope, on the east side of Mobile Bay."

"She's in Alabama?"

"For the last six or seven years. She moved over from north Florida after she quit college."

I was impressed by Benny and delighted with his news, but something seemed wrong. Why would a girl who won the National Spelling Bee drop out of college? I guess I'd always assumed that after her dramatic victory in our spell-down she'd go on to become president of Harvard or the CEO of some multinational corporation. Now I saw how narrowly foolish that assumption had been. In terms of intellect, the only thing that had separated the two of us was the spelling of a single word, and look how I'd turned out. My own career had barely risen beyond the library basement. Why should I have expected so much more of her?

"How do you know all this?" I asked.

He leaned back in his seat. "The truth is—and I say this without irony—it's a small world. We all know somebody who knows somebody. I made some phone calls, said it was urgent, and people got back to me."

"Why would you take that kind of trouble?"

"I wanted to win your contest." The wrinkles around his watery blue eyes deepened as he smiled. "Even a famous loser like me likes to come out on top once in a while. Turned out to be a pretty simple matter, too. One of my stable managers down in the Florida panhandle knew her family. I'm a horse breeder by trade, in case you didn't know."

"No, I didn't."

"Yeah, I got stud farms all over—Florida, Alabama, Georgia. I was always a keen judge of horseflesh. That's what made me a good jockey. After I quit the track, I started my own business." He leaned toward me and winked. "Can't make a living just running for office, you know."

"Sounds like you're doing pretty well."

"Son, I'm rolling in it. It's funny, but when I started out, I thought politicians got paid big bucks. Now just about every horse I own makes more money than the governor."

"So why do you want my paycheck?"

He laughed. "Lord, boy, I don't want your money. I want that plaid sport coat you was wearing on TV. You said it was part of the deal."

"Don't tell me you were a fan of Bubba's game show."

He started to answer, but caught himself. Then he drew in a slow breath and tried again. "Not the show, so much," he said, watching me closely.

"You're a Bubba fan?"

Benny blushed. "Bubba Wilkins and I were very close," he said, and I could tell he was choosing his words carefully. "That coat has sentimental value for me."

"That's fine," I said. He was clearly uncomfortable, and I didn't want to press him. But Benny kept on talking.

"Bubba and I had a lot in common, you know. He used to be with the rodeo, so we both knew horses. I met him in the hospital the time I tore up my leg." He shook his head. "Hard to believe that was thirty years ago."

"I know a lot of people respected him," I said, and Benny looked almost relieved to hear it.

"I still remember that hospital," he went on. "Bubba was laid up longer than I was because he'd been gored by a bull. But I kept coming back to see him. I guess you'd say we hit it off." He trailed away into a quiet sigh.

"This isn't exactly a press conference, is it?"

"No," he admitted, patting the shirt in front of him. "Alacast was the only outfit I called. I knew they'd send you because you're the new guy."

"Then why did you bring all these T-shirts?" I asked.

"Parting gifts for the legislature. This is my last campaign. I'm moving to Florida after the primary. I guess that's why I'm talking to you now." He looked at me sadly. "You know, I was the reason Bubba quit the rodeo. He didn't want me to have to worry. Cowboys are a pretty homophobic bunch. They'd have killed him if they found out."

"The coat's at the dry cleaners," I said. "It had some mileage on it."

"You can see why I wanted this chat off-the-record," he said. "Some people knew, of course, about him and me. But I wouldn't want it to be common knowledge. People might think ill of him."

"If you like, you can pick up the coat tomorrow morning," I said. "I'll be at the studio a little after eight."

"I'd rather pick it up at the radio offices," he said. "Bubba's only been gone a year. Things are still a little touchy between Landerman and me."

"Landerman?"

His face flushed. "Bubba wasn't perfect," he said curtly. "Sometimes he strayed."

_/

So either it was about love, or it was about something else. If I could keep myself clear on that point, maybe I could sort my way through to the end.

Meanwhile, I had busywork to take care of. After I left Benny to his task of distributing T-shirts to the desks of the legislators, I stopped at the pay phone outside the Capitol pressroom and called my story in to the network. I told Sarge that the lieutenant governor had cut the wires on the legislative clock so he could hold the lawmakers hostage. Not sexy enough, Sarge told me, and then he hung up.

I walked outside into the sunlight and stood among the enormous pillars, taking in the view from the top of the Capitol steps. Around to my far left, beyond the side lawn, was the old Jefferson Davis home, the only Presidential Mansion of the Confederacy, now a museum sanctifying all the bitter failings of that unforgotten war.

Not many realize it, but the War Between the States began right here in downtown Montgomery. The order to attack Fort Sumter was sent by President Davis from a telegraph office on Dexter Avenue, just at the foot of the Capitol.

Other wars had spiraled out from this place, too. Nestled in among the old white bureaucratic buildings stood the Dexter Avenue Baptist Church. For over twenty years that redbrick building had served as the rallying point for the Civil Rights Movement. The famous nonviolent march from Selma had ended on its white wooden steps. Martin Luther King Jr. had preached there, in that very building, for nearly six years.

I thought about the Montgomery Baptists from my boxcar ride and wondered if this had been their church. It was certainly possible, and maybe even likely. In all the South, this church was the one that had forged the most powerful link between politics and religion. Its congregation might well have climbed into boxcars for a dangerous trip north, to the center of a government that had not yet taken their side. The church was quiet today, no one going in or out.

I wondered about the differences between their church doctrines and my own. Historically, I was a Methodist, so we all read the same book, certainly. Maybe we highlighted different passages. They probably carried the red-letter edition, relying on Jesus to keep them all on track, while I still thrashed in the icy grip of the Old Testament. In the Book of Daniel, to be specific. As a child in Sunday school, I was fascinated by the story of Daniel being delivered from the lion's den. But there was a passage in Daniel that came to haunt me in subsequent years:

He revealeth the deep and secret things: he knoweth what is in the darkness.

We all struggled with secrets. Benny, me, everyone.

Three tiers below me, at the head of Dexter Avenue, with the Baptist Church to his left and the State Judicial Building to his right, my cousin Billy addressed a throng of journalists and television crews. I could see Danny Larson among them, tape recorder clipped to his breast pocket, pen and notepad in hand. He and all the others were listening intently to this serious candidate for attorney general. I couldn't hear what Billy was saying, but the reporters were writing it all down. I could read it in the paper tomorrow morning.

I smiled when I realized that Billy would surely tune in to watch himself on the evening or morning news, and if he looked closely, he'd see me standing at the top of the steps behind him. I thought about moving down closer, descending slowly into the picture, step by step, until he couldn't help but recognize my face floating there beside him on the screen. But it would have been pointless. Too many years had passed, and now Billy wouldn't know my face from any other in the crowd. Better, maybe, just to stand there. An anonymous figure waiting at the statehouse door.

Chapter 16

On the drive to my father's house that night, I tried to imagine what Billy's response might be to my weatherman debut. The old Billy would have come straight at me, without a thought in his head but to shut me up for good. The born-again Billy was a different animal, a reincarnation as mysterious to me now as he'd been at his mother's funeral. Back then religion had taken him over like a virus, but maybe the virus had finally run its course. Maybe there was a third version of Billy to contend with.

I'd tried to glean some insight by rerunning the tape of his press conference before I left work, but there was no clue in his delivery. He was smooth as a countertop. It's easy to read a hothead, but a man with a calm voice could be thinking almost anything. In any event, I didn't have to wait long to find out what was on Billy's mind. Lucy had invited him for dinner.

He'd called the house trying to track me down, saying he wanted to congratulate me on my new job, and Lucy had been more than happy to play a role in bringing us together. Billy was the family celebrity, as far as she was concerned, and the idea of feeding him barbecued brisket at her own dining-room table had been more than she could resist. He'd graciously accepted her spur-of-the-moment invitation, even though it meant a long drive.

So when I trudged through the side door at dusk, planning nothing more complicated than a raw Pop-Tart followed by a sudden free fall into bed, I was stunned to find myself in the midst of a celebration in my honor.

"Surprise!" Lucy yelled, swooping awkwardly toward me down

the hall, her smile so broad I could have counted all her teeth. She was heavily made-up, even by her standards, and she wore a poofy yellow dress that umbrellaed down to her knees. Her high heels proved a poor choice for the orange shag carpeting, and she had to negotiate her footing as if she were stepping over bodies.

She grabbed me by the end of my tie and tugged me forward to the living room. My father, dressed in one of his loudest golf outfits, sat propped in his blue vinyl recliner with a napkin tucked in his collar to catch his drool. Steve, for once free of his hospital scrubs, was decked out in khaki pants, a blue blazer, and, inexplicably, a glossy-brimmed sea-captain's cap, as if he'd just dropped anchor in the yard. He posed at ease by the recliner, ready to intervene should an unexpected seizure tip my father over.

"Here's our prodigal boy," Lucy announced, drawing me forward into the room. "Home from his day on television!"

Alone on the gold brocade sofa sat my cousin Billy, with his white shirtsleeves rolled to the elbow and his tie loosened just enough to show he felt at home. I froze when I saw him, while years of bottled panic flooded through me. But as he rose and stepped around the mosaic-tile coffee table to offer me his hand, I recovered myself, realizing how different things were between us now. The seesaw had shifted. He was much smaller than I remembered, several inches shorter than me, with no hint of malice in his ruddy face. If anything he looked concerned, worried—maybe even apologetic for his sudden reintroduction to my life.

"It's good to see you, Taylor," he said, grasping my hand with both of his own.

"I guess you're here for my vote," I said, and Lucy and Steve both laughed.

"It's high on my list," he said.

"He's here for my barbecue," Lucy chirped. "And a dose of fine conversation."

"How's the conversation been so far?" I asked.

"Educational," Billy said, nodding graciously to Lucy.

"Golf and septic infections," Lucy said. "Those are the mainstays around here. Taylor, you wouldn't believe how much medical knowledge Steve has. He could go on a game show."

"I just always had an interest in that stuff," Steve said shyly.

"Well, you've turned it to fine use," Billy told him. "Looks like you're taking real good care of Bob here."

We all looked at my father, who stared unblinking into the middle distance.

"Bob's not septic, though," Steve informed us. "He won't go toxic for a while yet."

As if to assert the final remnants of his own free will, my father chose that moment to evacuate his bowels.

"Oh, dear," Lucy said as the room was suddenly awash in inappropriate sounds and odors.

"No problem," Steve assured us, taking immediate command of the situation. "Bob's got his rubber drawers on tonight. I'll have him cleaned up in a jiffy." With that he scooped him effortlessly from the chair. My father's expression never changed, but he coughed out a stream of phlegm that trailed beyond his napkin and down his shirtfront. "See there?" Steve said. "Long as that cough reflex is working, Bob's still in the game." Then he whisked my father from the room and carried him nimbly up the hall stairs.

"We'll wait dinner for you, Dad," I called after them.

"That's my cue to set the table," Lucy said, the bubble back in her voice. "I'll leave you two to get caught up. But don't talk about your day yet, Taylor," she added, patting me on the cheek. "We all want to hear about that." Then she stumbled away toward the kitchen.

"If you don't mind," Billy said softly, "I'd like to talk about certain parts of your day before we sit down to dinner."

"If you want to enter my contest, you're too late," I said. "I've already got a winner." I moved past him and settled myself onto the sofa just as Lucy stalked back into the room with a purple aerosol can.

"This'll fix everything," she said and waved the hissing can above our heads. A cloying mist of liquid lilac settled over the couch, coating us in sweetness.

"Thanks," I said, but she was already gone.

"I need to explain some things," Billy said. "I'm afraid you've got the wrong idea."

"You might start with Clay Hartsell," I said.

He sighed and squatted down in front of me. "Do you believe in the death penalty, Taylor?"

"I don't know. I never gave it much thought."

He stared at me for a long moment before he spoke. "Well, I have," he said quietly. "God's given me an insight in that regard. I believe it's wrong to take a life."

"You ought to know."

He laced his fingers and let his gaze drift to the carpet at his feet. "Exactly right, cousin, I do know. That's a weight I carry every day."

"Then you picked a mighty odd career path," I said. "Most capital cases get referred to the attorney general's office, even I know that. You people hand out death sentences like store coupons."

He raised his head and smiled. "We haven't prosecuted a death-penalty case since I've been there." He stepped around the coffee table and sat beside me on the sofa. "Taylor, do you know what kind of people get sentenced to die in this state?"

"I'd imagine being poor and black might have something to do with it."

"That's right," he said, "and so far I've kept a dozen minority offenders off death row. I've also set up a few prayer groups in the maximum-security facilities."

"Interesting form of atonement," I said. "But Clay Hartsell doesn't exactly fit the minority profile."

He leaned in close. "Three years ago Mr. Hartsell raped and murdered a nine-year-old girl up in Gadsden. But we never took it to trial. I offered him a deal to keep him out of the electric chair."

"And help yourself out in the process."

"Blackie's was the only open case I knew I could control. Look, Clay Hartsell is a guilty man, and I've seen to it that he'll spend the rest of his life in jail. There's no moral dilemma in that."

"But you've broken the law to do it, Billy."

"The letter of the law, not the spirit. Everything I've done serves the greater good."

"Why all the phony witnesses? Why didn't Hartsell just plead guilty?"

"False confessions don't always hold up in court. I figured it was safer for Mr. Hartsell to just keep his mouth shut and let me prove he was guilty."

"But he wasn't guilty."

Billy let out a long breath and patted my knee. "You're my blood kin, Taylor, and you know better than anybody how far I've come. So you be the judge. Open up any can of worms you want, I won't lift a hand against you." He paused. "But be careful. Not everybody out there's been redeemed."

There were holes in his thinking, that was obvious, but before I could frame an argument, Lucy reappeared in the doorway.

"Bob, are you about ready, sweetheart?" she called toward the stairway.

"Be right there, hon," came Steve's cheerful voice in reply.

She turned her smile toward me and Billy. "I trust we've got no vegetarians here."

"Only Dad," I said.

"Oh, I wouldn't make your father do without his protein," she said. "I put ground beef in his Jell-O."

Steve marched sure-footed down the stairs and entered the room carrying my re-outfitted father, who was now asleep.

"Everybody to the table," Lucy ordered. "Don't want anything to get cold."

Billy and I rose together from the sofa and moved into the dining room, where the table was crowded with bowls of food arranged around the centerpiece of Lucy's barbecued brisket. She'd fixed turnip greens, creamed corn, fried okra, and biscuits. Scattered among the larger bowls were relish dishes piled with spring onions, celery, green olives, and sliced pickled beets, all on my mother's best china. It was a feast. At the head of the table was my father's quivering red cube of meat-filled Jell-O.

Steve settled my father onto his chair and stretched a bungee cord across his chest to hold him upright. The rest of us then took our seats around the steaming meal.

"Billy, I'm sure Bob would appreciate it if you'd say grace," Lucy said.

We bowed our heads. "Bless this food," Billy said somberly. "And forgive us our trespasses."

"What a lovely thought," Lucy said, and she passed him the bowl of creamed corn.

"It's never a mistake to ask forgiveness," Steve offered. "You never know what's coming next."

"Amen," Billy agreed.

"So, Taylor, tell us all about your day," Lucy prompted me.

"I saw a dead boar hanging off the side of a truck," I said. That pretty well covered the gist of it.

Chapter 17

They say hindsight is twenty-twenty, but they're wrong. Sometimes history can take on a life of its own, mutating further and further from the truth. That's one reason Benny was right not to trust the general public with his story. When biography enters into common knowledge it's more susceptible to corruption, and suddenly schoolkids wind up believing that George Washington chopped down a cherry tree and refused to lie about it to his father. We're all suckers for an uplifting story.

I nurtured my own share of childhood misconceptions. I used to think that dogs in real life could be as smart as dogs on television. I used to think all people in authority were put there to make my world a better place. I used to think Jesus loved me. I used to think Jerry Lewis was funny. I used to think my life would have turned out better if I'd won the National Spelling Bee.

The rest of the week unfolded without any more surprise visits from my cousin Billy, which was fine with me. I was busy with the ordinary pressures of learning my new job—mastering the equipment, writing stories, delivering broadcasts, making the rounds to all the arcane agencies on my beat, and covering the press conferences of various unimportant candidates. And of course there were the forecasts.

On Wednesday I predicted a high-pressure system would soon bear down on the state capital. And I said that Clay Hartsell was innocent of the murder of Arvin Wilson.

On Thursday I predicted dangerous radon levels in many

government buildings. A new weather category, but an important one. And I said the witnesses in the Arvin Wilson case had all lied.

On Friday morning I predicted fireballs within the week, probably before the Tuesday primaries. And I said I'd been there when Arvin Wilson had been shot.

On Friday afternoon I predicted an end to weather as we know it. I promised a revelation come Tuesday.

Alf had been right about my potential as a conversation starter. My weather reports became the hot topic at backyard barbecues throughout the Channel 11 viewing area. Some people suspected I was crazy, while others thought I was engaged in some sort of avant-garde performance art. Some thought I was trying to catch the eye of big-time network executives in hopes of landing my own talk show. Nobody, that I could tell, simply took me at face value. But everybody tuned in.

My cousin Billy kept quiet through all this. He wasn't the same hothead I'd known as a kid. He had learned to be careful—otherwise, he'd never have made it this far—and I was protected by the spotlight now. If something suddenly happened to me, everybody would want to know why. For all Billy knew, I had a backup plan to get the word out in case I unexpectedly broke my neck in the bathtub or disappeared down a mine shaft.

But there was also the chance, however remote, that Billy was merely keeping his word and allowing me to decide for myself what his fate ought to be. If that were the case, there was a sad side to what I was doing. Arvin Wilson's last day was cold history now, and if I chose to drag it forward, the consequences would go well beyond the jailing of Billy Hatcher. Other lives would be altered, and not necessarily for the good.

I couldn't let that tempt me, though. No matter who Billy was these days, my debt was to the past, not the present or future.

My first day off was Saturday, when the network affiliates replayed Friday's broadcasts all day long. I got up early from the army cot in my father's basement, disarmed Lucy's alarm system so I could leave the house without alerting the police, and began the long drive down to Fairhope.

Eventually, I found myself on Alternate Route 98, winding along the sparsely populated eastern shore of Mobile Bay. The town itself was little more than a speed reduction on the highway, and I drove back and forth several times along the same sand-covered stretch of the narrow coastal road looking for the address Benny had given me. The homes here, modest beach cottages mostly, were set back from the highway in lush palm and mimosa groves, and Spanish moss hung low from the older, spreading trees. No house numbers were visible. I finally stopped at an isolated office complex perched on the precipitous shoulder of the road to ask for directions.

From the highway side, the place appeared to be a simple flat-roofed building no bigger than a mobile home, but as I stepped into the main lobby I saw that it was far deeper than it looked, with stairs to a lower level and a two-story annex that extended out toward the water. It wasn't an office complex at all, it was a medical clinic of some sort, and the sign at the counter said it was operated by the Sisters of Mercy.

The entryway was crowded with overgrown rubber plants and false papyrus, which at first masked the odor of the facility. But when I emerged from the alleyway of greenery to approach the main desk, I couldn't help but notice the pungent smell of alcohol and pine detergent that dominated the cold air of the reception area. A woman in a light blue uniform and a tight nurse's cap sat behind the counter, smiling benignly. I couldn't tell if she was a nurse or a toned-down nun, or maybe both. She had a straightforward quality about her, no makeup at all, and a smooth, dusky complexion that suggested healthy doses of the sun. In other circumstances I might have thought her an outdoor type, a woman more at home chopping wood than filling out forms for the sick and disabled.

"Can I help you?" she asked, her voice friendly but hushed. A dull, prolonged cry drifted up from some distant room in the lower annex.

"I'm a little lost," I told her. "I'm looking for forty-one-seventeen."

She brightened and rose from her chair. "This is forty-one-seventeen."

I checked the piece of paper, thinking I'd misread Benny's handwriting. But the numbers checked out.

"On Highway 98?"

"Yes. Villa Mercy. Do you have a loved one here?"

The obvious sympathy in her voice unsettled me. "No," I said. "I don't think so."

Her smile shifted slightly, still sympathetic, but also encouraging. "Do you have a relative you'd like to bring to us?" She pulled out a blue application form from a cubbyhole behind the counter and set it on the white Formica between us. "We have a waiting list." Her voice dropped to a whisper. "But naturally we have openings coming up all the time."

"No, I'm just—looking for someone."

"Oh, please, look around all you want," she said, gesturing toward the stairwell. "We understand. Long-term care is a big step. You need to be certain it's the right thing to do. And I'll be glad to answer any questions."

Long-term care. I knew what that meant. We'd looked at a few long-term-care facilities for my father, once it was clear he couldn't be saved. But Lucy had resisted that final act of resignation. The patients in these places were usually beyond all medical hope. They were terminal.

My mind raced through the possibilities. The most hopeful was that Benny had given me the wrong address. Or maybe he'd just lied to me to get Bubba's jacket. Or maybe it was all a prank set up by Alf or Sarge to break in the new guy. The option I didn't want to consider was that Alissa really was a resident here.

"No, I mean I'm trying to find someone," I said, my voice suddenly weak with uncertainty. "I was given this address." I held up Benny's note as proof.

"Oh, I'm sorry," she said, the pity easing naturally into her voice.

"I'm looking for Alissa Powell," I said.

Her expression darkened, and she stepped around the counter toward me. She stood without speaking for a long painful moment, and I understood clearly that the news wouldn't be good. She narrowed her eyes and stared as hard into mine as anyone ever had.

"You're Taylor Wakefield," she said carefully.

"That's right," I said, surprised that my weatherman fame had spread all the way to the Gulf.

"I'm Alissa Powell," she said. Then she slugged me hard in the face.

Chapter 18

Baby Angela was still alive at the age of six months, which surprised even the nuns who had named her. She'd been born with spina bifida, and shortly after her birth she'd contracted meningitis. That sort of double affliction isn't easily survived, not for very long anyway, but Baby Angela hung on, day after day. The nuns kept a round-the-clock watch over her condition because if she so much as caught a cold, that would surely be the end.

But the end of what? The Sisters of Mercy had become used to seeing lives flicker out. They dealt with it daily. But those were lives coming to rest after a journey. Baby Angela had never smiled or laughed. She had never cried, which may have been the most disturbing absence of all. Her brain was a withered mass of nerve endings. She swallowed food on occasion, but other than that, she offered no sign of consciousness, no proof she comprehended any portion of the world around her. And because Baby Angela could neither act nor react, she remained a question mark. Whether she possessed even the rudiments of self-awareness was anybody's guess. It wasn't a case of seeing the glass as half empty or half full. Baby Angela's glass might well have been completely empty; but it might also have been completely full, the water so pure it remained invisible.

And so Baby Angela had become the focal point not only of the Sisters' fervent prayers, but also of their philosophical contemplations, which is to say their doubts. They discussed her in nightly staff meetings. Did she have a mind? Did some form of feeling inhabit her heart? Was she capable of longing? Did she have the ability to dream? And what was the condition of her soul? Was she innocent, or tainted like the rest of us by the hand-me-down scarrings of Original Sin? Was it a blessing to be denied all earthly knowledge? Was it a blessing to be severed from all manifestations of human love?

I learned about these ruminations from Alissa, who did a much better job of controlling herself after a passing nun had pulled her off me. The nun, a stocky pillar of a woman in a uniform similar to Alissa's, had ascended to the lobby from the lower level, two steps at a time, when she heard me knock over a chair and a potted rubber-tree plant on my way to the disinfected tile floor.

"We've talked about this, Alissa," the woman said, wrestling her away from me and forcing her into the seat behind the counter.

"I was welcoming Mr. Wakefield to the facility." Her eyes were flinty and cold, and she continued to stare me down as if I were the devil.

"Mr. Wakefield?" the nun replied, her eyes widening as she turned toward me. "Oh, my." She stepped across the cracked terra-cotta pot of the rubber-tree plant and extended her hand. "I'm Sister Margaret," she said, her voice suddenly soft and measured, the tone reassuring. "Please excuse Alissa. She's working through a lot of anger issues."

"Sure," I said, brushing potting soil from my pants. "No problem." She'd clocked me good, but I didn't want to complain. There's a certain embarrassment that goes with being sucker punched by a nun.

Sister Margaret smiled tightly and turned back to Alissa, who sat gripping the armrests of the swivel chair. "Alissa," she said sternly, "Three hours of baby duty. Now."

"What about this mess?" she asked, indicating the heap of dirt at the base of the broken crockery.

"I'll handle it," Sister Margaret told her. "You've got other messes to tend to."

Alissa rose and composed herself, then walked calmly from behind the counter. "Follow me," she said, and I did, through the back of the lobby to an alcove off the central hallway.

Baby Angela's crib was tucked away there, surrounded by pieces of electronic equipment I couldn't identify. Monitors of some kind, probably, although none of them were hooked up at the moment.

"I have to be here now," Alissa said quietly, "and while I'm here I have to let go of negative thoughts." She gave me one last sidelong look, then settled herself onto a tall stool beside the crib and began her turn keeping watch over the child.

"Baby Angela's a miracle," she said, her voice brimming with wonder and admiration. I couldn't see her eyes, so I couldn't tell if she were giving me her own view or merely echoing someone else's. "Nobody knows how long she'll last."

I peered into the crib at the narrow, dark infant. She was barely more than a foot long. She wore a tiny pink dress—a doll costume, it looked like—which fit snugly around her slim, curved torso. Someone had Scotch-taped little pink bows to her scalp among the few tufts of curly black hair. Her thin arms were clamped tight against her side, her miniature fingers cupped against the fabric of her dress.

And before she talked to me about another thing, before even explaining why she had hit me, Alissa told me about Baby Angela. The child had been here virtually its entire life and had become much more than just another patient, although I scarcely know what other words to use because some of them sound ugly. A curiosity, a surrogate, an object of pity. Maybe even a pet. At the very least, she was a test of faith for the Sisters, and everyone on staff at the facility—the nuns, the nurses, even the janitors—all took turns keeping vigil, so Baby Angela might never have to be alone for more than a moment.

When she'd finished telling me about Baby Angela, Alissa fell silent and sat with her head bowed. I couldn't tell if she was watching the child, praying, or simply letting herself drift away in thought. After a few minutes had passed, I decided to attempt a conversation.

"How do you know me?" I asked, softly.

"Lots of ways," she answered.

"Which one made you attack me?"

She was quiet for a moment, then turned to look at me. The rage had gone from her eyes, but a deep weariness had replaced it. "All of them."

I'm not sure what I'd thought might happen between us, but this wasn't it. I'd expected initial friendliness, at least, maybe a jovial nostalgia to start things off. We might have moved through a gradual discovery of whatever things we held in common, or what values we shared, or what hopes we still had hopes for. She might have confessed to the same feelings I'd had that day we faced each other in the finals. We might have come together like two long-separated halves of a piece of broken crockery. If I'd made a list of a hundred possible reactions Alissa might have had to my turning up on her doorstep, assault would not have been one of them.

But I was here, I was determined, and in spite of this unpromising reunion, I was still potentially in love. After all, if Benny and Bubba could strike thirty years of lightning in a single shared hospital stay, maybe it wasn't ridiculous to think Alissa and I had similarly found each other at the National Spelling Bee. Maybe our connection was as legitimate as I'd imagined and had merely been lying dormant from that day to this. It wasn't impossible. If locusts could crawl up out of the ground on a seventeen-year timetable, who could say what an unreasonable expectation might be?

As I watched her watching Baby Angela, it took no effort to imagine some form of love between us, or at least the prospect of it. True, I'd seen her only in the most limited contexts, but some things were clear already. She had passion and strength of character. There was a bright goodness about her. She was fearless. She was kind. She would fight if she had to. Her voice had deepened to a more lush and husky tone, and its soft, sultry power was stronger than ever.

Admittedly, there were certain obstacles. Alissa's bitterness toward me was monumental and could be divided into three basic categories—the past, the present, and the future—which left me little to work with. And of course there was the whole nun thing.

The past was the most difficult to get around because it was already a lost cause.

"You ruined my childhood," she told me. "The moment you misspelled that word, my life turned into a nightmare."

"But you won," I said.

Two roads had diverged. It never occurred to me that choosing one over the other might be irrelevant, that both roads might end in brick walls.

"What did I win?" she asked accusingly. "You took all the prizes."

I told her I had no idea what she was talking about.

"Yeah, right." She paused in her vigil to glare at me. "I'm sure the only reason you entered was your love of spelling."

"No," I admitted, but I didn't elaborate. Now did not seem the best time to talk about the problems of my own childhood.

"My father spent months getting me ready for Washington," she went on, "drilling those stupid words into my head. He told me that if I won, we'd never have to worry about money again. He said I'd be a star. Then you stole it all."

"I didn't steal anything," I said. "I misspelled a word. I lost."

She puffed out a short, disdainful breath. "Oh, come on. *Responsibility?* Nobody makes it to the finals and then misses on a word like that. You knew exactly what you were doing."

This was the most absurd thing I'd ever been accused of. She actually thought I'd taken a dive in the National Spelling Bee. I hardly knew what to say.

"What about *therapy?*" I asked.

"Don't be an asshole."

"No, *therapy*–that was the final word in 1940. The next year it was *initials*. In 1932 it was *knack*. Those are all easy words."

"People didn't take the Bee seriously back then. The competition wasn't as tough."

"I humiliated myself on all three television networks," I pointed out. "Why would anybody do that on purpose?"

"For the contracts," she said, as if it were obvious. "You made losing the Bee a bigger deal than winning it. You took over the spotlight."

"It wasn't like that," I insisted. "I was distracted, that's all. I had a lapse in concentration."

"Distracted? The place couldn't have been more quiet if it was underwater. Nobody even breathed."

"I was distracted by you," I told her.

I had hoped this revelation might soften her a little, but I could tell by the way her eyes narrowed that she thought I'd just accused her of cheating.

"That's a lie," she said.

"You were just so beautiful," I went on. "It had nothing to do with contracts or anything else. Just you."

"Oh, really?" Her upper lip curled at the corner. "Then how come you're the one who ended up with a syndicated radio show? How come you got to do TV commercials with Sugar Puffs Pete? It's like my father says, the White Man always finds a way to keep the Indian on the reservation."

I sighed. "You know, you're pretty cynical for a nun."

The muscles in her jaw tightened, and I thought she might smack me again. But she took a deep breath instead.

"I'm not a nun yet," she said. "I'm still in the counseling phase. Or at least I was until you came along."

"Why do you need counseling?"

"*I don't need counseling*," she hissed, then collected herself again. "It's just part of the process. Counseling helps them evaluate your potential. They're very selective. Not everybody's cut out to be a nun, you know."

I couldn't argue that.

"So, how long until you take your vows?" I asked.

"There's no specific time frame," she said, a slight hint of defeat in her voice. "Obviously, there've been setbacks. If I could just catch a couple of breaks from Sister Margaret, I might make novice by next spring. The counseling's gone pretty slow so far. They think I've got *issues* to work out. I thought once I converted, things would go faster, but so far they're still dragging their feet."

"You weren't Catholic?"

She glanced toward the lobby. "I wasn't anything. But you can't join the Order unless you're Catholic. They're sticklers about that."

The more Alissa talked, the more she loosened up, and pretty soon I learned enough to understand why she hated me. She'd had a hard life, much harder than my own, and even though I thought the blame rightly belonged to her father, I could see why it was easier for her to put it on me.

In the aftermath of the Bee, Alissa's father had driven her all over the country knocking on doors, convinced there was somebody out there waiting with a vault full of money. But nobody had wanted her. Alissa was right—I'd satisfied the national quota for child academic novelty acts, leaving no room for her.

Still, her father kept searching for angles. He took her to producers, managers, talent scouts, advertising executives, television sponsors, everybody. But nothing panned out, and none of the agencies would even take her on as a client. Spelling was just not a marketable talent in show business, and Alissa had nothing else to offer. She didn't sing or dance. She had the wrong look for modeling, the wrong accent for voice-overs. And unlike me, she wasn't enough of a car crash to snare the public's interest.

Mr. Powell had not fared well under the weight of his failure. His daughter had done her part, becoming National Champion, but no matter how hard he tried, he couldn't make her a star. Then suddenly the window of opportunity was gone. Another National Spelling Bee Champion was crowned, and Alissa's chance was gone forever.

Maybe Mr. Powell had been something of a desperate character all along, or maybe this was the turning point for him, I don't know. Maybe my cowboy persona was too much for him to bear. But in any case, the day after Alissa's sad reign was over, he broke into the broadcast studio on the top floor of the Dinkler-Tutwiler Hotel in Birmingham and vandalized the equipment for my radio show. It was the first in a long series of poor choices.

One of those poor choices cost him his job. Another cost him his marriage. Another cost him both his driver's license and his credit cards. Another cost him his left foot to just above the ankle. Another cost him eighteen months of probation. And another cost him twelve-to-fifteen years at the Holman Correctional Facility in Atmore, Alabama.

That's why Alissa had dropped out of college and moved over here by the bay. She wanted to live within visiting distance of her father.

I'm no psychologist, but I'd guess he was probably the main reason Alissa wanted to make the leap from Seminole agnostic to Catholic nun. A parent like that could leave any good kid thinking she had a lot to make up for.

Anyway, there wasn't much I could do about it now. The past was one of the few inescapable things about the world, and she'd probably need a lot of time to sort her way through it. Or maybe that was the glitch in her counseling sessions with the Sisters of Mercy. Maybe they were trying to tell her that misplaced hostility was the wrong starting point for becoming a nun. But either way, I decided to leave it alone.

I moved up beside Alissa at the edge of the crib and looked again at Baby Angela lying peacefully in her little doll dress. I admired her. She was quite an affirmation, it seemed to me. Not of justice or fairness, because her medical circumstance was wholly undeserved. But she showed how stubborn new life could be, even if it had nothing else to gain, nothing else to look forward to. Like a weed forcing itself up through a sidewalk, Baby Angela had staked a claim on her own small piece of real estate in her own small realm of existence. Who could say any of us ever accomplished anything more?

Chapter 19

Hail can come from a clear sky because the sky is never really clear. It's always cold, always moving, always building or spreading, piling factor on factor like a baby giant playing with its blocks. Hail bigger than buckshot can fall without warning because the seeds of hail, the ice crystals, are always there in the upper stratosphere, waiting for the right combination of winds. When the ice crystals drift down to a warmer band of air, then cycle skyward in an updraft, a layer of water forms and freezes around the crystalline core. If the ice falls then, there's no hail, only a cold rain. But if the ice gets caught in a series of updrafts, if it rises and falls repeatedly in the sky, the ice accumulates like the layers of an onion. When the updrafts can't support the weight, the hailstones fall.

The largest hailstone on record had a circumference of seventeen inches and weighed one and a half pounds. But records were made to be broken.

Alissa now had a fresh grudge against me because the nuns asked her to leave Villa Mercy. Apparently, she hadn't been making the kind of spiritual progress they required, and when she knocked me to the floor of the lobby, that was it, they wanted her out. A healing sabbatical, Sister Margaret called it. Alissa could return under probationary status once she had her demons in check.

Since I was the embodiment of those demons, Alissa decided to assign herself to me as a spiritual exercise.

"You're my trial," she said, following me out to the car with an overstuffed duffle bag and an open shoe box full of turquoise jewelry and crucifixes. She had changed out of her uniform into a pair of faded jeans and a denim work shirt with the sleeves cut off at the shoulders. She looked ready for chores on a cattle ranch, but feminine, too, and I found myself staring at her the way I had in the spelling bee, with a mixture of embarrassment and longing. It seemed suddenly ridiculous that I'd failed to recognize her. She had the same dazzle, and as she swung her bag onto the hood of my Maverick and turned to face me, I realized that this was the first time I'd ever seen her in full sunlight. "I need to confront you head-on," she explained. "It's the best way to cope with my loathing."

"This seems kind of sudden," I said.

"Sudden is what I do best." She plucked out a silver crucifix and hung it around her neck, then tossed the box through the window into the backseat. "It's your fault they kicked me out. You owe me." She pulled a brush from a pouch on the side of her bag and jerked it savagely through her hair. "You're obviously here for a reason," she went on. "I guess you're the bitter pill I need right now."

"I don't see how I can be the problem and the cure at the same time."

"God's very efficient," she said simply. Then she opened the passenger door and climbed inside.

I didn't argue the point. She was, after all, the reason I'd come to Fairhope, and with her father in prison she had nowhere else to go. Alissa was probably about as lost in the world as I was, and when people are lost, they'll go for just about anything. Some join cults, some change careers. Some take up golf or start making tile coffee tables. Alissa may have needed me for the same reason I'd needed Alacast: radical change. Sometimes that's the only answer. Even if it's wrong.

I also figured there was a chance she'd soon start to warm up to me. I was the guy who had ruined her dreams of stardom, wrecked her father's life, destroyed her family, and got her evicted from the convent. Her impression of me had nowhere to go but up. I put her duffle bag in the trunk.

The ride from the Gulf was pleasant. We took a slight detour through Atmore so she could show me where her father lived, but it wasn't visiting day so there was no point in stopping. Back on the interstate, she quizzed me pretty closely on my life. I told her about Alacast and the weatherman job, and then, to my own surprise, I told her about Billy Hatcher. I even talked about the unexpected qualms I felt over turning him in, the irrational sense that I was committing some kind of betrayal.

"We talk about dilemmas like this in counseling sometimes," Alissa said. "A choice between evils. The devil sets things up that way to make us feel there's no way to win."

I didn't much like having my options narrowed to a choice between evils, but at least the choice was clear. I'd kept quiet long enough to know that keeping quiet wasn't the solution.

"I'm afraid I set this dilemma up myself," I told her. "The devil just came along for the ride."

We rounded a long curve to the northwest, bringing the glare of the sunset through the windshield. Alissa rummaged in her purse and pulled out a pair of dark glasses with a missing stem. "Just wait and see what God's got in store," she said. She perched the glasses on the bridge of her nose and leaned her head back carefully against the seat.

"So you think everything will take care of itself?"

"God works through agents," she said simply. "That means somebody'll probably have to do something." She rolled her window partway down and spit out a wad of gum. "You just won't know what it is until the time comes."

"What if I'm a little slow on the uptake?" I asked. "What if the opportunity goes right on by?"

"Won't happen," she said. "We're all part of God's plan."

Taylor Wakefield, part of God's plan. That couldn't be right. If God had nothing better than me to rely on, the universe was on pretty shaky ground.

Naturally, I didn't mention my spiritual reservations to Alissa. Our relationship was still more or less undefined. She wasn't a full-fledged nun, but she obviously had strong opinions, and as we felt our way forward in the dark, I didn't want minor religious differences to louse anything up.

"So you think God will protect me?" I asked.

She scowled at me over the top of her sunglasses. "Of course not. For all I know, part of God's plan is for you to get chopped into small pieces and fed to lab rats. I just meant things will work out overall. You know, in the long run."

"I'm more focused on the short run," I said, "and being fed to lab rats is not my idea of things working out overall."

"Tough," she said, unwrapping a fresh stick of gum. "It's not up to you."

Again, I didn't want to argue. Living at Villa Mercy, even as an administrator, Alissa would have seen far more than her fair share of bad endings. As a daily routine, that would take a toll on anybody.

"I'm staying at your place, by the way," she informed me.

"You'd probably be more comfortable at a motel," I said, preferring to postpone certain introductions.

"I don't use money."

"I can give you some cash," I offered. "Whatever you need."

"I didn't say I *needed* money," she corrected me. "I said I don't *use* it." She took off her sunglasses and studied the broken frame.

"Is that like a vow-of-poverty thing?" I asked.

"Matter of personal choice," she said, tossing the glasses out onto the highway.

"How long have you been not using money?" I asked.

"About two months now." She folded her arms across her stomach and stared down at the floorboard. "Actually, it was Sister Margaret's idea. She says I worry too much about personal finances. She also thinks I don't trust people enough. She wants me to reach out more." Alissa sighed and slowly cranked up her window. "I'm supposed to learn that God will always provide. You know, *Consider the lilies of the field,* and all that."

"How's it working out?"

She shrugged. "Okay, for the most part. God's great at opening up people's hearts, I really see that. But he's no help at all around vending machines."

We rode for a while in silence, all the way to the southern suburbs of Birmingham. It was long past dark now. I made the turn onto Oxmoor Road, and block by block, the neighborhoods of my childhood began to form around me.

"My great-great-great-grandfather used to visit these hills," she said dreamily. "He was a famous chief."

"If his name was Powell, I've never heard of him."

"He went by his first name. Osceola."

"You're kidding—Chief Osceola was your ancestor?"

"I just said so, didn't I?"

Osceola. I was impressed. In grade school I'd been taught that, excluding Pocahontas, only seven Native Americans were important enough to be written up in the history books: Tecumseh, Sitting Bull, Crazy Horse, Geronimo, Chief Seattle, Chief Joseph, and Osceola. The first four were usually denounced as troublemakers, but Seattle, Joseph, and Osceola were always presented as wise and noble statesmen. Well, maybe not so wise in Osceola's case. After the Indian Removal Act, he was the chief who refused the government's order to take his people on the Trail of Tears, which triggered the Second Seminole War. For eight years he led a mixed nation of tribal stragglers and escaped slaves in a campaign of resistance in the Everglades. He was finally lured from the swamps to discuss a treaty and captured under a flag of truce. He died in prison.

"His name means *The Black Drink*," she went on.

"You mean like coffee?"

"No. God, you're such a White Man. The Black Drink was a cleansing ritual practiced by Seminole and Muscogee warriors."

"What kind of cleansing ritual?"

"Vomiting."

"That was cleansing?"

She sighed impatiently. "The black drink made them throw up.

That's how they purged themselves of bad spirits before going into battle."

A descendant of one of the great chiefs. Amazing. I wondered what it would be like to have such a living connection to history. None of my ancestors had done anything but reproduce and die.

We drove up over Shades Mountain, past the reservoir.

"I don't really have a place," I finally told her. "I've been staying in my father's basement."

She shifted in her seat. "Why doesn't that surprise me."

The rest of the short way to Cahaba Heights, I kept telling myself it would be better if Alissa checked into a motel. But I made no effort to find one, or even to convince her that I should, so I guess the matter was already settled. She had a strong will, that much was clear. If she thought it was in God's plan for her to stay the night, it seemed silly to argue.

So before long there we were, idling by the curb in front of what had once been my home. I didn't usually park on the street, but tonight I had to. An ambulance blocked the driveway. Its red and blue light strobed silently along the length of the well-manicured block, bouncing in bright flashes from the rows of aluminum siding and the sturdy, brickwork facades.

"What's this about?" Alissa asked, but I didn't answer.

I got out of the car and started toward the front porch, where Steve stood beneath the yellow bug light with his shoulders slumped and his hands shoved deep in his pockets. He stared down at his feet, and I thought he looked cold, even though the air was clotted with humidity. Tree frogs buzzed in the distance, and armies of crickets chirped beneath the dark front steps.

"Hi, Steve," I said. I put a hand on the wrought-iron railing and pulled myself slowly up toward the door, one heavy step at a time.

"Hi, Taylor," he answered, and from the way he said it I knew the score.

Inside, Lucy was crying loudly into the gold brocade of the lilac-scented couch. She was flanked by two men in medical garb, whom I took to be paramedics.

"I killed him," she wailed the instant she saw me. I looked at the older paramedic, a balding man with hairy forearms. He shook his head slightly to tell me that wasn't exactly the case.

"Where is he?" I asked.

"He's already loaded up," the older paramedic told me. "We just thought we'd see if maybe the missus here wanted to ride along."

He raised his eyebrows to tell me they'd been too concerned about Lucy to leave her alone. I could understand that. Only a year earlier, Lucy had put in a full week of hysterics when her cat broke its neck in a window fan.

"It's okay," I assured him. "She'll have people with her."

He nodded. "Sorry for your loss," he said, and headed back to the ambulance, easing carefully past Alissa, who stood watching through the glass storm door.

"Yeah, sorry for your loss," the younger one repeated. He handed me a round plastic knob as he passed by. "Sorry about the alarm system, too. We tripped it coming in. Mrs. Wakefield couldn't remember the deactivation code, so I sort of had to dismantle it a little bit to shut the noise off."

"Thanks," I said.

Alissa stepped through the door and looked around.

"They broke the alarm," I told her. It seemed so unspeakably sad. I held up the plastic knob to show her. She took it from my hand and examined it.

"Alarms are a waste of money," she said, and I understood what she meant. Something always gets in.

"I don't quite know what to do now," I said.

"I do," she said matter-of-factly. She put a calm, practiced hand on my shoulder. "I guess that's why I'm here."

✍

So for Alissa, it was just another day at the office. She made the necessary calls, guided us through the paperwork required by the hospital and the police, advised us about funeral arrangements, and gave Lucy all the spiritual support she could muster. She also handled the firing of Steve, though the actual decision was Lucy's alone. Steve and I were both surprised by that move, though I guess we shouldn't have been. Technically, his job was over.

Lucy had other reasons for wanting Steve gone. Apparently, he had borrowed my father's car that night—which was a usual practice since he didn't own one himself. But this time Lucy was suspicious because he'd showered first and put on aftershave. He'd been less attentive lately, she thought, and now it occurred to her that another woman might be lurking out there somewhere in the night. She decided to follow him and find out.

The problem with that was one of timing: she would have to leave the house immediately after he did, or else she'd lose him in the darkness. Unfortunately, Steve's moment of departure came while Lucy was still spooning my father his pabulum dinner. In her haste to get away, she dispensed with the rest of my father's normal meal and substituted a whole-wheat cracker. By the time she got back from the tavern—where she'd merely found Steve drinking beer with his friends—my father was long dead. He'd strangled on the fiber.

I wasn't sure what kind of grief I felt. In many ways, my father had been dead a long time already. This last step was inevitable and even expected. Still, I guess there's no way to be completely ready when that permanent hollow space finally opens up inside.

Monday morning, Alissa and I drove down to Montgomery and I delivered my forecasts as if nothing had happened. For the past week the sky had remained a wide unbroken blue, the air still and balmy. It had been calmer than the calm before the storm. But that kind of stasis couldn't go on indefinitely. Something had to change soon, anyone could see it, and I predicted hail. Tons and tons of hail. I knew the seeds were up there, rising and falling, gathering layer after layer of icy glaze. When the heft was right, the sky would fling them down, I was certain of it. I warned everyone to stay indoors, to board up their windows if they could, to keep the cellar doors ajar for quick retreats, to abandon all crops that grew above ground. I told them we'd see hailstones big as television sets, that bridges, houses, and cars would be destroyed, that foolhardy pedestrians would be struck down in their tracks. The five sacred trees of the Druids—oak, ash, rowan, willow, and hazel—would all be shaken to their roots. The sky would empty, and the wind give up its dead.

The network got a lot of calls from worried farmers. But I couldn't issue a retraction. Nothing can stop the weather from doing what it will.

Chapter 20

News does indeed travel fast. When we arrived at work Tuesday morning, there was a condolence card taped to the network-office door. It was an expensive card printed on heavy stock, with watercolor lilies on the front and *In Deepest Sympathy* printed in slender feminine script on the inside. In the blank space beneath the sentiment, Billy had scribbled his own personal message:

> *Sorry about Bob. Lean on Jesus*
> *in your time of tribulation.*
> *Also, be at my office at 8 a.m.*

Since Rusty Wilderman had already offered me a couple of vacation days to regroup after the loss of my father, I knew I could get away from the network that morning. I had no idea what Billy wanted to see me about, and I wasn't even sure I cared, but going seemed to make as much sense as anything else I might do.

I left Alissa at the network and walked the three blocks to the State Administration Building, a massive structure with a white stone facade, located just behind the Capitol. Billy's office was in a paneled suite of rooms in the basement. I introduced myself to the picture-perfect receptionist, a creamy young woman, all teeth and hair spray, who disappeared briefly into an adjacent office.

"Mr. Hatcher will see you in a moment," she said brightly. "He just has to make a phone call first." As she said this, the tiny red light on her telephone flashed on. We both sat down and watched it, patiently, like strangers idling together at a stoplight. After about half a minute, the light went out.

"Mr. Hatcher will see you now," she said, smiling warmly at the phone.

Billy's basement office was more basement than office. The cold, bluish light from the low ceiling panels seemed to sink away into the dark Masonite walls and dull concrete floor, dividing the room between shadow and glare. There were no windows and no decorations on the wall except a framed technicolor vision of Jesus delivering the Sermon on the Mount. A couple of tall filing cabinets flanked the door, but other than that all the office contained were two metal swivel chairs and a green metal desk. The desk held nothing but a telephone and a sheet of paper. Except for Jesus picture, the place looked like a Soviet interrogation room. I shut the door and stepped up to the front of the desk.

"Have a seat," he offered.

"Thanks for the card," I said, easing myself into the chair across from him.

"It's tough to lose parents," Billy said. He took a heavy breath and blinked down at the desktop. "Makes you feel like you've moved to the head of the line."

I had nothing to say to that, but he seemed comfortable with my silence.

"I'm worried about you, cousin," he said at last. He leaned back in his chair, which creaked loudly. "You're way up on a cliff right now. Somebody needs to put up a fence to keep you from going over the edge."

"You're worried about my weatherman show," I corrected him. "Today's the day for revelations."

"That's up to you. I said I'd accept your judgment and I meant it." He stretched his legs so his shoes stuck out from under the front of his desk and folded his hands over his stomach. "But here's the thing, Taylor: politics isn't about individuals, it's about teams. There's people behind me—people I've got no control over—and some of them are pretty hard sons of bitches."

"So you want to build a fence to keep me safe."

"I just want you to know what the consequences might be if you decide to give my name to the world."

"Somewhere along the line I stopped being afraid of you, Billy. That goes for your whole team."

"You're in a state of grief right now, and that's making you reckless." He took a sheaf of papers from his inside pocket and dropped it on the desk between us. "We're family, Taylor. I wouldn't do this except to keep you from getting yourself killed."

I picked up the papers and looked through them. They were requests for warrants to be issued against Lucy LaVonn Wakefield and Steve Rigotoli for the murder of my father.

"They didn't kill my father," I said.

"Bob was on his way out, I'll grant you that. But she did put the food in his mouth that choked him, and there's plenty of witnesses that she and that male nurse had a relationship going. You and me could both testify to that."

"It was still an accident."

"Judgment call, Taylor, and it's my decision to make. I can file these papers anytime I want. Tomorrow, next week, next year. I might wait till I'm a hundred. There's no statute of limitations on a thing like this, as I'm sure you know."

I sighed. He pushed himself up from his chair and rubbed his sides.

"Here's something I've learned from watching you, Taylor: fear works wonders in the short haul, but it does finally break down. Sooner or later, even a ladybug like yourself gets fed up enough to make a stand."

"Maybe I'm not as fond of Lucy as you think."

"Doesn't matter. You've got a soft heart, cousin, and that's a good Christian trait. You wouldn't ruin somebody's life just to embarrass me on your TV show."

"How do you think Jesus would feel about this kind of extortion?"

He smiled. "Religion's based on extortion, Taylor—act right or go

straight to Hell. It's all about arm-twisting. For the greater good."
He hitched up his pants and walked around to the front of the desk,
where he rested a calm fist on my shoulder. "I'm saving your life
here, cousin."

I was in no position to argue.

Chapter 21

Most people were disappointed that I didn't follow through on my promised revelation in Tuesday's broadcast. Rusty Wilderman was among the most irate, and he summoned me in to account for myself as soon as I got back from the TV station. Alissa was waiting for me, too, and she followed me into Rusty's office.

Rusty sat hunched over his desk with his shirtsleeves rolled, examining the gleaming pieces of his disassembled Walther PPK. A can of gun oil and an assortment of cleaning rags added to the usual clutter of his desktop. A fresh box of German-made ammunition waited between the sailing schooner and the silver railroad spike.

"I can put this thing together in under forty-five seconds," he said without looking up. He continued to scrutinize the pieces, but made no move to touch them.

"Am I supposed to say *go?*" I asked.

"No, you're supposed to say who killed Arvin Wilson. If, in fact, you know." He finally looked up. "Who's she?"

"I've acquired a sidekick."

"I'm Alissa Powell," she said.

He thought for a moment. "The girl from the spelling bee?"

"Yeah," she said. She folded her arms and fixed him in a dour stare. "What of it?"

"That's good." He looked at me. "Use her in a promo spot."

Then he explained the problem. As president of the network, he was delighted with the success of my oddball format, but as a candidate for attorney general, he was worried about his votes.

"People know I'm your boss," he pointed out. "If you keep quiet now, it'll look suspicious—like I'm the one who shut you up. I want you to settle this thing before somebody gets the wrong idea, and I mean pronto."

But people always got the wrong idea. Any journalist knew that much.

"Don't worry," I told him.

"Now we see through a glass darkly," Alissa added, *"but then face to face."*

He pursed his lips and nodded. "Okay then," he said and turned his attention back to the gun.

✒

But every storm has an eye, and when it passes overhead, a certain number of people will always be fooled, thinking now's the time for a picnic. On this particular afternoon, with nothing but blue sky overhead, those who misread the signs most drastically were Billy Hatcher, Arch Hathaway, and Wilkie Smith.

Just after the three o'clock live feed to the affiliates, while I was sulking in the newsroom and listening to Alissa explain the pros and cons of burial versus cremation, Alf came bounding in waving a press flier.

"The attorney general's office has called a press conference for 4:00 p.m.," he announced. Sarge and Danny both paused over their typewriters.

"I'll be there," Danny said.

"No need," Alf told him. "They've specifically asked for Taylor." Everybody looked at me. "It's got something to do with his broadcasts."

The barometric pressure was dropping. I could feel it in my bones.

✒

According to the wall directory beside the elevators, the attorney general's main offices sprawled through several rooms on the second floor, about as far away from Billy's office as could be. The conference would take place in between, in the pressroom at the back of the lobby on the main floor.

The room was dingier than I expected and was set up like a tiny amateur theatre, with a couple of overhead spotlights and black cloth draped across the rear wall. The audience end was cluttered with about fifty metal folding chairs arranged in crooked rows before a podium. Television and radio crews swarmed around one another, setting up their microphone and light stands and checking the sound levels on their equipment.

Alissa had followed me over, insisting that she had a right to keep an eye on me. She was making spiritual progress, she said, and hardly loathed me at all anymore, but she was afraid of backsliding if I left her alone with her thoughts. While I took a seat in the back row, she drifted over to a shadowy section along a side wall.

Someone suddenly clapped a hand on my shoulder and for a fraction of a second I thought I was under arrest. I turned in my seat, and there was a grinning Arch Hathaway squatting behind me like a gigantic toad. He kept a firm grip on my shoulder to keep from tipping over.

"Hoped I might see you here," he said, his voice low and conspiratorial. "There's been a development in your little pet project."

"What kind of development?"

"Front page, and then some."

"What did you find out?"

"Sorry, pal," he said, wagging a stubby finger in my face. "It's my story now. I give it to you, it'll be all over the evening news. You'll just have to read about it in tomorrow's paper, along with everybody else."

"You can trust me," I told him. "I'm not a journalist." I glanced toward the podium. "Besides, I'm not breaking any stories right now about Billy Hatcher."

"Cold feet?"

"Something like that."

This sparked an interest. He leaned forward and hooked his

arm over the empty chair next to me. "Moral ambivalence, maybe? Second thoughts about mucking up the family name?"

I didn't answer. He chewed the inside of his cheek for a moment, then stood up and stretched. I thought he was about to walk away, but instead he stepped around the end of the row and sat down beside me. He checked his watch and glanced around again, then slid his chair a few inches closer to mine. "Okay, sport," he said. "We've got a couple of minutes yet. I'll tell you a little of what I've got."

So in those final few minutes before the press conference, he explained to me how my cousin had orchestrated the outcome of the Arvin Wilson murder trial.

Arch Hathaway was a top-notch reporter when he wanted to be. That first day in his office, he'd been right about the futility of taking on the attorney general's office with no other ammunition besides my long-delayed testimony. But things were different now. My promised exposé had become a source of statewide speculation. Pretty soon every reporter within driving distance would be scrambling to verify the guilt or innocence of whatever candidate I finally named. When it dawned on Arch Hathaway that he was the only newspaperman in the state who already knew the answer, he decided to take advantage of that head start and snoop around a little.

He started with Billy Hatcher's tax return, which was on file with the secretary of state. What he found was that Billy had cosigned five bank loans the previous year, each one for ten thousand dollars. Each cosigner had then defaulted, leaving Billy to pay back the entire amount. It was a legal way to funnel money to people.

"Guess who the loan money went to?" he asked, barely containing his delight.

"The five witnesses who testified against Clay Hartsell," I said. Billy had told me that at Lucy's dinner party.

"Which is a clear indication of bribery. But here's the interesting part," he went on. "The defaulted loans got paid off by a big-time tomato grower down in New Orleans. Hatcher's got out-of-state people behind him."

"Why would anybody from out of state care about a fifteen-year-old murder case?"

"They don't. They care about Hatcher. He's not the *top* dog, sport, he's the *guard* dog."

"Guarding what?"

"Insurance fraud, racketeering, money laundering, anything these corporate vampires can get away with. Alabama's the only state with no consumer-protection laws, and that lets a lot of riffraff through the door. With their guy running the attorney general's office, they never have to worry about prosecutions. Your cousin's the most valuable asset to organized crime in the whole South."

The television crews that had come down from Channel 6 and Channel 13 in Birmingham finished positioning their cameras and their overhead mikes, and the last few stragglers of the Capitol press corps now settled into their seats. They all crowded up near the front, so they would be called on when it came time for questions. Only Arch Hathaway and I lingered at the back. I looked past him to Alissa, who had moved forward from the shadows. She, like everyone else, was now focused on the man approaching the bank of microphones.

We were maybe forty feet apart and separated by a roomful of reporters, but I recognized the look in Billy's eye. It was the one I'd seen at Blackie's when he had me in his sights.

He wore a white linen three-piece suit that glowed under the television lights. He seemed dapper, even a little fastidious, with a natural, radiant charm most politicians could only dream of. Before he spoke, he drew a handkerchief from his breast pocket and dabbed at his watering blue eyes, which hadn't yet adjusted to the brightness. His perfectly trimmed blond hair was neatly combed, his cheeks plump and ruddy, and as he gazed benevolently around the room with his thick-lipped smile and his teeth gleaming in the spotlight, he could have been a late-night talk-show evangelist offering affordable cures to the infirm and disabled. He deftly refolded his handkerchief and tucked it neatly back into his pocket, then cleared his throat. The room quieted at once.

"I want to thank you all for coming here today," he said, his voice rolling out in a deep, slow drawl. "I especially want to thank the gentleman in the back row, Mr. Taylor Wakefield."

He pointed me out to the crowd, and several people turned in their seats to look at me. Arch Hathaway smoothly scooted his own seat farther away.

"As those of you from Montgomery already know," he went on, "Mr. Wakefield has kept us all entertained lately with his unorthodox weather reports on Channel 11." There was some sniggering in the front rows. Billy arched an eyebrow and held up his hands to quiet the noisemakers. "Now, let's have none of that," he said evenly. "He's done this state a great service, which I'll come to in a minute. But first, I need to confess a little something to you folks." He stepped to the side of the podium, placing himself in full view. "Taylor Wakefield is a cousin of mine, I'm proud to say. We've been through some rough days together, isn't that right, Taylor?"

I didn't answer. I couldn't see where he was going with this, unless he was just trying to make himself the least likely suspect when I suddenly turned up dead.

"When I heard that he'd got himself a job with Alacast, I imposed on our family connection and asked him to help out on one of my cases." He eased back around behind the podium and leaned closer to the microphones. "You all followed the Clay Hartsell trial, and you know we nailed that son of a gun dead to rights. That part's beyond question. But I always suspected we'd missed somebody, an accomplice we'd never been able to charge. I asked Taylor to help me flush that accomplice out. That's what his broadcasts were all about."

I looked at Arch Hathaway, whose lip curled upward in a snide smile, and at Alissa, who frowned straight ahead, absently fingering the silver crucifix she wore around her neck.

"It was a strange approach, I admit." He smiled broadly. "But I'm here today to report on the success of that strategy." He looked carefully around the room savoring his moment. "Early this morning, that suspect turned himself in to the Montgomery County

District Attorney's Office. I'm pleased to tell you now that Harold Wilkinson Smith has confessed to a role in the 1963 murder of Arvin Wilson."

There was a full five seconds of stunned silence while everybody tried to process this new information. Then half a dozen print reporters all began asking questions at once, while the well-dressed TV broadcasters jockeyed for position for their follow-up interviews. The independent stringers for the wire services and those who worked in radio news, all of whom had shorter deadlines to work with, started the rush for the pay phones in the hall. Several of them offered weak smiles or halfhearted waves as they hurried by, my grudging welcome to the press corps. A chair tipped over. The room had come to life. Arch Hathaway began to chuckle. He reached over and slapped me playfully on the arm.

"Nice job, Sherlock," he said.

"Wilkie Smith was not involved."

"Then speak up," he dared me.

But I couldn't.

"You've got to give Hatcher credit," he said, flipping open his notepad to a blank page. "He tends to find a way out."

Alissa stepped away from the wall and perched on one of the metal chairs. She seemed lost in thought, but I couldn't read her expression.

I looked at Billy preening for the cameras at the front of the room, nodding, smiling, answering every wrong question he was asked.

This was an inexplicable disaster, but I couldn't dwell on it now. I had a dead father to worry about, and a stepmother who had come unglued because she killed him, and a girlfriend who despised me and wanted to become a nun. I had reservoirs of guilt and remorse and failure that I still couldn't find the bottom of. I also had a broadcast coming up soon, which meant I had isobars to analyze and thermal inversions to get a jump on before it was too late. Arctic air masses were suddenly on the move. It was up to me to put the word out.

Chapter 22

Not many people know it, but sometimes general elections are decided by the weather. If it rains, the Republicans have an edge, while the sunny days bring out more Democrats. That makes sense, if you think about it. The poor and the disenfranchised tend to vote Democratic, because traditionally the Democrats sponsor more assistance programs for those in need. But those in need are often less willing to go out in a storm—the elderly don't like navigating slippery sidewalks and single mothers don't like shepherding a gaggle of rain-drenched children. Bad weather keeps them sitting at home. So in some instances, in the tighter races, the winning candidate is quite literally determined by the heavens.

But heaven stays out of the primaries. They're a different game altogether because the parties aren't yet going head to head. Primaries are about local infighting, and calling in favors, and intimidating rivals at the precinct level. Primaries are about seed money and salesmanship. They're about weeding out the amateurs and gaining control of the machine. Primaries are about gaining ground and keeping it, come hell or high water.

Things can go terribly wrong in a primary.

When I woke up on Wednesday morning, I felt irrelevant in the world. Billy Hatcher was beyond my reach. My broadcasts had done nothing but give Wilkie Smith another opportunity to embarrass his parents. He must have known his phony campaign wouldn't make it past the primary, that he was reaching the end of the charade, and that he needed some new gimmick to keep himself on stage, something outrageous enough to hold the spotlight. I'd given it to him. He was the lead story on every newscast in the state. If I'd been a real forecaster, I might have seen it coming. Now, even though Alf had insisted I take the morning off because of my father, I would have to go down to the Montgomery County Jail and try to convince him that there were more important things in the world than blaming parents for their shortcomings.

My only comfort was in knowing that whatever story Wilkie Smith might ultimately stick to, it would have no bearing on Arch Hathaway's side of the case. Bribing witnesses would still get Billy arrested, and that was a start.

When I came upstairs to the kitchen, I found Alissa and Lucy sitting at the table talking quietly across a shoe box–sized package wrapped in brown paper and marked *fragile*. Alissa had turned down my offer to set up a second cot in the basement beside my own, and had instead spent the past two nights on the couch in the TV room. She'd really helped Lucy through the crisis, partly by listening, partly by assuring her that she wasn't to blame, and partly by sprinkling quotes from the King James Bible into the conversation. Some of the quotes were pretty unintelligible, it seemed to me, but that didn't matter. We were deep in the Bible Belt, after all, where scripture was always appropriate. Sometimes the most comforting passages were the ones that seemed to have no clear meaning.

"I don't want to open it yet," Lucy said, her voice raspy from crying. She stared down at her hands folded on the tabletop.

"There's no rush at all," Alissa told her. *"He that believeth shall not make haste."*

"But I already made haste!" Lucy said. A loud sob escaped her throat, followed by a series of deep, awkward hiccups, but she stopped herself abruptly when she saw me standing in the doorway. "Oh, Taylor," she croaked, wiping clumsily at her tears. "I made the wrong choice."

"What's the problem?" I asked.

Alissa turned toward me. She was already dressed and ready for the day. Her eyes looked brighter, somehow, and her cheeks had taken on more color. She might have been wearing makeup.

"Lucy changed her mind about having your father cremated," she said, her voice wavering between sympathy and annoyance.

"That's okay, Lucy," I said, tightening the terry-cloth belt of my bathrobe. "We'll do it however you want."

"It's a little late," Alissa said softly. She put her hand beside the brown package. "The funeral home brought him by this morning."

"Like he was a piece of mail," Lucy cried, and she began to hiccup again.

I stepped over to the table and looked at the small, neatly wrapped container of my father. This final version was unsettling, and I could understand why Lucy might start to second-guess herself. The leap was just too great to follow. One day you're a normal guy playing golf and everything's fine; another day you're wrapped in a shoe box on your own kitchen table. He was smaller now than Baby Angela.

But why *fragile*? It wasn't as if anything else could happen to him.

Alissa reached past the package and touched Lucy gently on the arm. "Would you like Taylor to do it?" she asked.

Lucy dabbed at her eye with a paper napkin and nodded.

I pulled the box toward me and slipped my fingers beneath the edge of the brown paper. I thought of all those Christmas presents my mother had made me unwrap with the utmost care so she could reuse the paper. This wasn't Christmas wrapping, but I still removed it carefully, gingerly peeling away the several pieces of tape and unfolding the end flaps.

The box itself was bluish metal, not at all what I expected. I guess I thought everybody who got cremated wound up in bronze urns. This looked more like the cash box at a yard sale.

Now that my father was out of his brown paper, it suddenly seemed wrong for him to be in the kitchen. He was out of place here among the spice racks and canisters and cutting boards.

"Why don't I take him into the living room for a while," I suggested and carefully lifted him from the varnished maple surface. He was heavier than I'd expected, which I found reassuring.

"See if he'll fit on the mantel," Lucy suggested.

I carried him to the living room and scanned the row of glass figurines flanking the Seth Thomas clock over the fireplace. "The mantel's full," I called back. "But I can clear some stuff off."

I heard her sigh heavily. "Just use the new end table," she said. "But put a newspaper under him, so he won't scratch the finish."

The newspaper was still on the porch, so I tucked my father under one arm and stepped out the front door. Another sunny blue day, and the heat was already beginning to rise. I stooped to retrieve the paper, which flopped open in my hand.

It was the *Birmingham News,* but both lead stories were out of Montgomery. The photos were horrific, and my stomach fell as if I'd crested the top of a carnival ride. A rush of light-headedness nearly tipped me over. I steadied myself against the iron railing and sank to the top step. If a freight train had lumbered through the yard right then, I'd have tossed my father aside and made a run for it. That was something I knew how to do, at least.

A journalist for the *Ledger* had been found dead in a burning car, handcuffed to the steering wheel. It appeared he'd been shot-gunned. There were no suspects.

The troubled son of a prominent local family was found dead in his jail cell, an apparent suicide. He'd improvised a noose by twisting together a number of strands of dental floss.

Arch Hathaway and Wilkie Smith were dead.

Chapter 23

The following Sunday morning I had an impulse to go to church. Alissa's influence, maybe, though her brand of spirituality wasn't the kind that typically attracted converts. Maybe the death of my father had something to do with it. His absence still seemed unreal to me. Maybe I needed a dose of ritual to help me close some final door.

Or it may have been something as simple as guilt, which was always good for packing a few more warm bodies into the pews. In my case, the sheer bulk of it was approaching world-class proportions.

But whatever the reason, I got up early, put on my workday coat and tie, combed my hair, and tried to remember where the Methodist church was. I hadn't attended any services since I was eleven, and I'd never had to go there on my own. I remembered it as about a ten-minute drive away, but when I pictured the white stone building in my mind, the neighborhood I imagined it in didn't seem familiar. For some reason I thought it might be near the statue of Vulcan, but I wasn't sure.

Then it dawned on me that I had other options. I could attend any church I happened across. The denomination didn't matter— any place with a steeple would do. I could just get in my car and drive, see where I ended up.

I told Alissa my plan and invited her along.

"No, thanks," she said, munching on a piece of burnt toast at the kitchen table. Lucy was still in bed.

"Why not?"

She shrugged. "I might be needed here."

"Lucy took Valium. She'll sleep all day."

"I'll still pass," she said. "Church isn't really my thing."

"But you're trying to be a nun," I pointed out.

She frowned and put down the toast. "That's a separate issue," she said stiffly. "Spirituality doesn't have to be tied up in ritual."

"It does for Catholics," I said. I was beginning to see why the Sisters of Mercy had kept her in counseling for so long.

"Today I'm off duty."

"I thought being a nun was pretty much a round-the-clock proposition," I said.

She took a slow breath. "Then let me spell it out for you, Taylor," she said. "I've spent the past year helping people die." She jabbed a serrated spoon into her grapefruit half. "I don't need hymns and collection plates to bring me closer to God." She blinked a few times, then picked her napkin from her lap and blotted it to the corner of her left eye. Either she'd squirted herself with grapefruit juice or she was starting to cry.

"I'm sorry," I said quickly. "You're right—church shouldn't be an obligation for anybody."

"I just need a break, is all," she said. She reached out and brushed her fingertips along my forearm. "But you go ahead. I get the feeling you might need it."

"All right then," I said, slightly disconcerted at the thought of going alone. I'd never gone to church alone in my life. Then I had another idea. "Maybe I'll take my father," I said.

Alissa carefully spooned a wedge of grapefruit into her mouth and looked at me. "He'd get more out of it than I would," she said.

⚡

A few minutes later I was driving over the mountain into Homewood with my father buckled securely into the seat beside me. I still didn't know where I was headed, but each time I came to a larger cross street, I took it, and before long I'd overshot all the regular neighborhoods and was barreling down the Greensprings Highway to the I-65 interchange. I accelerated through the curve of the on-ramp like someone had dropped a flag to start the race, and soon, without even thinking about what it meant, I'd sped past Vestavia, past Hoover, and was gaining ground on Montgomery. Maybe it was habit that put me on the same set of roadways I took each morning to work. Or maybe I knew all along where I really wanted to go.

A few minutes after ten o'clock I turned the final corner downtown and drove slowly up the long, gentle slope of Dexter Avenue toward the Capitol building, which loomed large before me. The street broadened at the foot of the Capitol steps to accommodate two lanes of parking spaces, and I pulled carefully in beside an ancient black Ford Fairlane at the end of the row. The Fairlane was a classic, still in mint condition, and so highly polished that when I climbed out of my own car I could see myself in its deep, dark shine. I felt suddenly self-conscious of my mud-crusted yellow Maverick.

With my father tucked beneath my arm, I crossed to the south side of the street and walked up the wide wooden steps of the Dexter Avenue Baptist Church.

I pulled open the thickly varnished wooden door and stepped inside to the relative darkness of the outer hallway. A small, elderly black man in a light brown suit stood like a sergeant at arms in front of the heavy, dark doors of the sanctuary. A hymn I vaguely recognized filtered out around him.

"I'm Deacon Tilestone," he said, stepping forward. "May I help you?" His voice eased out in a low rumble, much deeper than I would have expected.

"No, sir, I'm fine," I told him. I started to move past him but he put his hand on my arm.

"The reason I ask," he said softly, "is we get a lot of tourists here. Folks come from all over to see where Dr. King gave his sermons. Sometimes they even take pictures. That's fine on a weekday, but not when we're having services. Too disruptive. So I'm obliged to ask if you're here for worship or for sightseeing. If it's sightseeing, I'll have to ask you to come back on Monday."

"I'm not a sightseer," I told him.

"Well, that's all right, then." He released my arm and gently tapped the metal box. "But I'll trouble you to show me what's inside here."

"I've never opened it," I said. "It's my father."

He seemed to think this over.

"Reckon I'll still have to see, if you want to bring it in the sanctuary."

I understood the necessity of keeping a close eye on things, especially here. Black churches still got bombed, and this one probably figured high on any psychopathic redneck's list. In some ways the Dexter Avenue Baptist Church was just a normal house of worship serving a normal congregation. But it was also the centerpiece of the Civil Rights Movement, a spiritual museum enshrining our difficult past. To complicate things further, the Park Service had declared the church a National Landmark four years earlier, and that kind of spotlighting naturally attracted a steady stream of gawkers, any one of whom might prove to be deranged.

Maybe I was one of those gawkers myself. I hoped not. I hoped I was here for a good reason, even if I didn't understand what it was. I wasn't black and I wasn't Baptist, but this still felt like the most appropriate church for me to come back to. If coming back was even possible.

I set the metal case on a tall side table beside the sanctuary doors, next to the donation box for the church's restoration project. I gently flipped up the clasp and raised the lid. Deacon Tilestone and I looked inside.

He was a smooth surface of ash marked by small, partially buried fragments of bone. A miniature landscape, like some seventh-grader's version of a far-flung corner of an African desert. A faint cloud of him rose above the blue steel lid.

"So that's your father," Deacon Tilestone said reverently.

"I assume so," I said.

"What's his name?"

"It used to be Bob Wakefield," I answered.

"Still is," said Deacon Tilestone. "Being dead don't take away a body's name."

We watched him for a moment, this gray residue of a completed life, both of us mindful of our breathing so as not to further disturb his rest.

Deacon Tilestone gripped my shoulder like an old friend. "You can go on along inside now," he said. I thanked him and closed the lid.

He handed me the church bulletin for the morning services and stepped aside. The final strains of organ music and a prolonged "Amen" were just dying out as I opened the heavy doors, and I entered the sanctuary in the lull between the hymn and the sermon, as people sank back into their pews and the minister—Reverend Branch, according to the bulletin—stepped up to the pulpit.

I scanned the sanctuary for a place to sit down, but there was no room left in the pews. All seventeen rows were crowded with the faithful. The two pews of the choir platform, left of the pulpit, were packed with blue-robed singers. To the right of the pulpit, on another platform set off by a wooden railing, several rows of old movie-theatre seats sat empty behind the small organ, but I wasn't about to walk down front and climb the rail to sit there. I moved quietly to the left side of the sanctuary, to the eastern wall, and stood in the multicolored light from the first of five stained-glass windows.

The windows were touchingly simple. No Biblical scenes of Jesus, just a randomly patterned mosaic of small, colored squares. Blue, yellow, red, green, violet. But no orange, which struck me as peculiar.

As soon as Reverend Branch began his sermon, I understood my mistake in coming. His voice was resonant and full of grave conviction, but I couldn't listen to what he was saying, not yet, not in my perpetually fallen state. My mind was still racing through chaos and static, and as I stood there in the checkered squares of light, I couldn't concentrate enough to absorb his words, to follow what he was saying. Too much unfinished business still cluttered my mind—too many rifts between what I should have done and what I ought yet to do—and even after fifteen years, it seemed that my return to church was sadly premature. I was little more than an eavesdropper straining to hear noises through a motel wall. I was an intruder with no right to be comforted, no moral defense for being here, for disturbing this orthodox community with my un-necessary presence. The deacon had let me pass, and I was grateful for that charity because I had learned something from it, but there was still a rift in spirit that kept me from belonging here. I thought about my boxcar ride from Birmingham and realized there might be people beneath this roof right now who had shared their space with me that day, and here I was again, barging through their door with all my sins intact. My father had been purified by fire, but I was still the same old outrider, a long, long way from home.

Chapter 24

By the time I crossed the street and made my way up to the rear driveway around the side of the Capitol, the building had already been evacuated. Razor-brimmed troopers manned the makeshift safety barricades of ropes and highway-department sawhorses, while scores of displaced state employees idled together on the scorched slope of the side lawn, quiet as cattle, squinting back at the high plaster walls. Happy tourists milled through the crowd snapping pictures of anyone who looked haggard enough to be important. Children draped themselves against the barricades and called questions to officers standing guard around the governor's limousine. One boy darted underneath the barrier and smudged the tinted window with his palm.

I scouted the grounds for Alf, thinking he might be taping interviews with some of the bystanders for the next broadcast, but he was nowhere around. My own recorder was still back at the network, so I figured the best thing I could do was stake out a spot and wait for him, and maybe talk with a few state troopers in the meantime. I climbed across the barricade, press pass held high, and asked one of the officers what he could tell me about the bomb threat.

"Not a thing," he said and walked away.

I moved down the line toward the governor's limousine and tried the question on another trooper.

"We're not allowed to comment," he said politely. "You'll have to talk to our public information officer."

"Where can I find him?"

His brow furrowed and he shook his head. "I'm not sure," he said. "I think he's in Louisiana until next Friday."

I'd run into that sort of answer all week. In the days following the primary, a lot of the people I needed to talk to had gone on sudden vacations or business trips to other states. Some had gone even farther. After certifying the election results, the secretary of state had gone camping with her husband in the Yucatán. The attorney general was now bicycling through France, in celebration of his own victory in the gubernatorial primary.

I couldn't blame them for leaving town. The election stink had taken over, creeping into every conversation, every interview, every question from the press. The electoral process appeared to have malfunctioned, and no one in the government or law enforcement was doing anything about it.

The gist of it was simple: in several of the statewide races, discrepancies had occurred between the original vote totals reported by the probate judges and the final results certified by the secretary of state. These changes occurred in eight counties—Pike, Randolph, Taledega, Houston, Lauderdale, Mobile, Russell, and Covington— and were too selective to be blamed on miscounts. For example, of the twelve candidates in the race for attorney general, only two were affected. In every instance the projected frontrunner, Bo McMillan, lost votes to the dark horse, William Hatcher. Hatcher won the nomination by less than a percentage point.

Naturally Bo McMillan and a host of others all cried foul. Protests were lodged, demands were made, investigations were called for. The airwaves were filled with angry interviews. But nothing happened. According to the secretary of state, the figures reported to her office had to be accepted at face value because she had no investigative authority. By law, election challenges fell under the jurisdiction of the attorney general.

"We'll definitely look into these statistical anomalies," William Hatcher had told the press. When asked if there might be a conflict of interest in his heading up the investigation, he took the high road. "I will not allow my personal involvement to deter me from performing the duties of my office," he had vowed. But so far the case had proven to be a real baffler, and he'd made no headway whatsoever.

I edged along the barricade toward the limousine, getting as close as I could to the trooper watching over the governor's wheelchair. Once the bomb squad issued the all clear, there might be a chance to get a quote or two from the governor himself before they wheeled him back inside. Maybe I could get in a question about election fraud. Now that he was retiring from politics, the whole state was seemingly up for grabs. He surely had opinions about the chaos.

The rear door of the limousine suddenly swung open and the troopers all shifted their attention to the crowd along the barricade. Cameras clicked behind me as quick-draw tourists tried to bag themselves a candid souvenir.

But it wasn't the governor who emerged from the backseat of the car. It was Alf.

"Thanks for the chat," he said, stepping out in a cloud of air-conditioned cigar smoke. A murmur of disappointment rippled through the crowd. Alf gave a friendly wave to the boy who had smudged the car window, then strolled over to join me at the barrier.

"Pretty nice car," he observed. He pulled the Lanier recorder from his inside coat pocket and switched it to rewind.

"Is that the governor?" I asked, nodding to the figure in the back of the limousine.

"Yeah." He stopped the tape and pressed the playback button. "Listen," he said, holding the machine up between us.

". . . *might get me in hot water,*" came the low, gravelly voice. "*It's not really mine, you see, it belongs to the office.*" Alf hit rewind again, and the tape whirred erratically through several bursts of high-pitched chirping.

"What was that about?" I asked.

Alf smiled and leaned back against the cross-rail of one of the sawhorses. "I tried to borrow his limo for the weekend. Limos are real babe magnets. But I got other stuff on here, too." He pressed the playback button and the voice returned.

"*. . . so I do feel election reform is needed. But in all honesty I don't think it'll happen.*" Alf clicked off the machine and put it back in his coat pocket.

"Sounds like a cry for help to me," he said. He blotted his forehead with the back of his hand and squinted up at the sky. "It's too hot out here," he said. "Come on, I'll buy you a Coke."

He was halfway up the side steps to the Capitol before I caught him.

"What are you doing?" I asked.

"There's a soda machine on the second floor," he informed me, pointing past the trooper at the top of the landing.

"You can't go in there," I told him.

"Sure I can. That's what press credentials are for." He presented his identification card to the trooper, who nodded and stepped aside for us both. "If reporters didn't cross barricades," he went on, "we'd never get the real story on anything but flower shows."

I hesitated on the top step. "What about the bomb?"

"Don't take it so seriously," he said, tugging on the massive bronze handle. The door swung heavily open, and a cool breeze swept out across the porch. "They have bomb scares here all the time. It's no big deal." He glanced over at the trooper. "Besides," he said, lowering his voice, "this is a good time to poke around."

I eased across the porch as if it were mined. "Poke around for what?"

"News." He stepped blithely through the doorway and disappeared into the relative darkness of the hall. I followed him inside and clanged the door shut behind us. The echo settled slowly into the stillness of the empty building.

I blinked away enough of the shadows to make out the dim silhouette of the brass light fixture hanging outside the governor's office.

"What happened to the lights?" I asked. "It's like a mausoleum in here."

"The power's off. They're afraid of electrical fires. That's the real danger if a bomb goes off."

"Apart from getting blown up, you mean."

"Relax. Ninety-nine times out of a hundred there isn't even a bomb. When there is, the bomb squad usually takes care of it." He thumped his fist against the sturdy plaster wall. "Anyway, we're not talking about some Palm Beach condo that'll fold in a high wind. This place has over a hundred and fifty rooms and the walls are over a foot thick. Any bomb small enough to carry in couldn't knock out more than a room or two. You couldn't get hurt unless you were in exactly the wrong place at exactly the wrong time. You're more likely to get struck by lightning."

He paused by an unmarked door and tried the lock. "We're in luck," he said, pushing the door open. A wedge of light fell across the hall floor and up the opposite wall. "Come on, I'll show you the governor's office."

"Are you crazy? We can't go in there."

"Sure we can. We've got the whole floor to ourselves. The bomb squad won't be out of the basement for another twenty minutes."

"How do you know where the bomb squad is?"

"Taylor, this isn't my first bomb threat. I know their whole drill. They don't just wander around the building, you know. It's a systematized sweep. First they clear the halls, then they check out the legislative chambers and the rotunda because that's where the public has the most access. After that they go right to the basement."

"Why the basement?"

"That's where the building supports are. The treasury vaults are down there, too." He ventured a few steps into the governor's office. "The basement takes a long time because of the kitchen and all the janitors' closets."

I followed him through the doorway. The office was narrow and deep, almost like a hall itself. The drapes were tied back with velvet sashes to let in the sun, but there was still a dark, subdued quality to the room. The walls were paneled in rich mahogany, and the ornate desk and high-backed chair had the polished gleam of fine museum pieces. Built-in bookcases, overstocked with leather-bound volumes of history and law, lined the left and right walls, and two delicate antique tables, littered with expensive bric-a-brac, sat like frail spinsters in the corners. At the center of the room a crystal chandelier hung above a pale blue Persian rug that seemed never to have been walked on. It was a perfectly manicured office, steeped in ceremonial opulence. Clearly, nobody worked here.

"This is what I love about bomb threats," said Alf as he settled comfortably into the governor's chair. "All the red tape disappears. We've got free access to everything." He began to rummage through the desk drawers.

"If you really want news," I said, "we ought to look somewhere else."

I felt uncomfortable in this room, and not just because we'd arrived uninvited. Too many fateful decisions had been made here. The place was a vortex of history, the calm center of countless storms. From Jefferson Davis to George Wallace, the darkest campaigns of the Confederacy had all been orchestrated from within these walls.

"Where would you rather we looked?" Alf asked me, propping his foot on the side of the desk.

I sank onto the satin edge of a spindly antique chair. Alf flecked a piece of dirt from the heel of his shoe.

"I don't know," I said.

"Okay—the Tuskeegee City Council is in trouble over sewer-line construction projects. We could sneak a look at the report in the state auditor's office."

"We've had that story since noon."

"What?"

"Danny phoned it in before lunch. Half the council is under indictment for rigging bids on state contracts. Try listening to a broadcast sometime."

He shrugged. "So pick another scandal." He leaned back in the chair and closed his eyes.

"How about secretary of state?" I suggested.

Alf sat up straight. "I'm glad I brought you along," he said, and headed for the door.

The secretary of state's inner office was just a few doors down the hall and around a corner from the governor's, but there was a world of difference between them. A network of cracks slivered up the bright plaster walls, and ominous brown stains spotted the high ceiling. The furniture was functional and anonymous—a small blond desk, half a dozen filing cabinets, bracketed wall shelving— all piled haphazardly with file folders, papers, and ledgers. I closed the door behind us and began to examine some paper-filled cardboard boxes balanced along the radiator.

"What exactly are we looking for?" I asked.

"Something incriminating would be nice," Alf said, pulling open a wooden file drawer. "Like the original vote totals, maybe."

"What about these?" I asked, tipping a box toward him.

"Those are just paper ballots," he said. "A few counties still use them. What we need are the summaries from the voting machines. They're bound to be here somewhere."

"What would they look like?" I asked.

"I'm not sure. They might be in a folder. They might just be a few stapled sheets of paper. We know Hatcher's race was tampered with, so look for anything that says 'Attorney General' on it."

I picked up a thick, loose-bound volume from a card table by the radiator. "How about *Third Quarter Budget Report, Office of the Attorney General*," I asked.

"That wouldn't be here," he said, without looking up. "Budget reports are kept in the state budget director's office. Figures for the third quarter won't be released until December."

"But it's right here," I said.

Alf stopped shuffling through the disarray of folders and took the report from my hand. He studied the cover for a moment and shook his head.

"Makes no sense," he said. "This report ought to be under lock and key in the office next door. Hatcher would probably have a stroke if this leaked out before the general election. Hell, he'd get rid of it altogether if he could."

"Why? What's in it?"

"Evidence of misprision of funds, for starters. This thing details all the expenditures connected to the attorney general's office. Shows where all the financial bodies are buried." He scanned the table of contents, then thumbed through to a middle section of the book.

Here was the unexpected virtue of a lumbering bureaucracy. Every department had to account for every nickel it spent or it couldn't get a budget for the following year. Now column after column of budgetary overruns showed clearly how my cousin Billy had manipulated the system.

"Look at this," Alf said, flipping back a few pages to compare figures. "He's run his branch of the A.G.'s office two million dollars over budget since the start of his campaign. In the last three months, he's hired forty special administrative assistants, but the number of prosecutions coming out of his office is down by more than half. It looks like he put his whole campaign staff on the state payroll."

"Can't he go to jail for that?"

"He could, but he won't. All cases that have anything to do with the misuse of state funds are automatically referred to the attorney general's office. Nobody else can prosecute." He dropped the report back on the card table. "You can see where that leaves us."

"We should still tell the attorney general."

"Ted Stricker isn't about to fly back from France to file charges against his own office." He shoved a stack of ledger books aside and sat on the edge of the secretary of state's desk. "Taylor, even if the attorney general isn't involved—and that's hard to know at this point—he won't do anything until after the general election. Arresting his most prominent assistant would blow up his own gubernatorial campaign."

"We can't just wait until after the election. Billy Hatcher might be attorney general by then."

Alf thought for a moment. "Well, I suppose we could make a copy of the report and send it to somebody at the U.S. Justice Department. They can't arrest him because he hasn't broken any federal laws, but they might send in poll watchers to keep him honest in the general election. If Hatcher loses that race, whoever beats him can open a legitimate investigation."

"Then let's make a copy."

"Copy machines won't run. The power's off, remember?"

"We could stash it in the pressroom overnight," I suggested, "then run it through the copy machine in the morning."

"That'll work," Alf said, pushing himself up off the table. "The secretary of state's still off in Mexico someplace. I can sneak the original back in here tomorrow, no problem."

I picked up the book while he eased the office door ajar and peered outside. Faint voices echoed from a distant part of the building. Alf checked his watch.

"They're just up from the basement," he told me. "Right on schedule." He swung the door wide and stepped out into the hallway. "They'll do the other wing first. We've got plenty of time."

He pushed through the swinging doors of the stairwell opposite the office, and I followed him into the nearly total darkness. We climbed awkwardly up the stairs.

"I'm still puzzled about this budget report," Alf said from somewhere up ahead of me. "There was just no reason for it be there."

An odd thought crossed my mind, an absurd notion about why it might make perfect sense for all the documentary evidence against Billy Hatcher to be gathered together in one run-down vacant office during a bomb scare. But before I could think it through to a logical prediction, the world behind us shifted in a flash and roar, and the darkness shot past us, thundering upward through the floor and walls. I pitched forward up the steps, knocked headlong by a ball of air so thick and compact it felt solid as it broke across my back. A cloud whirled over me and I froze against the rail, holding my breath. The stairway shuddered as the main shock spread beyond us. When I finally opened my eyes against the dust, the well was dark again.

"Are you still there?" Alf whispered.

"I'm here," I said.

The sound still pounded in my ears. Neither of us moved. After a moment we heard voices in the hall below.

"Shut off the water main!" someone shouted. *"It got some of the pipes!"*

"Maybe we'd better get off these stairs," Alf said.

"Up or down?"

I blinked the grit from my eyes. The dust fell gently now, like snow. Alf stifled a cough.

"Down, if the steps are still there. But take it slow."

We crept down the long flight, testing our weight carefully against each worn marble slab. The bottom steps were littered with debris, and streaks of light streamed in around the swinging doors. Water pooled across the landing and spilled off into the darkness of the next descent of stairs. We pushed our way out into the hall and found ourselves standing in sunshine.

We stood staring at the gaping hole where the secretary of state's office had been. The blast had sheared away the outer wall, and now the ragged edges of the room framed the bright view like a giant television screen. The spray of a ruptured water pipe spewed from the ceiling, arcing a small rainbow above the radiator's twisted remains.

Beyond the rainbow, seventy-five yards away, rose the clean white facade of the State Administration Building. Lounging at the side door, with his hands shoved in his pockets, stood my cousin Billy, calmly watching the show. A thousand bits of paper swirled between us in the breeze.

Chapter 25

Cyclone. The term was coined in 1848 by H. Piddington in his *Sailor's Handbook,* and was derived from the Greek word *kukloma,* which meant "the coils of the serpent." In the northern hemisphere, cyclones spin to the left, in the southern hemisphere they spin to the right, and any cyclone that drifts across the equator immediately cancels itself out. Hurricanes, tornados, whirlwinds, waterspouts, and whirlpools are all examples of cyclones.

Most weathermen don't count whirlpools as a type of cyclone because they think weather only happens in the air. But they're wrong. Weather can happen anywhere, and a cyclone is any spiraling power strong enough to cause destruction. Cyclones can even be manmade. A bullet, for example, as it rifles from the barrel of a gun.

My time as a weatherman was coming to its natural end. At first, Rusty Wilderman had been willing to keep me on after the primary, even though his own election loss left him free to resume his old duties. Maybe he just needed some time to recover from finishing dead last in the twelve-man attorney general race. Or maybe he was swayed by my ratings, which for a while had climbed higher than Bubba's game show.

But after Wilkie Smith's confession, my viewer-share began to taper off. The mystery, it seemed, had been solved, and with no new plot lines developing, my show began to grate on people's nerves. I was like one of those street-corner prophets who seems fascinating at first, but soon becomes just one more annoyance to tune out on the way to work.

My appeal did rebound slightly after the Capitol bombing, I guess because people wanted to see the weatherman who got himself partly blown up. The blast had driven a few slivers of what might have been a filing cabinet into the backs of my legs. Nothing serious—I hadn't even registered any pain until I got outside the building. But there was blood, and that's what the TV cameras focused on.

The resurgence of public interest in my show was short-lived. With no new high-profile murders to spread rumors about, I quickly devolved into yesterday's novelty act, and by the time my bandages came off, my ratings had thudded permanently back to earth. It was the Sugar Puffs Kid all over again. For the second time in my broadcasting career, I'd burst on the scene as the most original freak show in town. But freak shows can't endure, even on television. In the long run people prefer normal.

Alf tried to intervene, but once I'd lost my audience I was done for. Rusty said he'd keep me on through the end of the election season. After that, he would have to let me go.

The only bright spot in my life remained Alissa, who appeared to have settled in at my father's house for an extended stay. She'd gone from hating me to bringing me ham sandwiches for lunch, a transition spurred forward by her belief that I was keeping quiet about Billy Hatcher for spiritual reasons dictated by God.

I don't know that God had much to do with it, however. It's true I didn't want to be the cause of trouble for Steve and Lucy, but I wasn't sure that was the whole story. Personal motivations become difficult to sort out once people start turning up dead in jail cells and burned-out cars.

The evening of the bombing, when I arrived home covered in plaster dust, still bleeding in spots and with a detailed snapshot of the explosion tattooed across the back of my sport coat, Alissa wept uncontrollably. I was glad she did because it saved me the trouble.

"I'm very confused," she said, both arms wrapped tightly around my neck. A fresh wave of sobs broke from her throat. We were standing in the living room next to my father, who now rested on the new end table with cork drink-coasters under his corners. The coasters had watercolor prints of famous golf courses on them.

"I got into the governor's office today," I told her, and she sobbed again.

"Close calls are so difficult to interpret," she said softly, her face still pressed against my chalky lapel.

"Not for me," I said. "Anytime I don't get killed, I take it as a good sign." I held her tight against me, and for the first time since I'd known her, she started to relax.

"Nuns don't have boyfriends," she whispered.

I kissed her lightly on the temple, then the cheek, then the lips. It was the completion of a gesture begun in my mind when I was twelve years old, and now fourteen years of anticipation flooded through me in a moment of undiluted relief and gratitude. She seemed to go along, settling her body softly into mine, and all those fires that had burned against me for so long abruptly changed direction, opening up a moment of unexpected intimacy, a moment in which all my inadvertent trespasses against her life were scoured away, a moment pure and true enough to define the world thereafter. I could finally answer Benny Bibberly's question: it was indeed about love.

She sighed and looked up into my face. "This'll probably add a year to my counseling."

At least.

She joined me in the basement that night, and even though she shivered at times like there was still too much to be afraid of, she didn't run away.

She came to work with me every day from then on, saying God didn't want me taking on my cousin Billy alone. Her presence made no difference to anybody at the network, except possibly Frank Landerman, who still worried about blows to our dwindling professionalism. But I liked having her along. Of course Billy didn't really figure into it, as far as I was concerned. In principle I hated him more than ever, but in practical terms, he still had the upper hand. Given the circumstances, I was happy to steer clear of him altogether.

Billy, it turned out, had other ideas. He didn't know what to make of my silence. I guess it never occurred to him that he'd simply won, that I was in no position to rock his boat without capsizing too many others. My plan, if I even had one, was to serve out my network time quietly and without incident, and maybe hope for a change in the weather.

But there was one question mark Billy couldn't tolerate. After the bombing, Alf had made a point of mentioning the budget report in several on-air interviews, without ever going into detail. Billy didn't know if we had the report or not.

In fact, we didn't. Alf had dropped it in the explosion, and as we huddled there on the dark, groaning stairwell, wondering if the entire structure were about to come down around us, neither of us had felt inclined to sift blindly through the debris looking for it. By now it was probably in a landfill somewhere miles away. But for Billy that report remained a troublesome loose end.

Seven days before the general election, when I was down to my final week as a weatherman, Billy called me at the network. When Alf handed me the receiver in the newsroom, I had to sit down to talk.

"I think we need to meet," he said. His voice was edgy, and I could tell it annoyed him to make the call.

"I'd rather not," I told him.

"I don't blame you," he said. *"But there's a lot of bad news in the works. I figured you and me could maybe put a stop to some of it."*

"What kind of bad news?" I asked.

He laughed. *"How many kinds are there?"*

An infinite number. There were as many kinds of bad news as there were of snowflakes, and no two were exactly alike.

"I know what Arch Hathaway knew," I told him.

"I hope not," he said. *"The Tree of Knowledge is a dangerous thing to climb around in."*

Billy had seen us talking the day of the press conference. He probably had a pretty good idea what I'd heard from Arch Hathaway.

"There's a limit to what people can get away with." Even as I said it, I wondered if it was true. In all my weeks as a weatherman, not one of my predictions had been right.

"Cousin, I'm disappointed in you," he said. *"You sound so pessimistic."*

Sometimes we have to put our faith in something that seems wrong. Like swinging a golf club easy to get more distance on the shot. Like steering in the direction of the skid, or blowing on a fire to make it hotter. Like standing your ground with a vicious dog because the worst thing you can do is make a run for it.

"When do you want to meet?" I asked.

"The sooner the better," he said cheerfully. *"I've got a chicken dinner at the Elks Lodge until about seven, but I'm free after that."*

"I'll be right here," I said. I figured not even Billy would be crazy enough to do anything violent at Alacast headquarters, even with no one else around. It would be strange territory for him, with too many uncertainties. He'd have to behave himself.

"At your network, huh? Well, that's fine, Talyor, it's just a friendly meeting." His voice sounded jovial, reassuring, and I could see why he'd done so well in politics. *"Oh, and one other thing,"* he added. *"Bring along your houseguest. I may have a little bad news for her, too."*

So he'd been watching us. Suddenly I thought how stupid I'd been in letting Alissa come up with me from the Gulf. I should have kept her out of harm's way, hating me awhile longer for ruining her childhood. Then I could have gone back later, after everything with Billy had resolved itself, and asked her out on a date. We could have gone to the movies, or to play miniature golf. We could have been in a normal situation together, or at least as normal as one could expect between a near-nun and a fake weatherman. Yes, if I had the choice over again, I'd leave Alissa in Fairhope and settle things with Billy first. Romance was tricky enough without a sociopathic relative lurking in the background.

But before I could form an objection to Billy's last instruction, he'd hung up the phone. That's when the true drift of things came back to me. What made me think I'd ever be able to resolve my problems with Billy? Even if Alissa were tucked safely away in Fairhope, patiently awaiting news of a tidy ending, I would have no idea how to orchestrate the proper outcome. As my father had been fond of pointing out, a golf ball could bounce from a tree limb into the cup, but that kind of ricochet wasn't something you could count on. I needed to focus. I needed to ask myself the right question. If it came down to a matter of choice, what choice did I now have that might somehow make a difference in Billy Hatcher's fate? Or in my own.

And as far as Alissa was concerned, what choice had I made that brought her here in the first place? I couldn't remember making one.

That was the catch in a universe of free will. One possibility always led to another, even on the most microcosmic level. Choice was not a matter of a few conscious decisions a day, it was a relentless barrage of overlapping options coming so fast we couldn't think through them all. Every waking moment was filled with a multiplicity of alternatives, and we chose automatically, intuitively, instinctively, unthinkingly, and we did so without ceasing. Choice was not a fork in the road, it was an ocean with more currents than we could ever know. The trick was to keep ourselves afloat.

But where did that leave the future? Still up for grabs, was my sincerest hope.

I put the receiver back onto its cradle and looked up at Alf, who stood waiting for a damage report. Since the bombing, he'd been as obsessed with Billy Hatcher as I was. I'd even say we'd both become a little paranoid, except I'm not sure the term applies when someone really *is* out to get you. In either case, our daily routine now included checking our cars for explosives before leaving work in the afternoons.

"He's coming by here tonight for a visit," I said. "He wants to see me and Alissa."

Alf thought it over. "That's probably okay," he concluded. "He wouldn't make his plans public if he meant to do anything drastic."

Alf sat back heavily against Sarge's worktable. "Maybe you can tape him," he suggested. "He might say something to incriminate himself."

Over the past few weeks, I'd come to learn that defeat was a huge portion of any journalist's job, and now I could hear it creeping into Alf's voice. Part of our daily frustration working in the news business was in knowing certain ugly truths we could never broadcast. It didn't take a genius to know that Billy had committed a raft of crimes, but we had no evidence, and since all the infractions came under the jurisdiction of Billy's own office, unsupported accusations would bring nothing but a libel suit. To the people of Alabama, Billy Hatcher was a crusading lawman dedicated to cleaning up the state, and any reporter who made wild, unsubstantiated claims against him would look like a muckraking crackpot.

There was also Billy's retaliatory power to consider. If we broadcast what we knew, he might come after us as an angry assistant attorney general with the full force of his office behind him, or he might come after us simply as a murderous psychopath. Either way we were looking at a bad outcome.

For now my main concern was Alissa. I didn't feel altogether comfortable bringing her into close quarters with my cousin Billy. I would tell her about the invitation, but if she didn't want to come, that would be fine with me.

She was out getting us Mexican food at the moment. Sarge had appointed her the network's first and only unpaid intern, using her to run errands and to handle rewrites. She was especially good at the latter. Each of our on-air stories had to be paraphrased a dozen times during the day so we could repeat them without sounding like we were recycling the same broadcasts. The chore called for someone with a large and flexible vocabulary, and Alissa's background as a National Spelling Bee champion figured in nicely. The work gave her something constructive to do while she waited for God to show his hand, and it seemed to take her mind off the situation. She had developed a new range of smiles, some demure, some friendly, some chagrined, some wistful, some amused, and some even straightforwardly happy, as she handed out her neatly typed alternate versions of the day's odd or unfortunate events. New depths of color had surged into her cheeks, as if her pulse itself had made a comeback from some deep hibernation. She seemed to have become radiant.

When she came through the newsroom door, her arms laden with leaky brown bags of enchiladas and burritos, she knew at once that something was up, probably because no one was grabbing for the food and because Alf avoided looking at her altogether. She carefully elbowed Danny's typewriter aside and set the bags on the table.

"What's happened?" she asked, looking from me to Alf, then back to me again.

"The assistant attorney general wants to meet with us this evening," I told her.

She narrowed her eyes. "Us who?"

I shifted uncomfortably in my chair and took a breath. "You and me. He said he had bad news for us both."

I don't know what reaction I expected from Alissa right then. A normal response might have been fear, or panic, or at least some indication of misgiving. But Alissa was in a phase of renegotiation with her religion, and people like that could be hard to predict. Freestyle believers like her—and Billy, too, for that matter—saw the world through the shaping lens of their own private notion of God, and that vision could vary not only by denomination but by personality. Opportunity, disaster, threat, deliverance, all conditions might wear the same face in a time of crisis, and any two zealots might have different readings of the signs. It was all highly idiosyncratic.

Alissa's reaction was to smile. I'm not sure what kind of smile to call it because I hadn't seen one like it before. I'm tempted to say beatific, but that seems overly grand. I guess I'll just say enigmatic and leave it at that.

Chapter 26

Seeding the clouds. That's a sore spot with some weathermen, those purists who view it as a form of cheating. If the sky itself can be manipulated to suit our temporary needs, prediction becomes a different game entirely. Forecasts become mere self-fulfilling prophecies, divinations with no basis in the divine.

In purely practical terms, there can be legitimate reasons for it, for spreading silver nitrate a mile in the air to generate a chain reaction among those drifting, listless molecules. When crops are dying, desperate measures are called for.

But still.

Alissa would say cloud-seeding demonstrates a lack of faith, which it does. But more than that, it reveals the nearly limitless dimensions of our own hubris in the face of God or Nature or whatever it is that organizes all the principles. It says to that Organizer, *Step aside, Bub, we'll take it from here.*

No wonder we're an endangered species.

Seven o'clock came and went with no sign of Billy. I should have expected that. He'd want to give us time to wonder and worry and second-guess. The calm before the storm.

Alissa sat thumbing through magazines at Darla Wilderman's immaculate desk in the reception area of the outer office, a bored veteran killing time between crises.

I mostly paced the hall and other offices, moving aimlessly from room to room, periodically checking the news ticker for any AP stories I might want to get a head start on for tomorrow's early broadcast. But nothing was going on in the world. No events, no eruptions, no quirky sets of happenstance. No change in atmospheric conditions either—nothing but a broad blue evening darkening to a broad black night. The usual smear of stars. No movement of air, no circulation. Heaven holding its breath. I straightened clutter, emptied wastebaskets, and fidgeted with stray pencils. I'd actually broken two of them by the time the knock came at the door.

Alissa set her magazine aside and folded her arms across her stomach. I took out my small Lanier tape recorder and turned it on, then slipped it back into my inside jacket pocket. The knock came again, and I walked past Alissa toward the door.

"Take a few deep breaths first," she said softly. "But don't hyperventilate. It won't help if you faint."

That gave me a moment of clarity—not about what would happen when I opened the door, but about Alissa's attitude toward it all. I knew she was a passionate woman, I'd known that since she first decked me in the lobby at Villa Mercy. Maybe I'd even known it years before, as I listened to the painstaking perfection with which she mouthed the infinitely jumbled letters of the alphabet. But now, in this moment of coming face to face with what might be honest-to-god evil, she seemed dispassionate, as unconcerned as a cat sunning herself on a window ledge.

But that wasn't it at all, I realized. Alissa was no sleepy cat on a window ledge. Her passive look, her relaxed attitude, weren't signs of disinterest, they were more like a reincarnation of something I'd witnessed years earlier, something I'd encountered on the streets of my childhood.

Righteous resistance.

Alissa was an inheritor of odd histories, a bitter Seminole Sister of Mercy who'd been trained to spell every irrelevant word in her non-native tongue. Her ancestor, Osceola, had been caught with his guard down, but Alissa was too savvy for that. She'd seen too many people die unfairly, had come through too many tempering fires, and now, in the aftermath of so much enforced Catholic pa-

tience and discipline, she had arrived at that rarest mutation of the
soul, the strength to weather her convictions. She was the spiritual descendant of those protestors in Birmingham, the nameless
martyrs who flickered across our television screens, people with
enough will to sit passively through the worst of what other human
beings would do to them.

Yet I still had no idea what she was thinking.

I closed my eyes for a few seconds, steadied myself, and opened
the door. Billy stood there, lounging against the opposite wall in an
ill-fitting blue blazer, casually picking Elks Club chicken from his
teeth with a yellow toothpick. At first he seemed every bit as relaxed
as Alissa, but as he shoved himself forward from the dark paneling,
his eyes darting back and forth to read the landscape of this new
environment, I saw how caged he was, how restless beneath that
thin mask of piety and goodwill.

"You're late," I said.

"My apologies," he answered. He paused in the shadow of the
doorway and nodded toward Alissa, a thin smile curling across his
upper lip. He walked past me to the newsroom door and peered
inside, then glanced around at the other rooms. "This place looks
like a garage sale." He pointed toward Rusty's soundproofed office
door. "What's down there?"

"That's the president's office," I said as I closed the outer office
door.

"Wilderman," Billy said, pronouncing the name with exaggerated contempt. "Clueless from day one." He turned and looked at
me directly. "Cousin, don't even pretend to think he'd make a better
attorney general than me. I may have flaws, but I'm no empty shell.
I believe in things. I get things done."

"Like you got things done with Arch Hathaway?" I asked,
thinking this would be a good thing to have him answer on tape.

"It hurts me that you'd think that," he said. "I had very little to
do with what happened to Mr. Hathaway. He just poked around in
the wrong places, that's all. Got himself tangled up with a zealot."

"A New Orleans businessman, maybe," I said.

He chewed his toothpick for a moment. "You're just full of good tidbits, aren't you?"

"I keep an ear to the ground," I told him.

Billy narrowed his eyes. "Good way to get your head stepped on." He tossed the toothpick to the floor. "But I'll concede the point. I do sometimes answer to a man in New Orleans. He, in turn, answers to a man in Miami. The man in Miami—well, who knows where it goes from there." He smiled. "You aren't the only one with a network."

"I want to know why I'm here," Alissa interrupted, rising to her feet.

She was here because I'd stupidly involved her. She was here to give Billy leverage.

Billy paused to look her over carefully. "You're here to serve, Sister, same as me."

"You said something about bad news," I prompted him.

"Well, it's not bad news, per se," he said, taking on a reassuring tone. "It's more like a forecast. I see bad things on the horizon."

"Sounds like you've acquired the gift of prophecy," I said.

He shook his head. "Doesn't take a prophet to see where you're headed, Taylor. Your future's shaping up to be a mighty short one. I'm worried about you."

"Forecasting is a tricky business," I told him.

"True enough. Sometimes the whole sky fills up with thunderheads, and not a drop falls. It all just blows over. That's what I'd like to see happen now."

He turned his back on us and walked down the inner hallway toward Rusty's soundproofed sanctuary, moving with a sense of authority that seemed to transform every step he took into a personal claim on yet another yard of ground. Alissa slipped her purse strap over her shoulder and marched stiffly down the hall after him. My pocket tape recorder hissed faintly against my heart like a broken pacemaker as I followed them into the office and shut the cork-covered door.

Billy settled himself comfortably behind Rusty's desk, slouching into the chair like a teenager. I stood directly across from him, while Alissa hung back by the tall gray filing cabinet next to the door, where she set her purse.

"Now, Taylor, caution requires that I ask you to put your hands on the desk and lean forward."

I did as he said. He stretched his left arm across the desk and deftly pulled the Lanier recorder from my inside coat pocket.

"This," he said, holding it up between us, "is an act of bad faith." He placed the delicate recorder on the brightly polished mahogany desktop, next to the radio schooner. Then he picked up Rusty's silver-plated railroad spike and brought a full-force blow down on the small machine, ramming the point all the way through into the wood.

"Rusty might wonder about the hole in his desk," I said.

Billy pried loose the spike and placed it precisely along the edge of the desk in front of him. "Vandals. They're everywhere these days." The Lanier recorder whirred through one last squeaky fragment of its inner machination, then fell silent.

"I guess vandals blew up the secretary of state's office," I said.

"No, I'm afraid public servants were behind that one," he admitted. "Some clutter had to be disposed of. Bureaucratic loose ends."

"Why not just carry it off somewhere?" I asked.

"Too much of it—whole filing cabinets full of records and reports, not to mention all those boxes of election material from the primaries. We'd have needed a forklift and a backhoe to get it all out." He squinted toward the window and chewed his lip. "Besides, that office was scheduled for remodeling anyway."

"People almost got killed."

"That wasn't the intent. You're my conscience, Taylor, I don't want you hurt." He swiveled his chair from side to side. "Look, politics is a contact sport. Sometimes things get a little out of hand. I don't much like it, but there it is."

"Blowing up buildings isn't politics," I said.

"Expediency, Taylor. That's politics in its purest form." After a calculated silence, he leaned back in the chair and propped his feet across the corner of Rusty's desk. "You know, you're lucky I was around when you were a kid. You needed somebody to throw you off a gym roof just to show you what the world was like." He stared at me, unblinking, for a few moments, then ran his hands up over his scalp. "Did I ever tell you how I got to be assistant attorney general?" he asked.

"Somebody must have put in a good word."

"No, this was a case of the Lord helping those who help themselves. Ted Stricker had just got himself elected attorney general. I knew he hadn't hired any assistants yet because he hadn't even been sworn in. Stricker's a real Milquetoast kind of guy, I don't know what the voters saw in him. Anyway, he lived alone out in the country—small farm, a few head of cattle—and one night a plane landed in his front yard. Stricker couldn't believe it, here was this twin-engine Cessna leaving skid marks in his flower beds. So he came running out in his bathrobe to shoo it away. Only it wouldn't shoo. Instead, three fellows in business suits climbed out—" Billy smiled— "and one of us had a shotgun. Well, Stricker knew something was up, so he started yelling that he was the new attorney general, he could put us all in jail if we didn't leave. But that didn't quite carry the weight he hoped it would. We just dragged him back inside the house, sat him down in the living room, and stuck the twelve-gauge in his mouth." Billy held up a finger, as if he'd reached a moment of particular instruction. "Now, this was all just theatre, you understand, nobody was really in danger. The gun wasn't even loaded." He swivelled slowly back and forth in his chair. "Then this runt of a cocker spaniel came running in from the kitchen. Couldn't have been more than twelve or thirteen weeks old. Little brown spotted thing, with his tail still unclipped. I guess he thought it was all a great game, so he started chewing on Stricker's moccasins, like he was trying to help out. Just about the cutest damned thing I ever saw." He shook his head and took a slow breath. "And it occurred to me that I could move things along a lot quicker if I just picked up that pup and snapped his neck. Intimidation's a skill, like anything else, and if you kill a man's dog like that, he'll know you mean business."

"Not exactly a Christian gesture," I said.

"Oh, I disagree," Billy said, leaning forward in his chair. "Animal sacrifice goes all the way back to Genesis. Abel slaughtered his sheep to please the Lord. That's why God preferred him over Cain." He leaned back now and folded his hands across his chest. "But I couldn't do it, Taylor. I'm not that kind of man anymore. I couldn't set my emotions aside, even when a point needed to be made. So I just leaned over and patted that pup on the head. Then I took the gun barrel out of the attorney general's mouth and said I hoped he might have an opening for me in his office. As you can see, the Lord rewarded me for my gentleness of spirit."

"I guess you pulled the same routine with the probate judges in the primary."

"Not everybody's got yards big enough for planes, Taylor. The primary was more a case of straightforward politics. You know how that goes—machines get tampered with, a few ballot boxes get mis-placed. Maybe the polls close early in a couple of key counties. It's not that hard to swing an election."

"Then you didn't really win the primary."

"Sure I did. The vote totals have already been certified, and after that there's no provision for appeal. I could drop dead tomorrow and you'd still see my name on the final ballot."

"I guess that explains why you didn't put much effort into campaigning."

"Waste of time. Just plant a few disciples on the election crew, and you've got yourself a landslide."

"The general election won't be that easy," I said.

He shrugged. "Not my concern. My backers will take care of everything. They stand to lose a lot if I get cropped out of the picture."

"You're working for criminals, Billy."

"I've reconciled myself to that, Taylor. Jesus himself set down the guidelines. I render unto Caesar what is Caesar's, that's all. So what if my supporters make a little profit here and there? Money has nothing to do with God's kingdom." He looked over to Alissa. "You want to back me up on that point, Sister?"

"Have no fellowship with the unfruitful works of darkness," she said.

"It's not darkness, and it's plenty fruitful. You ought to be happy for me. I found my true calling."

"Instilling fear isn't a calling," she said.

He reached inside his coat and took out a pack of gum.

"Why not?" he asked, pulling out a bright yellow stick and unwrapping it. "It's my God-given talent. I make sinners fear for the condition of their souls. Nothing wrong with that."

"God doesn't want anybody to do what you do."

"That's a prideful thing, Sister, to think you know what's in God's mind. I sure don't."

"Then you ought to read the Bible."

He smiled. "I do. I teach Sunday school every week. You seem to forget, the Old Testament's got a lot of moral ambiguity to it. David committed adultery and then had his girlfriend's husband killed. Samson slew just about anybody he could get his hands on. Joseph's brothers sold him into slavery. Lot got drunk and committed incest with his daughters. Old Testament heroes can be a pretty unsavory bunch. But I'm okay with that—I've got some Old Testament in me myself."

"You should try the New Testament."

"Jesus is my Lord and Savior, Sister, that's first and foremost. I just don't let people walk all over me like he did."

"Mister, the Lord has infinite patience, but he can also strike you down in a heartbeat."

"Is that the Lord God or the Lord Jesus? If you're talking about God, then you're right back in the Old Testament. If you're talking about Jesus, you're flat-out wrong. Jesus made a career out of never doing shit to anybody."

"You said you had a forecast," I interrupted.

"That's right, I do. Hand over the State Auditor's Report."

"That's not a forecast."

"Or else."

I shook my head. "Look, Billy, I understand the threat. But I don't have the report."

"Then your friend del Tasorian shouldn't have shot his mouth off about it. Look, I hate to be a hard-ass about this, but I don't have any choice. Certain people have put a lot of money into my future. They can't have that report show up on somebody's TV show."

"It won't. We never got it out of the building."

"No offense, Taylor, but your say-so won't really satisfy these folks." He breathed an almost wistful sigh. "You probably don't believe it, but I'm on your side. I might just be the last thing standing between you and a burnt-out Chevy. I'd like a little cooperation in return." He reached back inside his coat and drew out a dull, blue-black revolver. "Do you know how close you came to getting shot in the face fifteen years ago?"

"I should. I was there."

"You were there, but you still don't know." He held up the gun for my inspection. "I've carried this thing since I was fifteen years old. Found it in a footlocker in my mother's attic. Twenty-two caliber. This is the only gun I've ever felt comfortable with."

"You shot Arvin Wilson with a thirty-eight," I said. The newspaper accounts were still clear in my mind.

"Blackie, you mean. He'd have kicked you in the nuts if you ever called him Arvin. But you're exactly right," he said, nodding. "It was a thirty-eight. I'm glad you remember, because that gun was your guardian angel." He rested the worn barrel of the twenty-two against his cheek. "I hate thirty-eights. They're too heavy, they kick too much, they've got lousy range, and they're way too loud. But that particular thirty-eight I'd just won in a poker game the night before. Drew to an inside straight, which is a stupid play, I know, but that night I did it anyway, and damned if my card didn't come up. So that gun was my new toy, and that's the only reason I had it with me. Any other day of the year, I'd have had this twenty-two."

"Caliber doesn't mean much when it's an empty gun," I said.

"The twenty-two wouldn't have been empty." He opened the cylinder and showed me its crowded circle of bullets. "This here's a nine-shot pistol. You'd have been dead three times over."

So that's what my place in the world came down to. I was alive today because my cousin Billy had filled an inside straight. What can we do with information like that? Wonder how many times a week we would have died if not for something unforeseen and beyond our control? Wonder if today's survival hinges on yesterday's traffic lights or the faltering path of a three-legged cat limping through a distant neighborhood after dark?

Whose hands are we in when we aren't in our own?

"Here's the funny part, though," he went on. "I won the thing off Blackie. So he's really the one who saved you. Which is quite a feat, considering he was dead at the time."

Every event is part of a chain. Now I could trace my survival straight to Blackie himself. It was the most appropriate news I'd heard in fifteen years. Billy flipped the cylinder shut.

"I could still rectify the matter, I suppose," he said, waving the barrel in my direction and grinning. "But that's not who I am anymore."

I thought of the last time I'd sat in this office while a grown man played with his gun. The world had endured a lot since then, all of it unpredicted.

"I'm glad to hear that," I said. "But I don't see what's changed between then and now."

"I don't let my temper get the best of me anymore. Temper was my downfall with Blackie. It wasn't a race crime, you know. He owed me thirty bucks from the card game. That's all I came for, but he wouldn't pay up, told me to kiss his ass. I got mad and shot him, simple as that."

"You'll go to jail for it," I told him. "Family or not, I'll make sure it happens. I don't care how long it takes."

He laughed. "Could be quite a while, the rate you're going." He tucked the pistol back into the holster beneath his arm. "Why not just let bygones be bygones? Nobody really cares what happened fifteen years ago. The past is like a Third World country—nothing but filthy hotels and a bad exchange rate. Nobody goes there anymore."

"History's too big a thing to let go of, Billy."

He looked amused. "Taylor, here's a genuine prediction: you'll still be griping about me in the nursing home. Nobody'll listen to you then, either. I'm the law here, you keep forgetting."

"Voters could change that. The general election won't be as easy to rig as the primary, no matter how much help you've got."

"Voters forgive anything but sex crimes and physical deformity," he said. "I'll take my chances."

"Arch Hathaway was a big mistake. Word'll get around."

"Let it. I'm sorry for what happened to the man, but right now he's the biggest scarecrow in the state. It'll be years before any reporters come snooping around me again. Except maybe Alf del Tasorian, and he's got less credibility than you do."

"Alf's got more listeners than you think."

"Not after he gets himself arrested for hiding a pound of cocaine in his refrigerator. In one of those baking-soda boxes, maybe." He clasped his hands behind his head. "See how easy it is?"

"What about me?" Alissa said. "What makes you think I'll keep quiet?"

"It's not about keeping quiet, Sister," he said. "You can speak ill of me all you want, I don't care. But I do need that report back, and God's empowered me to do some ugly things to get it."

"How ugly?" I asked.

"Well, you know what'll happen to Lucy and Steve. After that I may have to close down Villa Mercy. I've got the authority to do that, you know. A lot of people died there this year. That might call for an investigation."

"It's a long-term care facility," Alissa said. "Of course people die there. That's the point."

"I'm sure you're right," he said. "But I still might have to pull their license while I sort things out."

"I won't let you do that," Alissa told him.

"Glad to hear it. All I need is that audit report back. Things'll clear up in a hurry. Won't be a cloud in the sky."

"I don't have it," I said again.

"Then you're totally screwed, cousin. And you won't be alone in it, either." He took another sheet of paper from his breast pocket and carefully unfolded it, then handed it across the desk to me. It was a list of transfers to the Holman State Correctional Facility in Atmore.

Alissa moved forward and took the list from my hand. A darkness settled across her face as she studied the brief catalogue of convicts and their crimes.

"That's a bad bunch I'm sending down to Atmore," Billy went on. "Capital offenders, mostly—and every one of them wants to stay on my good side. What that means, Sister, is your Daddy's life just took a profound turn for the worse. He might not even survive."

"He'll survive," Alissa said flatly.

"That's the spirit. Just use your influence on Taylor here. Help me get that report back, and your daddy'll be fine. I'll probably be elected governor in four years—maybe I'll give him a pardon."

"He's only got three months left to serve," she said.

"I wouldn't count on that, sweetheart. Sometimes inmates make mistakes that add time to a sentence. It's hard to say how long he'll be in there. We'll have to wait and see what the future brings."

"What makes you think you've got a future?" Alissa asked. The question sounded oddly rhetorical, but Billy missed that part.

"Just look at the signs. I'm living a charmed life by anybody's standards. God's working overtime for me."

"That's a stretch," I told him.

"How about what happened with Wilkie Smith?" he asked. "You probably thought I had something to do with all that, but I didn't. It was a pure act of God."

"Don't blame God for human frailty," Alissa said, her voice straining to a level I'd not heard before.

"Fair enough. But then you tell me how it is that your daddy and

Taylor's stepmother both got delivered right into my hands. Seems like divine intervention to me."

I couldn't argue. Events truly were unfolding in unexpected ways. Who was I to claim knowledge of what it might add up to? Maybe Billy really was some kind of chosen instrument of God. Maybe somewhere down the road he'd have a great awakening, a real conversion experience, and wind up in the pantheon of heaven's heroes. Maybe a deathbed epiphany would cleanse his soul and cancel out whatever atrocities he'd committed along the way. Wasn't that a crucial tenet of the Christian faith—that it's never too late for sainthood?

In college I read a medieval text by an Italian bureaucrat named Boethius called *The Consolation of Philosophy,* written in prison while its author awaited execution for political mistakes. The argument in the book was simple: fate was beyond our control, but not the attitude with which we faced it. For Boethius, free will was a state of mind, not of action.

"Pride goeth before destruction," Alissa said.

"A quote for every occasion, is that your deal? Well, how about *Love your enemies?* Better yet, *Resist not evil.* That's some of the best advice Jesus ever gave. If you can't buy into that, maybe you ought to give some serious thought to changing religions. Go back to doing rain dances and all that other heathen crap."

I'm not sure what the breaking point was. It might have been the second Jesus quote. I'd always wondered about that one myself. Why would Jesus tell us not to resist evil? It made no sense. Evil was up at dawn seven days a week trying to take over the world. If we all just stepped aside, everything would end up being run by psychopaths. Every system—political, economic, social—would crumble into chaos and corruption.

Maybe there was a problem in translation. Maybe *Resist not evil* meant that sometimes you had to give in to the violent impulse. Even Jesus lost control from time to time. Sure, turn the other cheek if you can. But if you find the money-changers camped inside the temple, feel free to go berserk.

In any case, whatever Alissa's breaking point was, Billy overlooked it. Charged right past it, in fact, oblivious to the hole he had just opened up in the universe, a hole exactly his shape and size. He'd grown so certain of his own invincibility that he'd stopped reading his audience and had simply blundered on, pressing every wrong button he could reach.

"You shouldn't call me Sister anymore," Alissa told him. "I'm all through with trying to be a nun."

Billy started to smile, as if this were one more victory to crow about, but his face changed suddenly to a look of surprise. It was the most sincere expression I'd seen on his face since the day we buried his mother. I turned to Alissa and felt my own rush of surprise.

I'd venture to say that any other day of the year, Rusty Wilderman would have put his Walther PPK away in his desk drawer. I'm sure in Rusty's mind there was a logical reason he had to leave it on top of the filing cabinet that day, snugly tucked inside its holster. But I suspect Rusty's reason doesn't matter. History provides reasons of its own, and maybe the only one worth considering is this: that Walther PPK, loaded with the ammunition I'd recommended to prevent misfires, needed to be on Rusty's filing cabinet for Alissa at precisely this moment of her life. Alissa herself must have believed that.

I still believe in free will. But I've also come to see the tapestry of choices that binds us in a common framework, the way one thing leads to another, the way threads that started miles and years apart will someday inevitably intertwine, weaving and knotting themselves together in ways that might have been predictable all along.

All this time I'd thought I was the one who was supposed to stand in Billy Hatcher's way, that I was meant to be his undoing, or else he would be mine. Now I saw that I'd been nothing but a go-between, that my purpose had been far simpler than I'd thought. No wonder I'd never gained a clear vision of how to stop Billy—my stopping him had never been in the cards. I was here to bring these two together, my Seminole nun girlfriend and my murderous white-trash born-again politician cousin, for the defining moment of their lives. That moment was the intersection of two roads, fate and free will. Alissa stood at the point of their convergence.

As she dropped the holster to the floor and raised the pistol with both hands, holding it at arm's length and sighting down the barrel toward Billy's heart, I could see the choice she'd made. There would be no hesitation, no contemplative moment of self-reflection. She would simply pull the trigger.

Billy realized it, too, I guess, because he pushed himself up from the desk and shuffled backward a clumsy step, bumping the chair so that it rolled sideways and thumped softly against Rusty's display case of trophies. The move slowed Alissa for a fraction of a second as she shifted her aim. Billy stuck his hands out in front of him in a reflex of self-protection.

I was taken over by a reflex of my own, one that came from somewhere deep in the programming of who I was.

I stuck out my hand. Like a shortstop lunging for a hard line drive I launched myself toward the line of fire, reaching as quickly as I could into that narrow corridor between Alissa and Billy, between love and family, between future and past. I heard the shot and saw the flare. I felt the impact in my palm, and for the slightest split of a second I thought I'd made an amazing catch. But before the thought could fully form, even as my fingers snapped shut around the slug, it was gone, exploding from the back of my hand to continue on its way.

But its way was now altered. In shattering the webwork of my handful of bones, the bullet glanced downward, not toward Billy's heart, not toward Billy at all anymore, but toward a spot at the edge of Rusty's desktop, the spot where Billy himself had meticulously placed the gleaming silver spike, the spike that Tippy Weaver had once presented in a ceremonial gesture of gratitude. Metal struck metal and a spark flew as the bullet ricocheted upward.

That ricochet haunts me even now, giving rise to thoughts that could have gotten me burned at the stake in a more medieval time. Because philosophically, I want to have it both ways. I want to say

I'm caught up in determined movements larger than my own and so absolve myself of any personal responsibility. But I also want to believe I'm more than just a puppet of predestination, more than a domino knocked from behind, forever falling forward with an assigned momentum. But here's the catch: if there's such a thing as free will, there's also such a thing as accident, a moment not dictated, a wild thread unraveling in the tapestry. Accident is an argument against belief, against faith, because accident, by definition, falls outside the scope of any plan, even God's. If we acknowledge accident, we open the door to chaos. And chaos, like its negative twin, the providential universe, frees us from personal responsibility. If disorder rules the world, there are no pawns, no queens, no bishops, no game pieces at all. No rules to play by.

The hope, I guess, is to find a middle ground between these absolutes. Someplace with reasonable footing.

Responsibility. I have to wonder if accident played a hand in my misspelling of so particular a word, or if that misspelling was determined even before the letters of the alphabet emerged from the Phoenicians' early fumblings with symbolic language—determined, in fact, at the very dawn of time, when nothing yet existed but the weather.

I'd spent my life worrying about how to color inside the lines, and now a simple ricochet made me wonder if maybe coloring outside the lines was the one and only impossibility in the universe. Maybe the lines were always more inclusive than we could imagine. Maybe the lines formed automatically around whatever we chose to color. Maybe everything was right where it belonged.

Of course, I didn't know at first about the outcome of the ricochet. All I knew was that my hand was in pieces and my blood was pooling on Rusty's desktop. Alissa might have been inclined to pull the trigger again, but seeing that she'd shot me made her stop. Billy, of whom I had only a peripheral awareness, sank slowly back into Rusty's chair.

Alissa took Rusty's souvenir baseball and pressed it into my palm. "Hold this," she said, but I couldn't make my fingers close around it. She closed my fingers for me and then dug through her purse and pulled out a roll of duct tape. She quickly wrapped my hand, taping the ball against my palm to slow the bleeding on that side and tightly covering up the exit wound on the back. Meanwhile, the surprise of the moment evaporated and my hand began to wake up to its new reality. Every nerve ending below my wrist began to scream.

"Keep your mind focused elsewhere," she said. "Otherwise, you'll go into shock."

That part was easy because I was still worried about Billy. I looked at him closely as Alissa wrapped my hand. He was breathing raggedly in the chair, and squirming slightly, as if he were caught in something he wanted to escape. His eyes were open, but there was no meaning in his stare. He looked lost in thought. A stream of blood ran down the side of his throat, disappearing beneath his collar.

"What about Billy?" I asked.

Alissa glanced toward him, but I could see she'd already sized up the situation and had dismissed him from her realm of worries.

"God put everything back in order," she said.

That, or it was just a lucky shot.

Chapter 27

Jackie Robinson's home-run ball staunched the bleeding almost completely, at least on the palm side of the wound. The duct tape took care of the rest. Still, it wasn't long before a cold wooziness came over me, I guess because of the shock to my system. I sat in the corner chair exploring the fringes of unconsciousness while Alissa called Alf to tell him what had happened.

"Shouldn't you call an ambulance?" I asked.

"I just did," she told me, and I realized that I wasn't as clear-headed as I might be.

"I thought you called Alf," I said.

"I did that, too," she informed me and touched the back of her fingers to my forehead.

I looked down at the bloody baseball bound to my hand. "Someone should call Jackie Robinson," I said. I don't remember what happened next.

The ambulance, I learned later, was for Billy, not me. Alissa had figured it might be best for us not to involve ourselves any further in this gnarled chain of events, so after alerting Alf to the fact that there was now a seriously impaired assistant attorney general in Rusty Wilderman's office, she somehow got me into my car and put us on Interstate 65 heading south. She drove us all the way to Villa Mercy. I wasn't the nuns' usual clientele, being just run-of-the-mill damaged goods, but they were equipped to take care of me.

So far they've done a great job. I've got some recuperation ahead, but I'll be all right. Eventually, the nuns will turn me loose, spill me back into the world to attend to whatever else I was put here to do.

I'm sure I can manage, too, even without full use of my hand. But I do have permanent gaps now. I can move my thumb and my little finger, but not the other three, so except for the Boy Scout salute, that leaves me fairly limited. The muscles can regenerate, of course, but the nerves and ligaments got blasted away for good. Bone damage is a problem, too. The skeletal system simply doesn't work well without all its parts, and apparently I left a few important pieces somewhere in Rusty's office. Probably scattered across the deck of his little radio schooner, like the picked-over remains of a crew of miniature sailors.

So I've lost my ability to point and my ability to make an obscene gesture. I'm not sure yet what the impact will be on my ability to wear a wedding ring. Still too soon to tell.

I also can't type up to speed anymore, so that narrows some of my options in the field of journalism. It's just as well. I've had enough news to last me for a while.

The news did, however, provide me with a final parting gift. When I finally came around, two days after the shooting, I had no idea where I was. My drug-fortified state made me groggy, and my vision was still blurred. My left arm was strapped in place along the side rail of the bed, and my hand was a mass of bandages. The baseball was gone. I couldn't focus clearly on the woman standing by my bed, but I assumed it was Alissa.

"You shot me," I said.

"No, dear, that was an accident." The voice sounded like my mother's. "You shot yourself."

Yes, it was definitely my mother. I was stunned. Rosemary Hatcher Wakefield, back on the scene after her record-setting disappearing act, cheerfully reporting the facts from her own peculiar world.

"Mom." I said. That seemed to cover it.

She put a cool hand on my immobile arm. "It's so tragic," she said. "I saw the story in the paper. Don't you remember?"

I remembered all right, but I thought it best to hear her version before offering my own.

"Maybe you'd better fill me in," I suggested.

And she did.

Apparently, a few strategic fictions was all it took to fix an un-fixable mess. Billy would have admired the expediency. The official account, issued by Attorney General Stricker himself and taken to heart by the people of Alabama, was a sad one indeed.

Rising political star William Hatcher, after a fund-raising dinner at the Elks Lodge, had dropped by his cousin's office so the two could go out for a beer, as they often did. The cousin, a well-known local weatherman, had innocently closed a filing cabinet, on top of which the network president had left a stack of ratings reports and a loaded handgun. The vibration of the closing drawer jarred the gun from its position on the stack of papers, causing it to fire. The weatherman, who had seen the gun totter from its perch, had instinctively raised his hand in self-protection, and in an unlucky twist of fate, the bullet glanced downward through his palm onto the desktop, where it struck a silver-plated railroad spike. The rico-chet was disastrous.

The witness to the accident was Alf del Tasorian, news director for Alacast, who had stayed to work late that night. Among all these details there was no mention of Alissa, and no explanation of how I wound up at Villa Mercy, nearly two hundred miles away.

At first I couldn't understand how a story with such holes in it could gain credence. Then I realized how perfectly Alf's account resolved matters for Attorney General Stricker. Now no one would ever fault him for his connection to Billy Hatcher because Billy's criminal life would never come out. He was probably thrilled to know that the man who had spared his dog but threatened his life was now out of the picture for good. So what if Alf's version was a little off the mark? Stricker was a politician on his way to the governor's chair, and he wasn't about to rock his own campaign boat by looking too skeptically at the details. Casting Billy as a victim of freakish circumstance was a strategy that worked well for everybody.

Only history would suffer. The official record would canonize him as a fallen hero, a reform-school success story brought to a premature end. Every article and editorial would pay him some saccharine tribute.

I won't say that's wrong. Billy said I was his judge, but I'm as blind as anybody when it comes to what's inside other people. I suspect he wanted a clean slate as much as any of us. But we all get distorted by what we encounter in the world.

At least there would be a story to tell—and maybe that's all history was, a collaboration among survivors to support the most useful version of events. Maybe Billy's case was typical. Maybe everything recorded for posterity was an imperfection, a skewed perspective owing as much to fiction as to fact.

For his part, Billy would never contradict the story. The rising bullet had passed through the soft underside of his chin, then broken through several barriers of soft tissue in his throat. It somehow missed his arteries, which some might say was lucky, but it did rip through the nerve mass at the base of his brain. The prognosis was grim. No more lucid moments, no sudden awakenings. Maybe he could still think, or even dream, but there was no way to know for sure. He would finish out his days as a warm lump of meat packed around a beating heart.

But that's not necessarily the end of his political career. Billy was right about the irreversibility of a certified vote total. State law makes no distinction with regard to brain-wave activity, so Billy's name will still be on the ballot in the general election. A ground-swell of sympathy might yet sweep him into office. That's certainly possible, and maybe even likely, given the sentimental nature of the gesture. If that happens, the new governor will be obliged to appoint a replacement. Maybe Rusty Wilderman because he looks good on camera.

Or maybe someone real might get the job, someone solid enough to go after the shadows, the phantom businessmen who walk the rich streets of New Orleans or Miami or wherever else they might be.

"Billy's our responsibility now," my mother said. "We're his next of kin."

"We'll put him here," I told her. "He had an interest in this place."

They were as unlike as any two people could be, Baby Angela and Billy, but I could imagine them side by side in the alcove off the main hall. Billy was a resident of her world now. Baby Angela could show him the ropes.

"What are you doing here?" I finally asked.

"I live in Mobile now," she said, as if that explained enough.

I suppose it did. Our estrangement wasn't based on anything in particular. There had been no catastrophic moment in my hapless teenage years, no personal crisis that had set this wall between us. We'd merely gone our separate ways. For a long time I held that against her, but not anymore. She simply hadn't been cut out to be my mother, any more than I'd been cut out to win the National Spelling Bee.

"Taylor, I heard about your father. I'm sorry."

"Thanks."

"I guess I should have come to the funeral."

"We didn't have one," I told her. "His ashes are still in the living room."

She frowned. "Well, maybe you'll have one later." She snapped open her purse and took out a small business card. "You can reach me at this address, if you think you'd like me to come."

She placed the card into my good hand. I blinked a few times, but my eyes couldn't focus.

"What do you do now?" I asked.

"I own a craft store," she said brightly.

I had nothing to say to that, so I let myself settle into the sleepy stupor that was washing over me. When I opened my eyes again, my mother was gone. No note this time. But no mystery, either.

The only real mystery left in my life was Alissa, who did leave a note. In large legible script she curtly apologized for having shot me. That was all. No word of where she was going, no hint at how I might find her. The nuns have been tight-lipped, but I suspect that's merely their natural state. They're probably as clueless as I am.

I'll find her, once I'm on my feet again. If Benny Bibberly could track her down with a few phone calls, I'm certain I can, too.

I might not rush it, though. She chose to disappear, and I have to respect that, give her a little time to think things through. Religion didn't pan out like she'd hoped, and I suspect a lot of new gray areas have cropped up in her life. But that's healthy, I believe. Nothing's ever really black and white.

In the meantime, I'll busy myself with other things. Maybe I'll drop by the Holman State Correctional Facility some visitation day and introduce myself to Alissa's father. I could bring him a craft project to work on. Seems like a proper way to start.

Maybe after that I'll take a trip, just get away from it all. Australia is a place I've thought about. Down under. I hear they've got a pristine wilderness there, a wildlife refuge in an unspoiled maze of mesas and valleys, somewhere deep in the outback. The weather, they say, is something you can depend on. The morning always comes up crisp. The afternoon turns warm, but never humid. Near dusk a shower drifts down from the mountains, then disappears, regular as clockwork. At night a soft breeze cools the canyons.

I'd like that, the certainty of it all. Things have been too shifty for me lately. I've put too many costumes on, too many sport coats and hard shoes and striped ties. Too many fright wigs and rubber noses. Too many masks in general. What I'd like now is to peel those layers off, maybe just go naked for a while. I need to spend some time out in the sun. I need to let the old skin burn.

Clint McCown was born in Fayetteville, Tennessee, and spent most of his youth in Birmingham, Alabama, during the racial conflicts of the early 1960s. Before turning to fiction, he worked as a journalist in Montgomery, Alabama, earning an Associated Press Award for Documentary Excellence for his investigations of organized crime and corruption in Alabama politics. He has twice won the American Fiction Prize. His novel, *The Member-Guest,* received the Society of Midland Authors Award; his novel, *War Memorials,* was designated for Outstanding Achievement in Literature by the Wisconsin Library Association. His short stories and poems have appeared widely, and he has published two books of verse. He is a former screenwriter for Warner Bros., and for twenty years served as editor of the *Beloit Fiction Journal.* He teaches in the creative writing program at Virginia Commonwealth University.

Book design by Wendy Holdman.

The text of *The Weatherman* has been set in Concorde
by Stanton Publication Services, Inc.
and manufactured by Friesens on acid-free paper.

THE S. MARIELLA GABLE PRIZE

Graywolf Press is delighted to award the fourth S. Mariella Gable Prize to *The Weatherman* by Clint McCown. The prize is named after a key figure in the College of Saint Benedict's history. Sister Mariella Gable began teaching in 1928 and was a strong believer in the transcendent values of literature. In 1942, she published a provocative anthology, *Great Catholic Short Stories,* which contained stories on race relations, abortion, and a story by Ernest Hemingway. In her subsequent anthologies and essays (1948–1962), Gable tirelessly promoted unknown but critically acclaimed authors, including the emerging work of Betty Wahl, J. F. Powers, J. D. Salinger, John Updike, Flannery O'Connor, and Irish writers. She was herself a well-respected poet and essayist.

The S. Mariella Gable Prize is one facet of the ongoing collaboration between Graywolf Press and the College of Saint Benedict, located in St. Joseph, Minnesota, that began in September 1977. Graywolf Press also plays a prominent role in Saint Benedict's Literary Arts Institute, funded by the DeWitt and Caroline Van Evera Foundation and the Lee and Rose Warner Foundation, which includes author readings and lectures in the Twin Cities and at the Saint Benedict campus; student internships at Graywolf; an author-residency program; and a Reader's Theater program, a collaboration joining Graywolf Press, the College of Saint Benedict, and the Jungle Theater.